making do

books by paul goodman

making do

by paul goodman

THE MACMILLAN COMPANY, *New York*
COLLIER-MACMILLAN LIMITED, *London*

© PAUL GOODMAN 1963

First Printing

THE MACMILLAN COMPANY, NEW YORK
COLLIER-MACMILLAN CANADA LTD., TORONTO, ONTARIO

Library of Congress catalog card number: 63–16105

Printed in the United States of America

with John

The weary-hearted ken
nae second spring again,
  tho the waeful may cease from their greetin'.
                —"Loch Lomond"

contents

part one

hammering out a rule of thumb

1

Amos, Meg's husband, swore he'd come back one night and shoot her, and we felt that this was probably for real. Amos *was* crazy, more than the average, and he did have a gun. Yet we couldn't call the police as other people would, because we were anarchists and pacifists and didn't believe in policemen, we did not want them messing in our lives which were innocent but in many ways illegal. We knew from experience that if you call a cop, one thing leads to another.

Harold and I agreed to stand guard on alternate nights. But supposing Amos did come with his gun, what were we supposed to do then? What exactly? It was hard for people like us to be practical.

I was too old for these strenuous games. I had too much real work to do in America to be exhausted by the inevitable fuck-ups of my young friends and these hang-ups of my older friends who should have known better than to marry crazy persons. Yet I could not stay away from their fuck-ups and hang-ups, because any vitality that there was in my work came from my contact with my friends, such as they were.

Monday night, both Harold and I were there when she whispered, "There he is!"

"No!" I denied it, and went to the window. "Where?"

"On the corner. Just outside the light."

Her coarse hair was hanging down in strings. I was looking at her in distaste. She was looking out the window too often, as if she wanted Amos to come back and make love. This put Harold and me in an awkward position.

Slowly she put her nails to her teeth and became speechless.

Peering nearsightedly out the window, I didn't know whether it was Amos or not. The middle-aged glasses for my overworked eyes ought to have been bifocals but they weren't. Since I was scared, there might have been a man standing there, and if there was a man it might have been Amos, since I couldn't see.

2

But Harold, to our astonishment, had drawn himself up stiff and narrow, back to the wall, and was looking askance out the window, like the burglar that he used to be. We were so surprised at his relapse into the habit of his youth that for a moment we forgot our danger. It pained me to see my friend making himself narrow, and Meg looked at him sorrowfully. Her hair became less stringy. It was beautiful, but in a way inauthentic, that the character of our friend was more important to us than our peril.

"No one there," he said, and went back to his engineering textbook in the big easy chair, whose stuffing was coming out. Unlike me, he wasn't afraid and his eyes were sharp.

Meg smoothed out her skirt with her palm, like a child who has caused enough trouble and doesn't want her skirt wrinkled too. She knew that I was very annoyed with her.

I could not catch my breath. I had once seen the gun, a black Luger. I looked at the clock. It was midnight. I assumed that in his psychotic system, Amos would be scrupulously punctual about the hour, and bang bang at the door downstairs. But it was not precise, it was not precise to me, what I was supposed to do when this happened. Maybe it was the kind of occasion of life that was *not* precise.

I counted off sixty seconds. One-and two-and three-and four-and, until I was satisfied that he would no longer come tonight.

In the other room the baby began to make live noises.

3

I waited till she went in. "She keeps looking out the window as if she *wanted* him," I said.

4

Harold stared at his book.

"You know what I mean," I said. "Maybe we're in the way." It was now the eighth night, and I was tired of it even before we began. I was tired, period.

I wasn't interrupting his studying. He was listening, but he stared at his book.

I wondered if he did grasp my primitive meaning. Harold tended to be impotent, even with the little hustlers he picked up, who picked him up, and he sometimes behaved as if sexual motives did not exist. To me they were always in the offing. In sizing up a situation I always looked at a man's crotch or where a woman's fingertips were wandering.

"Anyway, from now on you're it," I said. "I have to go to Columbus."

"No!" It got a rise. "When will you be back?"

"Friday."

He frowned. What else did he have to do with himself, I thought impatiently, better than waiting for Amos and studying electronics? (I liked to keep tabs.) I scowled at his book of formulas and his vertical frown. We were impatient with Harold. He *made* himself stupid, the way he kept the parts of himself out of touch with one another. He was inevitably going to get into trouble with his Puerto Rican boys. He was studying for an examination that would inevitably land him in a war industry. Yet one didn't have the heart to discourage either his sex life or his precarious ambition.

"She doesn't want to have sex with him," he said. "She has been too frightened."

This, I took it, was a projection of his own problem. *He* was no longer frightened, but he found it hard to get an erection.

Sharply I asked myself: "Why was *I* so frightened?" It was clear by now that Amos wasn't really going to show, and I almost knew why. Then why didn't I come across, and fuck her, as I used?

She reappeared, carrying the baby who was dry and serious-eyed.

I suppose that I didn't come across, as she wanted, because on these vigils I was doing my Duty. I was so tired of the world that I no longer had the spirit both to do my duty and also have any human or animal contact.

When she came back in, her eyes had her malicious look. Capriciously, mischievously, she dumped the little boy in my arms to hold, knowing that I loathed to handle babies; but she was careful not to touch me, annoy me. It was her way of taking a childish revenge for the wall that I raised between us. As I was, she could have broken down that wall simply by speaking her need, which was exactly what she speechlessly could not do. But she was sometimes embarrassingly giggly for a stately woman.

She was deeply, dumbly, permanently in love with me. She had been before she met Amos, and she was now. It was too bad. She loved me, I think, because I was sometimes kind to her and drew her out of her speechlessness. And unlike my wife, she seemed to respect and admire me beyond reason because I stood up for something—in the city. I was a citizen. If these were indeed the reasons why she loved me, they were dynamite, a powerful combination. But I couldn't help being as I was, citizenly and sometimes kind to people. The trouble was that I did not love her, and sex with her was therefore only of the order of the pleasant. I was uneasy about being so impractically important to her, and I was too old for her anyway. Yet I could hardly refuse, when occasion arose, to give her the excitement that required so little effort from myself and meant so much to her, as one throws a morsel to a loved family dog.

The little boy whom she had given me to share clung to me confidently, and he had a rather pleasant baby smell. Would Meg now pluck up her courage and touch me, as if accidentally, instead of staring at me with that big reproach? She had quite repaired her hair, and was pretty. I was one quick and easy to be sexually accepting, and quickly aroused when I accepted.

Harold's presence was no hindrance. In this way, our friends were not impractical. Life was too short. Naturally, any of us was jealous and blue if he was left out, but usually we were too decent to stand in the way of people having a good time. We could have fucked in front of Harold's face, except that he would have gone into the kitchen to make us coffee, for after we were done.

But Meg kept standing, speechless and immobile, about eighteen inches away, enough within the aura of my physical privacy to make me feel uneasy, balked from coming closer by my wall of refusal and control.

"I see I won't get much sleep tonight either," I said surlily. "I'm on the first panel after lunch."

She was so in awe of me that even my childish petulance made her feel guilty. She was injuring the commonwealth because of her personal problems! She looked at me with woe.

"Why don't you go home?" asked Harold reasonably, not looking up from his guided missiles.

"Oh it's O.K.," I said, "let's have some coffee." (I didn't know why, but it wasn't yet time to go.)

The worst of it was that, when I did get home, my wife would make me an unwarranted jealous scene.

5

As crazy people do, with their attempted suicides and threats of murder that do not add up to any meaning and yet cannot be simply disregarded, Amos had immobilized us like the basilisk. I guess that was what he wanted, to bore us. His psychotic system was grippingly uninteresting. One could die bored.

His purpose, he grandly announced, was to *form a Christian community,* and *therefore* he had to make a kind of building sacrifice of the sensual element, namely Meg. And rescue the baby, no doubt, from Tiamat.

So we are forced to share in other people's bad dreams. Our society consists largely of this. When it reaches the level of international crises about Berlin and Cuba, there are headlines in the papers and students phone me about flying to New Zealand.

The little one in my arms—just by being born he had tipped off his father's insanity—he was gazing with his sober animal face into my eyes, and I was looking into his and did not flinch. I had the impression, looking down into his eyes, that these babies had from the beginning an intelligence fully formed. They could structure reality, form figures and grounds, share in the one active intellect of all mankind. They lacked only sensations, muscles, experience. The little boy made sense. He was making it up apace.

He pissed and the diaper became damp.

Before this baby was born, Amos ought to have undergone *couvade* like the simpler people, to prepare him for the existence of something new.

Most of our friends didn't like Amos. But I could talk with him because there was something generous about his crazy longing for community, even if he had to call it a Christian community. Like myself, he could not tolerate that people should continue as they were: he generously had to offer them what they did not know enough to want. (Often I was as boring as he was.) He knew—we weren't people to have secrets—about the old relations of Meg and me; but he gave no sign of being jealous, and he wasn't jealous, only murderous. On principle.

Unfortunately, I didn't like Amos either, because he was insane. He made me feel animally uneasy.

6

I myself went into the kitchen to make the coffee.

And meanwhile—it was between midnight and one in the morning—the police of Vanderzee, in their station house four blocks away, were torturing the screaming children of the poor. On Hamilton Avenue and along River Street, they were butting in and preying on the business of life that was not their business. In the Night Court on Burr Street they were dealing out a mechanical justice that was not human morality. Not one of us was safe from them.

It was not prudent to invite people like that into our lives, even such as our lives were. The question was if, with all our prudence and ingenuity, we could keep them out of our lives uninvited.

The peace that they kept was not our peace. The police of Vanderzee, and of New York across the river, of Paris, Madrid, Warsaw, Moscow, were the instrument of the worldwide system of States in which a man was hounded from one baroque jurisdiction to another baroque jurisdiction, and he had no asylum or even exile. This system was crazier than any system of Amos's feverish brain. In the Cold War, it throve on crises that paralyzed the ordinary good instincts of people to pursue their happiness. It was poisoning the air and the milk, and collecting enough bombs to destroy mankind twenty and thirty times over.

Those were brute facts. We kept them out of our feelings pretty well in order to live on; but unlike most people, we at least took account of them in our behavior. We had no intention of giving to them the name of our friend, even though he was dangerous to us.

But the bother was that Amos had that gun! *We* had a very sharp kitchen knife. It had an old-fashioned bone handle. I hefted it without enthusiasm. It was hard to imagine a situation in which one—Harold—could use a knife like this that did not eventuate anyway in dealings with the cops. My role in the imaginary encounter consisted of gingerly, but probably adequately, tackling Amos at the knees.

It was absurd. I was trembling with fear.

7

Sitting at the round table, Meg was nursing the baby with a round breast.

"I'm scared shitless—" I began to say. But I understood

that this vernacular tone was a profitless way of getting by easy. I drew a breath and exhaled.

My teeth began to chatter. After a few breaths I was flushing warmly and I said in a pretty good voice: "I'm scared that Amos will get in and I won't know how to protect you. I'll be paralyzed."

Harold looked up with concern from his book. He heard that I meant it. "Where are you paralyzed?" he asked.

"Like—these days—I get in a funk even swimming out to the raft. It's in my arms. My arms get weak. Then I can't catch my breath and I think I'm going to drown."

It was rich and buzzing for me to be speaking in a natural voice to my well-wishers who courteously listened me out since the speech seemed to be useful to me to say. I could hear the sentences floating in the air.

"I manage to make it," I said, not to alarm them unduly.

Harold sat thin-lipped. He was one who would matter-of-factly wipe out a man if necessary.

But clutching the baby to her, Meg had arisen from the table and was circling about me, around the table, with blazing attentiveness, as she did when there was something interesting and important about her loved ones. She was now speechless with excitement. Then she came out, as she did, with one of her primitive, calm observations. "You're impatient. You want Amos to come in order to have it over with."

This was true. I took it to mean also, "So you won't have to come here at nights and be alone with me."

Downstairs there was a terrible pounding at the locked door. Harold jumped, but I was hardly startled. "That's not chum," I said. "It's Jason and Connie, and he's drunk." We crowded to the window.

It was Jason all right, but without Connie. Where was Connie? At once my heart bounded convulsively in my breast, and I began to be anxious about something else altogether. *Now was the time to go!*

"Take care!" I said, "I've got to get to New York," and I grabbed my pipe. I went down and opened for Jason, and I said "Hi!" to him and went.

Suddenly I was on the little train rolling back under the Hudson River to New York, and my soul was frantic because of a cry for life that I did not quite hear. Instead of sitting well-behaved and quietly taking notes—for a panel tomorrow afternoon in Columbus, Ohio—I found myself striding oblivious from one of the two bright nearly empty cars to the other. My heart did not stop bounding. It was extraordinary, as if my thoughts were thinking me instead of me them. Why didn't they dutifully arrange themselves into a lesson on one of the numerous problems of the Americans? (I could not remember which lesson.) When it was so late at night, and I *had* fifteen minutes to myself to think.

I was leading a stupid life, that was for sure. In the almost total confusion that I was in—but let me not exaggerate, my health was pretty good and my wife and children had food and shelter—I was not a man to be going about the country making public speeches. I went just because they asked me and I couldn't say no; or maybe I went because I was apprehensive that something might happen in my absence, although it never did in my presence. Even so, it was still important to me, going to a convention to speak, to have something sensible to say.

An urgent thing was trying to think me. Unlike Amos, this *was* for real. I had certainly got away from *there* fast. I hated fantasy, I was literal minded. Confused or not, I trusted implicitly my intellectual habit, to respond directly to the hang-ups of my daily life and deny them by dreaming up paradise, paradise anything practical instead of the world we live in. And so I stepped into the other bright car.

9

Aha! Connie was pregnant.

At once my agitation subsided, for it was only a fact.

Why shouldn't she have the baby if she wanted? I was indignant. If Jason wanted her to get an abortion, what Jason needed was a kick in the ass. What was the matter with Jason? He simply didn't want to be bothered with anything new! Was he in a panic about being fired from the University? (She was a student of his.)

How in the devil could these kids—young people in general—possibly calculate the advantages and disadvantages of a future situation unique in their experience? One of them says, "But we're not married." Another, "Wait till I become the assistant branch manager." Another, "How can we manage with only three rooms?" They claim that their freedom will be curtailed, not realizing that they themselves will be changed and have a different notion of freedom. Then, like Malthus, they extrapolate to the Population Explosion, in order to protect the Alliance for Progress. The middle class, 1962.

—In the one bright car had been no one but the old drunken couple rapidly passing from hilarity to anger—now sitting in pettish silence—and hard to tell, on the train from Vanderzee at that hour, whether she was whore or housewife. In the other car were two overalled trainmen with lanterns going home, having a cigarette with the white-haired conductor under *Smoking Prohibited by the Penal Code.* Walking back and forth between the cars was the old man oblivious, head bowed, muttering to himself.—

10

I noticed that I was smiling, because the question was interesting—especially by contrast with Amos's fantasies or the Cold War. I enjoyed thinking about something real; it was a great joy to me. The question was, when *ought* a young couple to postpone the first child? I thought I had a clue.

The clue was, what would well up—from the unconscious?—when there, uniquely, the baby *was?* For there it was. A unique event, a leap. Will the young man leap ahead and appoint himself father? Will he, on the contrary, resign from the future and identity with baby? Will he take the baby as a rival lover and proceed to make his home a jealous hell? Will he become an enemy of the entire coming generation and regiment them to the dominant system of society in order to put them down?

Will he be tipped off his rocker, like Amos?

How would one know how to predict such things about a friend?

Connie's response was more physiological and reliable. (Connie was O.K.)

Now my mind was rolling more smoothly and I stepped more leisurely back into the other car. To become a parent was a unique fact, a leap. The economic situation, the family background, the social conventions, might be more or less supportive, more or less labile; nevertheless, there was a unique event, a leap. "Are they mature enough?" asks the Marriage Counselor, but his question is unreal. One man *became* mature. Another man was Amos. (Jason was O.K.)

I had made up my mind for them. Nobody had yet asked me.

"I'll use it," I thought stingily, "for my next quarter hour on WLSR, the Listener-Supported Radio."

Providentially, the whole issue of choice was vastly exaggerated, since, at least for the first child, the young woman wanted the experience and that settled it. Somehow those new diaphragms rarely seemed to fit! So there we had a natural rule of thumb: have the baby and find out what you yourself become. Have the baby, Connie.

11

So, abstractedly, from one car to the other of the little train as it groaned and squealed under the deep Hudson River, I reacted to the horror and frustration of a week of bad nights by hammering from them a rule of thumb. That's what the experience had been about. Who could predict that?

And as the car slowed down to pull into Market Street, I had a peaceful certainty. (It was incidentally the truth.) By now I was humming the Harp quartet and was puffing on my pipe. I had jotted down a line of argument for Co-

lumbus—an improvement in public housing—and I knew
with a peaceful certainty that Amos had gone to Israel to
join a kibbutz. I wondered if, if he had been sane, they
would accept him, he being a gentile. Anyway he wouldn't
be bothering us for quite a while. (The next we heard, he
was in Haifa in an asylum.)

It is important to notice that some of our intuitive cer-
tainties, and apprehensions, are true and some are false. It
is probably useful to note accurately what each kind feels
like, under what conditions we experience it, for we cannot
do without intuitions.

And at Sixty-fourth Street, as I hoped and expected,
Connie was sitting on one of the lonely benches in the
waiting room. She was still weeping, where Jason had
brutally left her—or where she had refused to go with
him farther—or where (in fact) she was waiting patiently
for me, to talk it over. My admiration for the resourceful-
ness of this maneuver gave me a perfect confidence in her.
It prejudged our conversation. She looked so lovely, sitting
there, weeping.

textbooks

1

At Sixty-fourth Street, as he hoped, Connie was sitting on one of the lonely benches in the waiting room, still weeping—where Jason had brutally left her—or else she had refused to go farther with him—or (in fact) she was waiting for him. How resourceful she was! he admired. It prejudged their conversation.

Her face brightened when he wearily came up the ramp, and he straightened a little. She had big wide eyes, and he assumed, since she was a sophomore of Jason's at the University, that she must be about seventeen. Too young, but there it was. (It was painful to conceive of her at the University, so he never bothered.) She was nineteen.

"You're crying here, all alone on these benches," he pointed out.

She wiped away the tears with the back of her hand but she felt no need to fix her face. Naïvely, but she knew she looked equally well weeping or smiling. With a shock, he recognized that she had the same sober outlook that Meg's baby had had in his arms, even though she had made up a certain amount of experience.

"Come out and have an apple pie at Beck's," he said, and took her hand.

But she had caught his glance at the clock on the wall. "Oh, no," she said, "I'll take the train back, when it goes."

"Yes—when it goes." At that hour the little train used to drag itself into the terminal and slump down like an animal, asleep.

"You've been waiting for me," he pointed out, not sitting down on the bench.

Again the tears welled into her eyes. "If he's going to be brutal," she cried, "I wish he wouldn't decide to do what makes him guilty. And then he gets brutal."

"But he's always guilty, dear. Whatever he decides, he feels guilty."

15

"Oh, no, not always!" she sang. She was altogether loyal and somewhat sensible.

"No, he's guilty when he *decides*," he explained. "Then, as you say, he gets brutal. It's the same thing, deciding and being brutal."

She waited to take this in. "Isn't that so for everybody?" she asked. "Unless you are going to do something anyway, how *can* you decide and go through with it without forcing?" She seemed to realize, suddenly, that he knew the facts. Had Jason told him? And *he* was now certain that Jason had "decided" that she must have the abortion. But the thought, either that he knew about it or that Jason had told him, was immensely comforting for her, and she really burst into tears. The tired man sat down on the bench and put his arms around her and held her. Next moment she was positively merry.

"What's so funny?" he asked.

"He said that he would take responsibility for everything. Like Jack Kennedy for Cuba!"

This *was* funny. He burst out laughing for the first time since the last time they resumed the atom-bomb testing.

"No, let's be serious, Connie," he said, trying to straighten his face. Laughing did not echo pleasantly in the tunnel. "I really do have one question." He would, of course, decline to give Jason any advice, but it was pleasant to give Connie the advice that she wanted to hear and that she would act out anyway, whether he advised it or not. It increased the amount of comfort in the world. "For a moment let's just leave Jason out of the picture. Right, dear? And here's my question: Can you get along if you have the baby? I mean, how will you feed your face? Will your father support you?"

She again gave this a long thought. She tended to converse as if the purpose of conversation was to hear what the other meant and to say what she meant. When she answered, it was sadly: "It's the opposite. My father would *rather* have me and the baby—but I *can't* leave Jason out of the picture!"

16

"Do you love Jason, Connie?"

"Yes."

"There you are!" The tired man spread his hands, and the lights of the little train went on. "It's easy to be practical! Just let every ball roll downhill."

Eventually, after the lights went on, the train would begin to rumble as if it were warming up and about to start. Then it would subside. Sometimes the lights went out.

"Do you like Vanderzee?" he asked. "Miriam"—Miriam was Jason's separated wife—"says Vanderzee is death on marriages. She can ticket them off on her fingers! O'Neil, Walker, Simak . . ."

Connie didn't want to hear about Miriam. But she answered solemnly: "Yes, I like Vanderzee. I love you, and you come there. . . . I love Harold. I'm fond of Soren. Roger is remarkable." She also could ticket them off, but not on her fingers. "I can put up with Barry."

"*Can* you?" he exclaimed, astonished.

The train was now vehemently rumbling and shaking, with a new urgency. They spontaneously rose. It subsided. But he accompanied her to the empty car and put her on and kissed her on the forehead, and came away refreshed.

2

Waiting for her at the Amstel bar, Jason was trying to keep his high. But he wasn't drinking enough. This was partly because his cronies at the table—he stayed near the door—were on marijuana, which they puffed from time to time in the men's john. They did not clamor for service. But he wasn't smoking either. What he *was* doing was slowly heating himself up for a stupid brawl, that he could be ashamed of.

Jason belonged to our older generation in Vanderzee, the ones who came over from New York following Roger. Indeed, the only practical result of all our study of city planning was that in 1948 Roger figured out that Vanderzee was only twelve minutes from Greenwich Village by the

17

tube, yet must be a remarkable other world where there were big lofts to let and the rent was cheap. By and large, our friends came to settle, sometimes marry, and sometimes watch their marriages break up.

The potheads, however, were johnny-come-latelies. As the Empire City choked to death on automobiles and housing projects, she vomited up her drifters. Greenwich Village became neo-Glassic, and they drifted to the Lower East Side. The Lower East Side sprang up fortresses of public housing, and some of them drifted as far as Vanderzee. They were dropouts, from home towns, from colleges, from the army, from the corporations. They were not anywhere, did not intend to be, could not be. They did not sleep between sheets. The most plausible of them were the Negroes, whom our society had *dropped* out.

We were uneasy about the association between Jason and some of these notebook poets; if it could be called an association, for they did not care about him at all, anymore than about one another. They entirely mistook him. When he was sullen, they thought he was cool. When he was bitingly critical of society, they thought he was uprooted like themselves. They were offended when he parodied their versification. They were sincerely puzzled when, after long messy nights in his place, it became clear that they could not make it a pad to curl up through the morning. But this language is exaggerated, for words like "puzzled," "offended," or "thought" imply more meaning than they ever allowed.

Their vacuousness made them just the company that Jason often wanted. When he was sullenly resisting any demand on him, especially if it made sense and was his demand on himself, he either sat at home watching TV or he made the scene with the cats. The excitement was equivalent. Unfortunately, he was also lively and sexy, and the cats never did anything. They didn't play ball or play the races or read the *Scientific American* or hunt for cunt. At the Amstel he liked to have loud and learned arguments with the bartender about big-league baseball, and this left them nowhere.

The night before he could no longer work on his doctoral thesis, on *The Public and Critical Response to Sister Carrie and Jenny Gerhardt*. By morning he had decided that Connie and he would not have the baby either.

His way of coping with this crisis was, next, to cut his afternoon class, which he liked to teach and for which he was prepared, and in the utmost secrecy and anonymity to travel twenty miles to a peep show in Baxter where for ten cents apiece one could watch one-minute films of women with silk stockings and black garter belts, otherwise naked. When he had a lively hard-on, he furtively fingered it with his hand in his pocket. Finally, wildly, he put his left hand inside his pants and masturbated to orgasm, his head glued to the machine, his ass sticking out, while his right hand fed coins, of which it had a supply.

The dimes fell from his hand and rolled on the concrete floor among the machines. Panicky, he noticed that, during his moment of oblivion, Some One was watching him. With rapid dignity he walked out of the place, landed breathless in a bar three blocks away, and began to drink.

His doctoral thesis was a careful yet indignant analysis of the alternate slighting and hounding of the American novelist, especially by respectable critics who added envy to their anxiety and did not see life clearly and whole. For Jason, the subject had been a find. It fired his generosity and answered his desperate need to defy the three old women who had brought him up. By now, however, it was a thousand ways involved in his soul with his peep-show panic. He felt that it was an act of shame to present to the professors his careful documentation, cogent reasoning, and honest indignation. They would reject him.

(He was only partly right. Professor Cartwright would have smiled and asked whether he wasn't making an issue. Professor Wilson would have paternally restrained him from an imprudence that would jeopardize the future that the academic degree was for. Professor Storr, however, would have rejected the thesis because it had a subject.)

Rationally, Jason did not himself disapprove of his peep show and his black garter belts. They were a harmless vice, and he joked about them—blushing. They were *his* marijuana. He would not have indulged them if he disapproved them, for he was a moral young academic. But he conceded that the peep show was not a very restful or recreative sexual experience, under the conditions. One could not gasp. One could hardly breathe.

4

By 2:00 A.M. the cats at Jason's table were beautifully slow. They rose slowly from the table to saunter slowly to the john. And returning, a cat slowly staggered, while a whiff of pot came from the closing door. (The Amstel was well protected and the management did not bother.) He stood, and looked startled at the Swift, who occupied the world.

Unluckily, watching them from a nearby booth was a little clique of black silk jackets so puffed up with recognizing the odor and so stimulated by their own knowing comments that it was finally incumbent on them to act up and assert their own superiority to this riffraff. They laid their plans, and Schiller rose to his height.

The cats were quiet enough, under the illusion that they were with another. They thought that their communal soliloquy remarkably signified, though they spoke with so little vital energy that their sentences were often quite inaudible, except as phonemes for free association. But that too was very well.

"Like Out There," said the cat with startled eyes, "they swiifft. Like they swiiifft, man, Out There."

"Who needs 'em?"

Angela was stoned on horse and wasn't saying anything. She leaned. They propped her up.

"They breeze by, man. It's a gas!"

"Sssss," said the poet among them, "whiffed!" And he laughed, and slapped his thigh at the conceit.

The Tao was to let the Occasion arise, at its own sweet

will in the long months to come. But the Swift pushed on, advancing in black jackets.

The startled eye was transfixed by the calendar on the wall. That eye was sharp and could read the small numbers of next month. "Like July Swifth!" he whispered finally, "that's ma day. I got it *made!*" he resolved, in the future perfect tense, and he slowly raised his fists above his head like a punch-drunk victorious boxer, at which Angela, deprived of her prop, slowly hit her head on the table.

The others, however, wore little smiles and twinkling teeth in their stiff pinched lower jaws.

"Ah jes got to get maself together, man," said the seer of next month. "It's all there. All's ah got to do is get maself together. Jes get ma rent an'—"

"Ain't it some shit?" said another cat. "The man needs his rent." And he slapped his thigh, and laughed at his own unconcern.

From outside, one could watch them in their fishbowl like a kind of stupefied clowns. One could listen, if one held one's ear close, while they sweetly and very slowly discoursed on the new bit: like the way not to be hooked, man, was to dig like a wide variety of narcotics, some of which were legally available. Ephedrines, rauwolfia, amphetamines, lysergic acid—the talk was scientific, like the TV commercials. They were coolly swept along in the popular culture of the Americans during the terrible years of the Cold War, when the budget for the bombs rose annually 15 percent. What had once been a cult of the underworld, or of sacred rituals in organic communities, had been neatly organized into the machinery of the American system.

Nevertheless, through dark glasses, for they were pained by rays of light, they *were* enjoying the blue neons of the ceiling reflected in the mirror back of the bar, a small thing but all their own. Except Angela who stared like a zombie. They propped her up.

The black jacket was now looming a little too close.

He had sidled over with a broad friendly grin. Immensely in the know. Hip as could be. When a member, on his way back from the john, staggered and upset Jason's bottle in his lap, Schiller joined louder in the laugh than any. But one could not believe in his laugh, because his forehead was perpetually furrowed with deep perplexity about a question of life or death that he no longer remembered and could never ask. His eyes were close set.

The cats looked at him with bland appraisal as one more object in the shifting maya of the world. And they stiffened a little more, with impotent hostility.

But Jason was ingenuously sociable. He welcomed the newcomer, especially since the others were so boring. "Hiya!" he said, "sit down." Characteristically he regarded the hoodlums as Townies, and he was that kind of collegian who befriends them and tries to improve the zoning regulations. He moved aside his chair to make a place.

The youth stood frozen, thrown off his timing.

His usual gambit was to ingratiate himself by degrees, overcoming their initial coldness or distrust. To seem, by being knowing, to promise everything—his assumption was that something was always wanted. In the course of conversation, their degradation would be exposed completely. Then, at the exact moment, he would reveal himself in his own shining perfection, insulted and indignant by being for an instant mistaken to be one of *them*. And hiss, "You cocksucker!"—"Hopheads, get out of town!"—"Collitch boys!"—or whatever the case might be. A fight would then ensue, a knife would flash.

But Jason's friendliness had been too sudden. Thrown off his schedule, to which he clung obsessively, the boy lost his voice. He could have picked a fight with Jason's type too, but that required a different routine, more surly and argumentative. Having to respond, in the emergency, to Jason's invitation, it was half under his breath that he muttered, "Not with them niggers." Three of the cats were Negroes.

This too could have been good enough for a fight. Though it was not loud enough to be heard universally, to be the insult direct, the remark was quite loud enough for Jason's sickly masculinity to be affronted and rise to the challenge. (Jason would, of course, have said, "Step outside!" and promptly got a kick in the groin.) The cats stirred uneasily. They moved closer together. Since they

22

had no loyalty to Jason, they were certainly not going to get involved in his fight for them. Unsupported, Angela slumped forward and her forehead hit the table with a thump.

But at this moment Barry Conklin walked in the door.

Boiling with rage at his real enemy, Jason knocked over his chair and thrust his way past Schiller to confront Barry. The hoodlum was utterly confused.

5

By a freakish mischance, Barry was carrying under his arm a load of half a dozen of the very textbooks, shiny mint, that he was going to peddle to the Superintendent of Schools in the afternoon.

Seeing them, like a stab between the eyes, Jason realized, again and again, that the textbook racket happened also here. Since last talking to Barry, he had checked up. A week ago, passing the school, he had stopped to chat with a ten-year-old girl, to take a look into that grammar that she was carrying.

Barry Conklin had come to Vanderzee well after Roger, Harold, Meg, Soren, Jason, or the original painters. He had not come because of Housing, for he had money, $20,000 a year in the textbook division of Eastern Printing. When asked why he did make such a provincial move, he said lightly that Vanderzee was the new avant-garde and it was his professional duty to be in the swim. But he really came to hang around the fringe. He was lonely for a reality. He respected our friends. He couldn't be one of us, and he couldn't stay away. Naturally, he compounded with this dilemma by one-upping as hard as he could, but without superior airs—for he was not a fool, and knew that his airs would be held not even in contempt.

He was friendly and sometimes he tried to give us something; but he was not openhanded, and when he gave Meg a bed that she needed, it proved to have bedbugs, after Harold had carried it down two flights and up three.

Other times he liked to expatiate humorously and boast

of his prowess, and this is when his character made him stupid. For he could not perceive that our friends were more simply in the world than he was. He intricately described the pork barrel of the textbooks, but he could not notice that Jason was a loyal academic and that he was burning up. It would have been inconceivable to Barry that Jason would take the trouble to look into the kid's grammar, but Jason did it as a matter of course. In six years he might have her in his class!

For his part, Barry was glad to see Jason. Right off, therefore, he needled him with a question about the book on Dreiser that he knew he was fucking up.

But Jason's soul was furious only about textbooks. "What's this?" he said, and roughly pulled a book from under Barry's arm.

The load cascaded to the floor. "Hey, those are mint!" cried Barry reproachfully, and painfully bent down to collect the books before they were stepped on.

Jason held in his two hands the second edition of the same grammar that he had examined in the first edition. His grip was mighty, but his fists were shaking.

Barry persisted in trying to be friendly. "That?" he laughed. "It's the revision by the Assistant Professor at Normal of the original by the head of the English Department at Mackenzie. As a matter of fact, the original typescript was so illiterate that the book was written by a copy editor."

"Do you realize," hissed Jason, "that if they had printed off four million copies of the text they used in 1900, it would now sell for four cents?"

"There wouldn't be much money in that for anybody," Barry pointed out reasonably.

Again Black Jacket was standing up too close. Indefatigable, belligerently astride. But he looked with bewilderment from one of their faces to the other, as they spoke. It could not dawn on him that they were quarreling about a book. He felt he was being had.

"Oh, that one!" said Barry. It was an American History. "That one I wrote. It is recommended by the American Education Association. It stinks."

His replies were good-humored and intelligent enough. But as always, he could not grasp that Jason might be serious. And the incomprehension appeared on his round face as a kind of piggish stupidity. This triggered Jason off.

For the moonfaced stupidity was before him like an engulfing swamp. If that face, if that face was allowed to exist in the world, it was impossible for Jason to live and breathe. Chaos was come again. Chaos and night in undisputed sway.

Hard as he could, he punched the face in the nose. It spurted blood. And Barry sat down on his behind.

Connie walked in at the door.

The textbooks were again scattered on the floor. This time, Jason thought dramatically, he ought to trample on them or tear them apart. But instead he looked, blushing, at his fist, while Connie hung heavily onto his side to keep him out of further trouble.

Awkwardly Jason bent down and picked up the books and put them on a bar stool.

Schiller and the other hoodlums were looking at one another with superstitious fright. Had there really been a fight about a book? With moral certainty they had felt that the newcomers from the city were vicious and communists; they had not taken them to be beyond human comprehension.

The waiter and the bouncer helped Barry to his feet, handed him his books, and eased him out the door. Since Jason was a fixture at the Amstel, they did not know what to do about him, and did nothing. The bouncer pointed a denouncing finger at the sleeping figure of Angela. "Get that stiff outta here!" he barked. "At least prop her up; it looks bad."

6

Ashamed, still indignant, Jason sat down. The cats were coolly grinning. Once the danger had been removed from their immediate vicinity, they were appreciative spectators. When Jason had punched Barry in the nose and the blood spurted, it was an epiphany, and they said "Flak!" and snapped their fingers.

"I'm sorry," Jason said to Connie, almost whining. His voice rose, "How can Puerto Ricans afford that kind of money?"

"Yes, Jason," said Connie. "I hope Barry won't be angry with you."

"Is this trash to be the textbooks for our kids?" He began to shout. *"Is this why I have to teach freshman composition?"*

"Cool it, man. Cool it," drawled a black cat, whose hearing was wounded by the sound of the angry voice, just as his eyes were vulnerable to bright light.

"Flak!"

"It's a gas," drawled a white cat. "He knocks him in the snout about a grammar!"

"Aw, cool it, man," drawled the pained black cat, on whose face was a grin.

Jason looked from one grinning face to another. They were too many. His wrath began to leak away, and he began to withdraw into his apathy. Barry Conklin was a stupid man, but these cats were the mechanical America.

Resigning into humor, he said for the record, "You fuckin' leeches on the body politic! how would *you* dig the tax structure of the town of Vanderzee?

"You're too swiiift, man," drawled a white cat.

"Let me read you a poem," drawled the poetical cat— and quick as a flash he whipped out his notebook and read very very slowly (once they had you, they took their time): "A

drop of

waterrrrrr

SPLASHeszzzzzzzzzzzzzzzzzzzzzzzzzzz."
The z's, buzzing like a saw, were not beautiful in his mouth.

But Angela's soft snoring was pleasant. They had again propped her up. And by a tangential association with snoring, a black cat was deeply moved to bring forth a vol-

26

ume of a San Francisco author and was leafing interminably for the appropriate passage, which if he found would have been very very very boring. In a literary panic Jason tried to forestall him with a political remark, "You mother-fuckers will be glad when a white man's bomb kills you and me both. How stupid can you get?"

Predictably, a black cat drawled, "Yeeeah, white man's time is runnin' out." He was a religious fanatic; for a moment his eyes spoke. Another black cat slapped his thigh, and laughed and laughed. But the others just continued their chemical grin. Their impenetrability was a deadly offensive weapon.

It was not all-powerful. For suddenly, with a quiet certainty, Connie knew that Jason had reversed himself about the abortion. Indeed, after his punching Barry in the nose about the price of children's textbooks, it made little sense for him to balk about having the baby. With a deep sigh, she put her hands on his shoulders, and let fall

"like a horse her silent muzzle on his neck."

But her love for him was like powerful sunlight, and it penetrated despite them, even through dark glasses. The grins became thin-lipped. They didn't like it. They could not yet think how to defeat it.

One of them slowly shoved back his chair.

"Like this cat's a drag," he slowly but definitely drawled.

Others shoved back their chairs, and Angela fell onto the floor. They slowly shambled to their feet and toward the door, leaving her there. For Connie to take care of.

One black cat slowly hung around to mooch the fiver for mescaline, which was the reason they had been sitting with Jason all morning anyway. Jason didn't pay him any attention.

a conference on delinquency

1

Before the first panel began, I knew that Columbus was going to be a beautiful Conference. When the five of us, the section on "Urban Environment and Mental Health," took our places at the table, we were inevitably trapped by the microphones grinning down our throats. (There was a surprisingly large crowd of students.) Nevertheless, before the deep freeze could really set in, the bushy-eyebrowed and moustached man on my left—Warden Howard Green, I figured from the program—implored, "Can't we dispense with these fuckin' machines?" and the white-haired lady—Justice Amy Watkins of Sacramento—favored him with a benign smile.

I myself was not much inhibited by microphones; I never talked into them and was always being admonished by the managers. But I felt heavenly comfort because somebody else was taking some initiative and I didn't have to be the only one to make a pest of himself.

Irving, who was a friend of mine—National Council on Child Labor—leaned over to the student factotum and said something, with his usual sprightly gentleness. The kid responded with the flushed resentment of seventeen years of age, unappreciated in its solipsistically expert arrangements. He pointed out that there was an audience, as if we were blind and deaf.

Judge Watkins—she had a pink face and was still a little girlish—judicially decided, "Let them be," either to spare the boy his embarrassment or because the students were in fact so noisy.

"Let's just shove 'em back," I said, and pushed mine to the back of the table. I was quick at inventive compromises. "All I need is elbow room and so it don't jump down my throat." I went in more and more for bad grammar.

This put the fifth of us, Dr. Ben B. Blumberg—Associate Superintendent of Junior High Schools—in an awkward position. For four of us had pushed our microphones away, but he was still sitting well behaved, as he had been, with his microphone in front of his mouth. Students in the front let out a laugh. Blumberg was an earnest Pharisee who had developed, in my own big city, with heroic effort and a modicum of success, the Broad Outlook program for the "culturally disadvantaged," as we called them. He believed in the middle-class family, and his eyes were precise and a little hard.

All of us had foreheads worn with worry and perplexity.

Ungraciously, forced to cooperate in deranging his own conception, the seventeen-year-old pulled back Dr. Blumberg's microphone also. "Young man, if you think it's the wrong way to work," said Irving, "why don't you put up more of a fight?" The youth laughed shortly. It was hard for us to remember that we had crashing authority—except in the actual institutions, where we were powerless. (This we remembered exquisitely.)

I turned to look uneasily at the cop, the Warden, who was sitting at my elbow. I saw in his eyes that he was in despair, and I absolved him.

My euphoria was probably relief, after the night before, at being able to carry on a reasonable conversation, with my peers, in a safe academy. For I lived with a good deal of intellectual starvation, and in chronic fear.

2

I had little reasonable conversation. I had no office, and when I met my peers at a party, we did not really talk. One man would be looking for somebody more useful than me to talk to, and I would be looking for somebody more attractive than him to look at, gloomy because there was nobody. Under the formal conditions of being on a panel, however, there was nothing *to* do but listen and say one's say. I came to these conferences, as I have said, because they asked me, but once there I often learned something. I was unable to read social science, but here were the authors and right up to date.

Before the serried faces of the students and teachers, we had to talk out loud and clear, and not interrupt too rudely. Yet we spoke to one another and not to the grandstand, except Dr. Blumberg who spoke to the audience, not to upstage us, but because he was pedantic.

Irving's current statistics—he started right off—were, as each time, appalling. They confirmed what I saw with my own eyes on the street, yet I wouldn't have believed it. City by city, the youth unemployment was 60 percent, 65 percent, 75 percent.

Then he said, pointedly and quietly as he did: "But employment is not a gimmick. The jobs are mostly no good anyway. And given the disappointment and resentment with which these youngsters finally get them, they are often just as bad off employed." When he said this kind of thing, his Adam's apple moved, swallowing, in his long neck.

"What do you mean by that statement?" interrupted the Associate Superintendent. "The boy with a job can get married." He was suddenly angry and quite human.

"The boy can marry. The husband is an alcoholic," said Irving laconically. "Ben," he said, "I haven't worked thirty years to improve the conditions of child labor in order to feed kids to the present economic machine and call it vocational guidance. That's what I mean."

We looked to Dr. Blumberg to reply. There was a pause. Instead, he lit a cigarette, and immediately a hundred of the students lit up. They had been waiting for our permission.

The Warden was next, and started by describing children who up to twelve, thirteen, fourteen years of age had never ventured more than five blocks from home. For some reason Amy was visibly moved by this dreadful information. I refused to be moved, but suddenly cut in, as I do —parenthetically, so to speak—to make a point that, in my opinion, needed saying at once, if we were going to make sense and not waste one another's time. An "urban environment," I said, was *not* a city; "urbanism" was not city planning. If he was going to use words like that we could kiss good-bye to talking about human beings rather than administrative units; but surely that was not his intention—which was why I interrupted him, excuse me.

When I interrupted him, his right hand was outstretched in a broad gesture. He left it there and stopped to think of what I had said. Then abruptly he brought it down and with it skipped two pages of his prepared text that had been founded on an assumption that he no longer accepted. Because of a new thought, he had actually changed not only his mind but his speech, his public image!

Some of the students were visibly electrified. I could see their hair stand up like a dog's ruff in the presence of the uncanny. The students at the State University did not much believe in the existence of the intellect.

He proceeded to describe the panic of hardened diddle-dybops in the woods, terrified of the dark and small animals —he was the Warden of six forest work camps. He raised a laugh when he told of an encounter with a cow. Many of the students had seen a cow. "But it's not so funny," he said, to their surprise. "These kids are really afraid; but they don't know of what they are afraid." And he showed, in a thrilling example, how a skillful and sympathetic counselor had made use of this exposed nerve of panic to get past hostility and touch a profound castration anxiety.

At this I thought: There were 180 millions of people in the United States. And we poor dears who felt ourselves responsible and acted so—I doubted that we were, from coast to coast, more than a hundred or a hundred and fifty. And fifteen of us were here in Columbus! It was appalling. I was sitting next to the only manly cop in America; and the great State of California had one ordinarily decent judge, Mrs. Watkins there. There we were. The students had come out in large numbers to listen to the visiting grown-ups, as well they might, considering the box that they were in at the University.

It was ten-thirty! We had disregarded the question period. We were too absorbed in the subject and too interested in one another. Oblivious, we got up to go to Amy's room for a drink and carry on. The students crowded round

—"Judge Watkins!" "Dr. Blumberg!"—some of them raised their hands as if in class. I kept arguing with Ben and Irving, and we brushed past them and elbowed through the crowd, leaving the young with their mouths half open.

Out the corner of my eye, as in a picture, I saw a stripling hanging on the fringe. He attracted attention partly because of his flaming scarlet windbreaker, in the style of a juvenile actor of the time named Jimmy Dean, and partly because his face was contorted with unbelief at our unfairness. He was still trembling with the embarrassment of half an hour since he had thought of a sensible question to ask and was working himself up to stammer or blurt it out, while the waves of shame of exhibiting himself engulfed him, and the hostility that he felt at our eminence made him angrier and angrier and more and more unjustified.

3

I couldn't get to sleep even though I masturbated, which is usually an adequate sedative for me. There was too much unfinished business of the day. I oughtn't to have brushed past the students. The scarlet jacket flashed in my mind's eye.

I saw him. He was feverishly rehearsing, rehearsing his revenge—mentally, for he would not be telling it to his roommate. He was walking across the campus, hunched against the drizzle, at 2:00 A.M., and burning up what little energy he had. He was a sick boy. (Mononucleosis, the current style of student blues.)

By now he had quite forgotten the reasonable question that he had meant to ask. He was afraid that he was losing his mind. Indeed, a part of his hostility was that *we* had missed his proper time.

In order to ward off his panic, he attacked. I saw him single out—the Warden. (He was too sentimental to pick on Amy Watkins; and I, so far as I knew, was innocent.)

His daydream voice became high-pitched, and suddenly he was accusing the Warden of the execution of Caryl Chessman and throwing in the quotation that he had learned from Camus on capital punishment.

But he was pitilessly self-critical, and he saw (I saw) that what he was saying was incoherent hash. He was ashamed of the name-dropping. Thing was to be more cool. So he started across the campus in another direction and rehearsed it again, and this time he began by asking an insinuating question with a quiet leer: "What did Warden Howard Green think of the student body at State?" And then, the left-hook across, accompanied by an abortive gesture: "What did the Cop think about backhand-slapping my friend Earl and calling him a young punk?" Etcetera, whatever would follow. This had the advantage of establishing the right context, a gang vendetta. Thing was to use dialect—"fuzz" walking on our "turf." This established the ground rules of conversation in one's own favor.

But using the dialect, the unhappy youth knew that he must inevitably slip up and appear ridiculous before his internalized Model Hipster. He was bound to miss the nuance. And in the meantime the students were angrily shouting at him, "Dry up! Sit down!"

The shouts rang around me in my lonely room, and impulsively I climbed out of bed and pulled up the Venetian blind. The campus was gray in the moonlit drizzle. The illuminated clock on the spire said 2:00 A.M. And Jimmy Dean was frantically striding across the black grass with his head sunk woefully into his depressed chest. Since he could not breathe in that posture, he must have been shivering, drenched. Stoned, I saw his pale face before my mind's eye.

The University hotel, where they had put us up, was absurd, endowed by the Stilton chain to give an M.A. in hotel management. It was used to try things on for size. The bathtub had black safety-stripes that scratched your ass like carborundum. When the bellhop carried up my bag, I did not know whether or not to tip him, since he was only doing his lessons. He took the quarter.

Jimmy Dean was eclipsed by the Memorial Library on whose forehead, incised in stone, were MONTAIGNE SHAKESPEARE CERVANTES. I let the blind drop and went back to bed and to sleep.

4

For the next panel they had shuffled us around, though I was still with the Warden. The others were the sociologist who had written the brief for the Integration decision; the great houser who had been dropped by our governor and was now teaching at the Institute of Technology; and Harriet Young, again a friend of mine, the little fire-eater from the Harlem Settlements. In fact, we at this Conference were the star-spangled banner and I might well have been proud of being in the roster. Instead, I had already written us off.

Seduced, no doubt, by the academic surroundings, I now began to hear the voices pouring into the microphones as nothing but the styles of the modern Western world. The microphones were set up exactly as if we had not protested, and this time, naturally, we succumbed. Our fight was spent. The Warden covered my hand with his, in commiseration. (I think he was queer for me—for my type of spirit—but of course we were too old.)

The Negro sociologist was an upright Puritan. One could almost see on him the shining breastplate of Brewster or Bradford, and one could actually hear the mellifluous and law-abiding sexual tones that made it quite impossible to pay attention to his adequate second-rate remarks.—He wasn't any John Milton.—Historically, his righteousness was something like Dr. Blumberg's Pharisaism; but the Jew was more bitter and compassionate, more in contact with his own suffering, more able to tolerate it because he was more supported by community and learning.

During the sermon I had plenty of occasion, while my mind wandered, to look at the students' faces. Scarlet jacket was in the front row on the right, but he was now wearing a handsome chocolate velvet jumper that looked expensive and bespoke a loving mother. The tight black levis were the same.

Suddenly, startlingly, he interrupted the speaker, to point out that if Professor Wesley was going to use words like "delinquent behavior," we could kiss good-bye to talking about real youth, for it was the social context and not the behavior that made the acts delinquent. I flushed red. It was my style, but exactly. And what was remarkable about the imitation was that he had grasped the essence: that the interruption must be important, accurate, and needing to be said as soon as possible, otherwise it was rude.

At once Professor Ellis, who was the moderator, stood up to interrupt the interruption. "There will be plenty of time at the question period," he said. But the sociologist, with an affable wave of his hand to indicate that he was not offended, proceeded with his speech, using the words "delinquent behavior" just as he pleased, stupidly.

I was infinitely distressed. It did not seem to me that the boy was mocking me, because his remark was correct, and nothing comes from nothing. Yet it did not seem to me possible that anybody could introject another so completely, so quickly. My mind clouded over. I went into the past or the future, I don't know where. It was a couple of minutes before I returned, and by now the Warden was on his feet.

The Warden spoke like a Pragmatist, and I was more at home. Good, too; a composite of James and Mead, erotic, communal. I liked his warm touch, his brown face, his blue shirt, his gray moustache. He was more like a forest ranger than a cop!

Slyly I looked at Jimmy Dean, and he was again beginning to be in a panic of embarrassment because he was afraid of Professor Ellis. My heart sank. Again we had missed his proper time. What I should have done, what I should have done was to get up, walk around the table, hold him in my arms and say, "Don't be afraid, kid; you spoke well; you made sense. Go on." For what was the decorum of this Conference to me? But instead I pushed back my microphone a couple of inches and wiped my brow.

And next I could hear my own voice speaking. I was not speaking it, but my habits were excellent. I was the Enlightenment—reasonable, outrageous, not without a certain persuasive passion for the reasonable. I hated my voice. I was so tired of making sense! But one cannot be superstitious or a fool if one isn't. And as often, I was offering a practical proposal: to include in the public housing a youth dormitory, a kind of primitive Youth House, where the adolescents could get away from their mothers and their hostility to the frequently changing stepfathers. Where they could lead their own sex lives with freedom. In a trance of the eighteenth century, I heard myself developing the anthropology of the Happy Primitive. I was appalled at my idiocy. I sat down trembling.

In this crisis, the homey and familiar voice of little Harriet saved my life. She was a Quaker—out of Earlham College, by William Biddle—and as she spoke I could read off the description in the catalogue: "Underlying all that Earlham tries to do is the vision of wholeness—both worship and work, both discipline and freedom, respect for the individual and concern for the group. This vision Earlham does not wholly achieve, but there are many among her sons and daughters who strive for it, and at least they know when they have failed because they have a standard by which to judge." And there she was, failing, but with her eyes flashing. She half turned to me, to quote something I had just said, and I had an odd experience: I understood for the first time since I read the words at age fourteen, the relation between Enlightenment and *Illuminatio*. For years it had vaguely disturbed me. Harriet was an *illuminata*, and she assumed, of course, since we both had common sense, that I was too.

Our last speaker, the great houser, was hard to place. He began with the joke, the inside anecdote, of reformist political power, Gladstone, Woodrow Wilson, the New Deal. I could see that many of the students were deeply impressed, to hear our message from professional authority, and I prepared to tune out. But how was it, then, that his message was not the law of the land? Why was he politically in such hot water? What took place at that unpublicized meeting at the White House that concluded in his resigning in disgust? Suddenly I began to hear the scornful overtones, throwing caution to the winds, exposing himself naked, the fatal disposition to end up with his head, like Münzer, on the block. Aha, he was an Anabaptist! From time to time there was a little nervous laughter, from those —the teachers—who caught the bearings of what he was saying. By the time he sat down, everybody was uneasy.

We had left plenty of time for questions! A dozen hands shot up.

5

To my surprise, Jimmy Dean was one of the first volunteers. This was not cool of him, to ask for the floor so soon. But he was not able to control himself. His outstretched arm was white out of his rich chocolate blouse.

Professor Ellis said, "Yes, Terry, now you can have your turn."

For ten long seconds, that must have seemed to him like long minutes, he could not get out a word. The attack when it came—I had miscalculated—was not against the Warden but against me. *"You!"* He nodded his head at me to bear the brunt of his respectful inquiry. "Explain how you sit there holding hands and playing footsie with that cop. That's my question. Let me expand it. I can respect him. He comes on like a psychologist, but in the showdown he will act like a cop, so we know where we're at. Last night he tells us how he conned a cat out of his castration complex to make him less of a pain in the ass to IBM. No sweat. He's an artist, I salute him!"—and he sketched a snotty Nazi salute at the Warden. "But what are *you* doing? Here you give us something about balling with jailbait in a Youth House. See? Fuzz. Jailbait. Fuzz. Dig?"

All this was delivered in a throaty intense tone that we could just about hear—he was not giving us the time of day; and only two or three rows back the students began to call, "Louder!" "We can't hear you, Terry!" "Give him the mike!" "Dry up, Terry!" I had the impression that he meant to talk in a more haphazard style, which would have been more narcissistic and insulting, but he was betrayed by the syntax and the logical structure of an intelligent middle-class home. I took it that the Nazi-salute bit came from Norman Mailer. I prepared to answer.

"Louder!" they sang at me before I said a word.

"The young man," I said in a loud voice, "wants to ask a question of me. He objects to my playing footsie with Warden Green whom, however, he respects as an authentic cop, although a phony psychologist. But I, he claims, am phony through and through because I talk like an outlaw as a conversation piece. Is that your point, young man?"

It certainly was his point, and yet this résumé entirely missed the point. For his point was that we were an in-group and he was excluded; it was that we had "made" it, and he, in a losing battle with his accumulating woes, was never going to make it; it was, most fatally, that we, whom he looked to, were impotent to accomplish anything, and this threw him into such a panic of insecurity that he defected to the enemy, to any enemy, whether the cops or the robbers. But these things he could not articulate; he knew them too vaguely. The result was that he could not shut up, for he had not really said his say. And so he got up again and launched, now in a loud, leering, and monotonous voice, on his phonograph record. We had to hear about Caryl Chessman and listen to the quotation from Camus. To the Town-Gown fight that neither the dean nor the police could handle, but he, Terry, brought about a truce. Next, by an inner logic, he was bitterly extolling the pimp who peddled him marijuana, although this was certainly an imprudent confession in front of Professor Ellis. Evidently he had to blurt it out to prove his authenticity, as a man tries to demonstrate that he has a sense of humor.

To me all this was new and boring on even the first

hearing. It was delivered with an interminable incoherence in a mechanical groove. Pretty soon I had had it and I held out my palm.

"Shut up, Terry," I said. "Let me answer your question." He sat down. I don't know if he listened.

"My guess is you don't want an answer. Once you turn on that phonograph record, you already have it all figured out. But let me tell you this. The men and women invited to this conference—" and I proceeded to launch on *my* phonograph record, though newly minted only the night before. "There are 180 million people in this country, and we a hundred, we a hundred and fifty, are wearing out our eyes and our hearts trying to do something for it, for you. *And* we expect we aren't going to succeed, but we do it anyway. What do you think about that?"

Unfortunately I spoke this in an earnest and ringing voice that evoked a thunder of handclapping. I was shocked. I had not meant to win a victory. What I had said was honest enough, but so irrelevant as to be almost a lie. For as the case was, nothing was relevant at that moment but to come across and take care of the youth's sick body and soul, preferably beginning with the Infirmary. What was the use of defending against attack? I pointedly cut into the applause. "Look, Terry," I said appealingly, and he did look up.

"Please," said Professor Ellis, rising.

"One moment, Professor. I have not done the young man justice. You're a lousy hipster, Terry, because you don't get anything out of this for yourself. Supposing you're right and you publicly expose us for a lot of crooks and morons. You win the satisfaction of a spiteful victory. Big deal. Wouldn't it be more useful to mourn, because we are no good to you?"

This was fantastic. How to convey to a young person that it is useful to mourn? How can he afford to hear that?

"May I explain something to the young man?" said the Warden, "Since I am responsible for the execution of Caryl Chessman. Let me describe my professional activity. It consists in putting on different hats. When the doctor comes and wants a report, I explain what the patient is complaining about. When the boy is in my office, I explain to him what the magistrate thinks the magistrate is doing. When the legislator shows up, I outline what the poor tenant is too speechless to say. I'm what they call an administrator. I'm by no means convinced that this process of communication, as we call it, has any value whatever. But it's the best I know."

Terry courteously waited until the Warden had finished speaking, and then he got up and went rapidly up the aisle and out.

6

I called at the Infirmary and inquired about him. They assured me that they were treating him, or trying to. But when he was supposed to rest, he entered the handball tournament and wore his hands bloody. He missed two meals a day. There was no doubt that he was using marijuana. He couldn't hand in a finished assignment in class, though he worked hard in the library and took pages of notes. In brief, they were going to have to give him a leave of absence, till he got himself in better shape.

"Till he got *himself* in better shape—" I echoed. I wondered what clear and distinct idea was expressed by that form of words. But I said, "How will the other students take his being dropped?"

"The other students?"—Evidently it did not occur to them that there was a community of students.

"Won't they object?"

"You are misinformed," the counselor told me. "He's unpopular with most of the students. They won't miss him."

I doubted it. It was next to impossible not to put up with Terry. But I said, "Thank you," and went to have dinner with Irving, as apart from the rest as could be.

Irving was, as always, cheerful, though not about any foreseeable future.

I asked him for his formula. "How do you keep pitching, Irving, given what you know? You say, Stop! What you're doing is a catastrophe! And you even point out another direction. You see them continue just as before, only worse."

"It won't be in our time!" said Irving cheerfully. "Less than a hundred years ago small children were working in factories fifteen hours a day. There was no workmen's compensation for injuries. Trade unions were illegal. The Socialist platform for 1912 asked for women's suffrage, the forty-four hour week, the conservation of natural resources."

Irving was useful to me at a conference like this, when he touched my arm and cautioned me to bite on my pipe. He said that I was more effective when I kept my temper and behaved like a teacher, which I was, rather than a prophet, which I wasn't.

7

For three days we fifteen conferred and quarreled, framing a body of sentences that we could agree to and publish. It came out that there was only one thing that we knew, but we did know it, and it was this: All these problems—suburban flight and urban housing, narcotics and narcotics laws (as usual the laws were more of a problem than the delinquencies), lifeless jobs and a phony standard of living, traffic congestion and bad schools and segregation and the lapse of citizenly initiative—all these were only properties of the kind of community that we had. We came back to the same point. It was a peculiar experience to re-create that community out of statistics and personal frustrations, hour after hour for three days.

And the city sprang alive around us. As when the pigeons in their hundreds suddenly fly down from the eaves. Recollected, but not in tranquillity as in a poem, but in quarreling. Among friends.

8

On Thursday night, seated before the University at a very long table, we knew that we had come to a terrible Conference. We were like the Estates-General with their *cahiers* on the eve of the French Revolution. Every expert among us was convinced that, in his own department, the system of our society was unviable, it did not work, it could not last. And here we came together and it added up: *all* of it did not work, it could not last. This was terrifying. Yet not one person among us believed that we must be on the verge of a mighty revolution. There were no signs of it. Where was the impulse of fraternity that must sweep across the country (if only for a day) on the Fourth of August? and there would be dancing in the streets. Where were the people with their cannon trained on our chamber, demanding a solution of every problem before they would let us rise?

The students and the younger teachers had been conferring too, and they asked us some hard questions that we could not answer. Nevertheless, they bore with us patiently while we floundered. The probability was very high that most of us in Clarence Kellogg Memorial Hall were going to be killed by the blast, fire, or radiation of atomic bombs. Was this the cannon turned on our deliberations?

Some of the young people kept threatening to destroy themselves, even before the bombs. But this kind of blackmail stopped thought; it did *not* invite it.

Terry—this time he was wearing a gray woollen sweater and ordinary loose-cut jeans—they must have been to him like sackcloth and ashes—was sitting in the fourth row. He was close enough to listen intently to what we said in our natural voices, undistorted by the electrical devices. It seemed that he himself did not intend to say anything. Perhaps he no longer felt like an outsider and was not looking for the weak chink in our armor in order to strike. (I did not realize that at supper he had been given notice of his suspension from the University.) But finally, modestly —somewhat awkwardly, for he was not used to modest gestures—he raised his hand.

"Yes, Terry," I recognized him at once, assuming that, of us fifteen, it was my special role to recognize Terry.

He stood up, but even before he could speak, somebody from the back called "Dry up!" He winced, but began anyway in his unvital murmur.

"Louder, Terry," suggested the Warden from the middle of the table.

"Louder? Louder than this?" he asked, his face contorted with pain. He tried, but really could not be heard any better.

"No, no," said Irving, from my side. "You only think you're speaking louder. You're not giving it any breath."

"Try throwing your voice *away*, Terry," suggested the Sociologist, in his trained baritone. "Awaayyy—" he sang, exhausting his breath to the diaphragm.

As for me, I was buzzing with pride of us, of our band, who, although public men, were able to attend to what really mattered. Breathing.

And Terry obediently took a breath and spoke out clear and normally loud, though his voice was drenched with anguish, the following question that he had carefully prepared: "If I—and I don't think I speak only for myself—if I can't make it in this school and have to leave—and this school is not much different from the rest of American society (maybe it's even better)—what do you advise me, us, to do? Is my question clear?"

"Yes, Terry," said the Warden, "it is quite clear. The communication is perfect."

"Would you like to take that one, Judge Watkins?" I called out to Amy at the far end of the table.

"Noooo," she said. "I think I'll let that one pass too."

"Are they dropping you from the University?" asked Dr. Blumberg, surprised. "That's too bad. You're a bright boy."

"Yes, sir," said Terry, and raised a laugh.

"By the way," I asked, a question I was afraid to ask, "how old *are* you, Terry?"

"Twenty," said Terry, and sat down. The unaccustomed breathing, the use of his normally loud voice, had felled him with a wave of vertigo.

His answer hit me in the solar plexus. It was worse than I had feared. This callow youth, so excellently endowed, was not a boy of fifteen as he looked. He knew so much, he had never learned anything.

Yet he *had* asked a good question. And we up front were wise enough to know we did not have a good answer. Perhaps this was a step in the right direction, though it was not exactly dancing in the streets. At least that was Percy Shelley's theory, "If Winter comes, can Spring be far behind?"

9

My following, my particular students, crowded round me, to take me downtown for a beer. But I was due at a reception for us at the President's House, a prospect of futility and boredom.

Terry hung on the fringe, pretending to himself that he was observing, but wistfully including himself.

"Let's go," said Shep. "I'd be honored if you come in my Chevy." I loved him, he had strong black hair.

I said, "No. I have to go to the President's reception."

"Oh, no! Not tonight!"

"But you're going away tomorrow, dear!" said the darling girl hanging on my arm. She was, ironically, the daughter of Dynaflow Bombers.

"Don't press me, kids. You know I'd rather go with you."

"Then why don't you?" Immediately I felt the accusing look of them all (I thought) because I was not choosing freely as they expected me to (I thought).

"It's polite; he has to," said the darling, coming to my rescue.

"No, that's not the reason," I said, and I kissed her on the brow and shook her off.

The reason, alas! which I could not tell them, was that in my calamitous picture of myself I had to be their bridge, between them and the World. I was theirs but I was irrevocably a grown-up. I would be their champion; I was not their accomplice. By assuming this thankless role I took the joy out of my life. To myself, my excuse was that thereby I had survived.

Biting his lip, Terry turned away up the aisle. He could not take comfort in his peers.

I pushed past them and called, "Terry!" He stopped. Irving and the Warden were waiting outside for me, to drive me. "Did you want to speak to me?"

"Yes, sir."

"My plane leaves at eleven. I'll meet you at the book-store at eight-thirty and we can have a couple of hours."

Terry made a circle of approval with his thumb and the tip of his forefinger, like an ad for some beer or other; and this seemed to me so brainwashed, that I assumed he would not show. But he held the door for me politely enough.

10

It was only at our last breakfast, when we were taking down addresses and struggling with our bags, that we knew, wistfully, that it had been a beautiful Conference. When we were let down from our rational give-and-take, that came often to agreement—because we respected one an-other's honesty and wanted to satisfy his reservations—into the absurd mindlessness of the United States of America, the ignorant armies clashing by night. When we faced the bleak prospect of the unnecessary facts.

We clung to one another. We did not know the solu-tion of most of the problems that we had discussed, but they were not such very difficult problems but that we could pretty quickly improve our cities. Except that, in the cold light of Friday morning, we were not going to. We did not have the power, and it was not power that was needed, but public concern, intelligence, willingness to *do* it. We spoke in warm tones and touched one another's bodies.

It was Howard Green who said, "It's been a beautiful Conference," and we could have broken down and wept. I noticed that the despair that was in the back of his eyes when I first met him was in the back of his eyes when I shook his hand good-bye.

Harriet, however, seemed to carry our dismay lightly. When she casually shook my hand—I would soon run across her in New York—she suddenly pressed it, and she said, in a voice that I never forgot, the words, "We shall prevail."

11

I stood around the bookstore for over an hour, but Terry did not show.

burglars

1

At the airport, Harold told the three boys to go out on the Observation Deck and watch for the plane that his friend would arrive on. It would have two engines, and not be one of the giants. But Henry had already drifted away.

Chico was indignant at being exploited. Asked to look in the sky for an airplane.

With a quick lookout for the guard, Ramón was under the turnstile and up on the deck.

He was enraptured.

The airfield was full of airplanes. A jet was rapidly descending like a gigantic silver fish. Its roar from the distant runway swept across the field. A turbojet was rising like a yellow fish. The boy gazed in wonder. Though he was fifteen—his birth certificate said sixteen so he could drop out of school—he had never before seen the airplanes.

Tall and skinny, Chico—certificate eighteen, but unskillfully forged—decided that he might look in the sky anyway. But he disdained to duck under the turnstile because that was cheapskate. When Harold gave him a dime, he put it in the slot and stalked upstairs, like a tourist, a dandy in his narrow-cuffed purple suit, sharp tie, and hat with a three-quarter-inch brim. Unfortunately his character did not allow him to pick up English—one had to stumble in speaking and be laughed at—so he was humiliated instead by not knowing English. Yet his eyes too lit up at sight of the planes. He had to admit that they were impressive.

The sky was hazy blue; the planes like fish were pointing up and down the air, chalk-white, silver, red, and green. It was like a carnival. A little oil truck darted forth to meet the jet rolling in. The men stood ready to climb aboard her with their hose. Little Ramón was now down among them on the field, watching everything.

Harold roamed frantically about the concourse in search of Henry, who was not quite bright. Only last winter,

Henry had flown in on a plane, from San Juan, but he spoke neither Spanish nor English, being dumb. One could never tell from his gentle brown eyes and olive face whether he was uncomprehending or shy or sly. At last Harold found him, in a long corridor For Passengers Only, pissing against the wall, skipping back to keep his shoes dry. Maybe he didn't know which was the house and which was the street. He didn't know that people in the United States don't piss in the street either. There was always too much to explain to Henry. Harold was not sure if he grasped what one explained anyway.

In the middle of the concourse Ramón was calling wildly for help, wincing in the grip of a gray guard. He had lit a cigarette on the field.

"*Qué pasa? Qué pasa?*"—Harold hurried to the spot. The guard loosed his grip.

Henry came slowly after, his penis hanging out, still buttoning his fly.

"How in hell did you get down in the first place?" cried the guard.

Ramón had a glimmering of light. "Ooooh! I climb down de pipe!" he said proudly. He still could not understand the uproar about the cigarette. "I sixteen year old!" he protested. "*Mirá!*" He searched in his wallet and showed his document.

"Wha' hoppen?" said Chico. "Wha' hoppen?"

The board flashed Flight 701, from Columbus and Harrisburg.

"That's ours," said Harold.

"O.K., just go away," said the guard.

In his schoolteacherly way, Harold used to take them to see the world. Chico was the only one who never caused him trouble, but he was boring and not good-looking, and Harold predicted that he would be the first one to be addicted to heroin.

The tired man was, as always, touched by Harold's thoughtfulness in coming to meet him. But how did he come to be off work?

Harold explained that it was a Jewish holiday, the Feast of Weeks. Harold was not conceivably Jewish, but he had calculated that this was the most practical choice on the personnel form. He existed in a network of illegitimacies, many of them not even shrewd. A chronic mild anxiety protected him from cracking up completely.

Chico took the wheel, with a flourish, and with a sinking heart the tired man wished that Harold hadn't come to meet him. It was not that Chico was a bad driver—he was—but that he had no license, he was probably under age, and Harold simply could not afford to be stopped and questioned.

Harold began the sharp harassment of the youth that he considered to be a driving lesson, bumper-to-bumper, on the Pulaski Skyway, at fifty miles an hour. Below, the salt marshes and their industries stretched to the horizon. The dumb boy gazed.

In the back seat, Ramón was frantic to chat about the car thieves. He was in a frantic mood. (The old man wondered, and waited for him to break.) Pedro had stolen twenty-six cars! He was good at it because he went to the High School of Electric Trades and knew the ignition circuits. Carlos was envious of him, so he was too rash, and he was caught at the seventeenth car. Some of the others did not really compete. Chico—Ramón was a good observer—was not interested in the cars, but in rifling the glove compartments, in lighting the cigarettes and trying to read the letters, like a big shot, like the owner.

Chico didn't like to be talked about, and he said, "*Maricón!*" but he didn't dare take his eyes off the road.

"How many have been arrested all together?"

"Six." Ramón looked up with white eyes at the ceiling and ticketed them off. "*Dos por verdad.*" Two were not given probation.

Henry absentmindedly opened up the glove compartment and pocketed Harold's cigarette lighter.

"Put it back," said Harold. *"Dámelo."*

Henry looked at him with wide dumb eyes and gave him the lighter.

"You drove with Carlos; how is it you weren't caught when he was?"

"I di'n' go the last time. I see he is nuts. I was scared."

"Isn't Pedro scared?"

"No."

"No? Isn't he scared they'll catch him? I'd be scared."

"No. He don' care."

"Is that what he says? Or is that what you think?"

"Both. He say so. I think so."

"Why did *you* go ten rides, Ramón?"

"What else is there to do?" Ramón said, depressed.

3

He turned his head and looked at Ramón. The youth's false animation had subsided, had been deflated, just by being talked to, by being asked and answering a few questions with a coherent structure and some kind of relation to facts, instead of the vaunts and threats that the teen-agers spoke to one another as their only conversation. This much reality was too much for Ramón, and he was on the verge of a deep depression.

"What's the matter, Ramón?" the man said, and put an arm around him to comfort him. They headed toward, and past, a giant billboard, of a shiny blue Buick and an immense pink face. It proclaimed that thus was one competent and manly.

Ramón began to cry.

"All of them in this city," thought the tired man wearily, "if I hold them in my arms, begin to cry. They aren't comforted, they don't become jolly, they don't get sexy."

"Mi hermano se ha marchado," sobbed the boy.

Harold turned sharply around; he hadn't known.

"Maricón!" shouted Chico out the window, at the driver in whose way he had pulled out without a signal,

the moment that Harold was not holding him with his steely eyes. In Chico's opinion such drivers were cheap-skates and should be wiped off the road.

4

One could piece out Ramón's story. Whenever his father was dangerous, he used to take refuge at his brother's. There he slept on the floor. Through the peephole of a missing faucet in the wall, he could spy on his beautiful sister-in-law on the toilet. Once he saw her entirely naked. Once she saw (he thought) his gleaming eye looking through the peephole.

But it was finished, because they were dispossessed to build the new cooperative housing.

The tired man winced, knowing the particulars. On that site they were replacing 1,200 low-income units with a mixed-income project, to contain 150 low-income units. More than a thousand families were to be dispersed. En-riques, of the Puerto Rican Cultural Office, had organized the threatened tenants. They fought City Hall. They sat in at the Board of Estimate. They picketed the office of the Promoter. And the result of a year and a half of hard work by 500 mothers and fathers of families, was an increase of the 150 low-income units to 200 low-income units. Señor Enriques was deeply humiliated and lost face among his people. The tenants had done everything except the one thing they should have done, unite and refuse to budge. Now it was too late.

In disgust, Ramón's brother and sister-in-law boarded a plane and went back to Puerto Rico.

"Pull over," said Harold to Chico. "*Dejále la vez a Ramón*. It's Ramón's turn." He could not give attention like the older man, but he gave what gift he could.

The tired man started in alarm. Now there was a child at the wheel! The first squad car that passed would stop them, though Ramón was, in fact, a competent driver.

They were near the entrance to the tunnel, on the outskirts of Vanderzee. "Just drop me at the tube," he said, to cut his anxiety shorter. "It doesn't pay for you to take me all the way to New York and back."

5

Harold was glad to be rid of him. He had felt a twinge of jealousy when the older man put his arm around Ramón, and thereby he understood that Ramón was going to live with him in Vanderzee and become the center of his affections. Just to have somebody with him in his bleak home whom he could love, in the way possible for him. To talk to, worry about, eat with, and touch.

The ones that Harold could love were unpromising. They were the ideals of the period before his own growth was arrested by the Ice Age of the prison. Indeed, as his despair of happiness and his fear of impotence grew worse, the young fellows tended to become younger, seventeen years old, fourteen years old. Ramón was fifteen, but he stood only five foot three.

For Harold, felicity would have consisted in one of these kids sharing in the household work, washing a dish, not stamping out a cigarette on the floor. In being able to trust one of them with a couple of dollars to have supper ready when Harold came home from work. Such felicity was not to be had. The money was pocketed and the supper unbought as if the kid had forgotten that Harold existed.

With Ramón, Harold's sexual satisfaction had been feeble at best since the boy had hustled him on Union Square. It would now become worse, when Ramón moved in, and the little devil began to express contempt for Harold's frequent impotence, and to presume on Harold's effort to keep him there by making him come off. In this department, felicity for Harold would have consisted in one of the youth's wanting to go to bed at the hour that Harold had to in order to get to work in the morning. But it rarely worked out that way. Harold lay awake in resentment, and the boys tortured him because they hated the feeling of being pressured, and to prove their power over him.

Yet it was not possible for them really to be contemptuous of Harold; for instance, they never robbed him. Because his kindness to them was powerful and authentic.

He knew Ramón's father. (When the boy stayed in Vanderzee, it would be in due form.) Once when Ramón was missing, and not to be located even on the police blotter, Harold had driven his father up and down every block in Spanish Harlem, looking for him. He got him to the clinic all five times to cure a venereal disease. Another time he paid for a lawyer. It wasn't clear—it never could become clear—if the parents knew that Harold had sexual relations with Ramón. Maybe they took it for granted. They certainly had no illusions about Ramón's innocence. Most probably the case was that, since they were going to respect Harold as a solid citizen who helped them out, it was necessary for them not to think of him as sucking cocks. It was not easy to bring up a boy in Spanish Harlem.

Harold believed absurdly that each youth in turn would reform and get a job, and look forward to a practical future. He wistfully thought of one or another bright boy going back to school. If they stayed away from hustling Times Square for a week, he took it as a capital sign of improvement, not realizing that they were keeping away because of danger or terror, having rolled someone or because an alarm was out; and they would drift back at the chance of profit or excitement or for no reason; just as they drifted from sniffing model airplane glue at twelve, to smoking marijuana at fourteen, to taking heroin at sixteen. But Harold was careful never to let them have more than half a can of beer.

Like everybody else, Harold was all of a piece. At his work in the factory he practiced the same exquisite self-deception. His job was to inspect radio tubes, and he was expert. When he had the tubes all neatly ranged in front of him, methodically he could show you which bench had been at fault. He knew every different style of bad work. He was worth a big salary; he could have made the plant famous for precision. And if the defect happened to be in the machines, he dramatically reported it and always called the shot. Mostly, however, the defects were in the workmen, and Harold was unwilling to get anybody fired; so he settled for routinely reporting an average number of rejects in a plausible range of categories.

Yet he worked at this job contentedly anyway, while he patiently prepared himself to work on guided missiles. He was astonishingly lacking in vision. The job was meaningless to him, but he never conceived what it would be like to be a technician in a meaningful job in a meaningful world.

6

As soon as the car stopped, they again lost Henry. But Ramón, Chico, and Harold came upstairs and opened the door.

"Get—that—out—of my house," said Harold tightly.

Four of the gang were lolling in the kitchen, and in the middle of the floor were piled half a dozen cases of liquor that they had stolen early in the morning. They did not budge.

Harold blew up—in his manner.

They had opened one of the bottles—it stood half empty on the table—and the tall fellow, tilted back on his chair, took another sip from the cup without a handle. It was Pedro. Harold smashed him across the cheek and knocked him into the middle of the room.

A youngster, who was sitting on the floor leaning against the refrigerator, went green and vomited his pizza all over the floor.

"Clean it up," said Harold to Chico.

"*Yo?*" Chico was truly amazed. He had been faintly amused. "I di'n' do nothin'," he whined.

Harold slapped him across the face, briskly but not hard, just enough to hurt. "Go in the bathroom and puke," he said to the green boy. "Here's the mop," he said to Chico. "The pail is under the sink."

But Chico, though cowed, really did not know which end of the mop to use, while also gingerly trying to protect his cuffs. Ramón burst out laughing and took the pail out of his hands.

Harold corked the bottle of whiskey and put it away on the top shelf in the cupboard. There was no sense in wasting half a bottle of Forester. He was now at the top of his rage. He kept an ear cocked for strange feet coming up the stairs. He was thin-lipped. If necessary he would have wiped one of them out.

Shambling they began to carry the heavy cases through the front room to the door.

Purposely Ramón splashed the floor to get them wet, and they jumped. *"Maricón!"* But they restrained the automatic punch at the smaller, for instinctively they knew that he was the favorite.

The green boy flushed the toilet in the bathroom.

As he carried his box, Pedro muttered under his breath a threat that got louder by the square of the distance. But this was quite indifferent to Harold. "Where in hell do you think you're taking it now?" he said quietly. And his anger vanished away. "First take it up to the roof," he directed them.

7

With Pedro, who was now following an adored leader, he stole up to the roof. There was a little dumbwaiter-penthouse, good enough to hide the loot for a few hours. The gang began to carry up the cases. The sick boy had gone home. Ramón was wringing out the mop. Chico was sulking over his spotted pants, and soon he too got up and left. The two small boys kept watch at the stairs.

Once the stuff was out of his apartment, Harold discussed half a dozen techniques to dispose of it. But the bother was, he saw, that they were all such cool and hip performers that their manner screamed out their identity louder than if they wore silk jackets with embroidered totem tigers. He advised them to adopt the modest plan of staggered individual trips with a few bottles carried in paper bags. All that was necessary was to post somebody on the roof across the street, to watch for the cop on the beat, and signal.

They eagerly assured Harold that the fence was going to give them a splendid percentage. He suspected that they needed a manager. But it did not want to occur to him that they were swapping $150 worth of bourbon for a fix for three of them and a little sack of hasheesh for the baby.

He gave Carmelito, the little one, five dollars to buy sandwiches for lunch and pick up some extra bags. He knew that this money would not be stolen. For in the situation that he was not dreading his impotence, he was in control. For the first time in months, perhaps because he had blown up (in his manner), perhaps because he had seen Ramón good-humoredly mopping the floor, he was strangely calm.

8

Pedro tugged him into the other room, to be private.

Harold liked Pedro, not sexually. He recalled what he had overheard in the car, that Pedro was the champion of the twenty-six car thefts. He was impatient that such an intelligent youth should play such childish games, but they were always surprisingly childish. They fitted so poorly into our city that the best of them never learned anything. It was evident to Harold that Pedro must be successful with girls and perhaps even enjoyed his conquests. So Harold's habits would be a subject of neither temptation nor contempt to Pedro, so Pedro was not attractive to Harold.

"*Qué quieres, Pedro?*"

"There is no fence," said Pedro. "It's for shit." He spoke fluent English.

"Why are you telling it to me?" said Harold. "Don't you know to keep your mouth shut?"

"I don't know why I tell it to you," said Pedro. "You're my chief."

Harold deeply frowned. He was deeply disturbed. And at this moment Pedro would have cut his throat for Harold, because the chief was concerned for him.

Finally Harold said, "Look, Pedro. You're never going

to have enough money to support a habit. Then what? Every day?"—he gestured to the roof. "For *you*, Pedro, it's not necessary. *No es necesito.*"

And Pedro looked at him with the eyes of a horse who is praised. And he said, as if with conviction, "I'll kick it!" This Harold carefully did not believe.

Loudly Carmelito burst in, with the sandwiches and the correct change. "Is change!" he said proudly, giving it to Harold.

Pedro slapped him hard, to teach him not to interrupt the grown-ups.

9

As he watched at the window while one by one they carried away the bags, Harold was hot with his thoughts.

Stationed on the roof across the street, Carmelito was busily watching them fly kites. When he would turn toward the red kite, Pedro or Jaime would saunter out of the doorway, each time going in a different direction and looking as natural as could be. Harold had forbidden Ramón to take any part.

What a fortune he could make with a crew like that! thought Harold wryly. In a business that he was good at and that was stimulating, instead of inspecting radio tubes and studying for an examination in electronics. Only thing was—it wasn't respectable. It was *not* thus that he must return from the dead.

The carriers came back in about fifteen minutes, wherever it was that they went with the bottles.

It was a pleasure to watch especially the young ones, how they *used* the streets, the basements, the cars, the city, the store they robbed. Since everything was private property (and they had none), almost everything that they did was illegal; yet mostly they went with a vivacious air, a guiltless air, alternately paling with terror. Best was when they had reason to be proud. Then they shone. But the older adolescents were already boring, conceited, hip, one of them like another, stalking or playing it cool. They had lost the city. The city had lost them. They had no faith. Sexually, they came off in the head, like epileptics.

The Mayor's sound truck went rolling by, barking *Blah blah blah blah blah.*

Watching at the window with him, Ramón was bursting with pride because he was the insider, the favorite. At this moment he loved Harold as much as it was given him to love anything. He had a strong erection and began to rub against Harold's hand.

There went Pedro again, quietly descending from the roof. Then he came out the doorway below and disappeared around the corner. And Harold recalled the conversation he had overheard in the car: "Pedro, he don' care if he's caught. He say so. I think so."

At this moment Harold believed that Pedro would kick the heroin, simply because it was too trivial for him. Nevertheless it would not make any difference! He would get them to catch him anyway! to preserve his sanity, unless— unless there opened to him a path of glory. But Harold was unable to imagine any paths of glory, neither for Pedro nor for himself. He himself existed as if under a hood.

He was conscious of Ramón's lust and began to be anxious about his own.

at the lawyer's

1

Being a crowd, we were loud. We had come in force to the
lawyer's to help Meg win custody of the baby. Roger and
Harold had each brought a carload. Others kept arriving.
The lawyer, the distinguished white-haired dean of Meg's
distinguished family, was overwhelmed by the invasion. He
was impressed that the little girl had so many loyal friends
who were willing to swear under oath for her character,
even though we did carry on like in the lobby of the Living
Theater at one of our openings.

His office was conspicuously modest—some of the leather
worn off the chairs—like a rare great publisher's, where a
man of letters is still treated as a human being and possibly
a gentleman, rather than as a property or an accomplice in
manufacturing commodities. The name was Duyckman—
he retained the *u*—a cousin on Meg's mother's side, and he
was the kind of conservative who gave his time gratis to
cases of civil liberties. The signed photographs on the wall
were of Hughes and Taft. (Warren was still too green on the
bench.) There was, inevitably, a friendly inscription from
Holmes and, astoundingly, a niche for Hugo Black, a mere
babe.

We, on our side, had agreed that it was acceptable for
Meg to sue for legal custody of the child to avoid future
trouble. This put nobody in jeopardy and made her family
happy. Only Ray Johnson kept objecting. He was a pacifist
with sparse champagne-mouse hair, whom we never felt
easy with, and he kept insisting that we could not conscientiously sue in "their" court. But he had come along anyway, and was now the center of attention.

The counselor needed only three or four witnesses.
Meg started to introduce him around, to the tired man, to
Roger, to Harold whom she had come with, to Connie, to
Mrs. Fortescue, her oldest friend. But we were more than
twenty, and the lawyer said, "Come on, let's get going and

get this over with." He picked out Harold, who was well dressed, and he and Harold and Meg vanished into the inner sanctum.

There was a hush as the door closed. Next moment we were louder than ever.

Over at the window, we were quarreling around Ray Johnson. The window had a lovely fan and the room was lined with Constitutional Law. For some reason, Reggie Cameron was along—he was in the East for the first time in thirty years—and he was vehemently opposed to Ray's dichotomy between "their" institutions and "ours." From Magna Carta on, orated Reggie like a Wobbly, the court had been won by freedom-loving men with bloody sacrifice and stirring eloquence (his own was a ringing high baritone); therefore, we appealed in *our* court, even though at present injustice was being done there. No man had the right to renounce the inheritance of 750 years! The estate was entailed! Many of us had never heard Reggie; he had retired to Montana in 1932, when he decided that the communists were fraudulent. It was not clear if he intended to appear as a character witness for Meg, who was born after he left.

But he had hardly begun his tirade when the inner door opened and Harold reappeared.

"That was brief," we thought.

"Send Roger in, he said," said Harold.

"What went on?"

"I was disqualified by two years in Walla Walla," said Harold.

This announcement we greeted with a shout of delight.

2

Even at their introduction, the old lawyer had been impressed by Roger's brusque and manly way of shaking hands, as if he meant the amiable gesture—which Roger did, impressed by the lawyer's record. And when Roger took a seat and looked at him with his brooding and rocky face, the lawyer thought how powerfully that face would work on a judge or jury. He would get him to shave.

At the first questions, however, he found that Roger had the defect of his virtue. He was simply too honest to appear in a court of law. Asked what he did for a living, he explained that he got some of it by making bookshelves and some of it by stealing from the supermarket. Asked if he was married, he explained that he often couldn't stand his wife and so he bashed her on the jaw till she left him. But since he was very eager to testify for Meg, the counselor tried to explain to him that, in answering a question under oath, it wasn't necessary to be quite so explicit—suddenly Duyckman became ashamed.

"You're not a good witness," he said briefly. "Send in somebody else."

As usual, Roger's feelings were hurt.

"Try Mrs. Fortescue," said Meg. "I've known her for ten years, and that should be long enough."

"Look, Roger," said the lawyer, and insisted on walking him to the door, "you're *not* a good witness. I have to judge that as a professional. It's nothing against you. Do you play bridge? Why don't we get together some evening?"

"Yes," said Roger. "I like you," he said frankly.

3

Our tired friend, back from Columbus, joined the political discussion over by the window. The view was worthwhile.

It was Central Park South. The window looked out across the little lake, the Shakespeare theater, the trees of June.

"No, Reggie," he cut in, "you don't understand Madison and Jefferson. They weren't members of society, they *made* society. It was theirs. They made a revolution, and now they set to making up a world. They got their friends together and *did* it. That's what the Declaration of Independence meant: We—now—do it! it's only decent to tell everybody our reasons."

Reggie listened to this with an edge of contempt. He was convinced that intellectuals didn't understand the facts of life. "I'm interested in the man in the street," he said shortly. In 1932 he had organized the unemployed, until the Party stole the funds.

"Oh, maybe there weren't so many streets!" said the other impatiently. "Maybe there were more men." He tended to think of the citizens of the heroic age as congregational anarchists, speaking at the meeting, fighting a guerrilla war and going home to plow and harvest. And it was still, it was always, the heroic age. But it was not clear to us whether he thought of himself more as the Citizen or as the Guerrilla.

On the present occasion he felt, sadly, out of place. He would have liked to be a character witness for Meg, but there was no use in even interviewing him. For although he was widely respected in the schools and even in the middle-brow press, his unconventional life and his unconventional views were entirely public, and an opposing lawyer could have torn him to pieces.

Mrs. Fortescue reappeared. At once it was evident to all of us that it had been absurd to consider her. She was a large, good-looking woman, mother of three, properly married, and with a fine record of employment in the hospitals. But she was, quite obviously, a Negress. This sudden insight at once disposed also of Fred Stokes and Abe Jacobs, for they were quite obviously Negroes. (Abe was a Yemenite.) Not that they were not respectable people, nor even that there was a strong prejudice in the court against Negroes; but how did Meg happen to have them as such old friends?

Waldo turned pale. He too was disqualified. He was the secretary of the Greeley Society, a homosexual protective association. Among our friends it did not much occur to him that he was sexually deviant; but of course that would loom larger in a court of law.

Indeed, it was the reappearance of stately Mrs. Fortescue
that awakened us to the pattern of events in Counselor
Duyckman's inner sanctum. The truth was—it was not our
scene. One look around and it was plain as the north light.

By and large we were fine people. The lawyer would be
the first to say so. Many of us were useful members of a
pretty useless society. As a group we were even exception-
ally citizenly and responsible. Our great turnout showed a
fine loyalty to one of ourselves in need. (Ordinarily friends
appear like that from nowhere only at the funeral.) Yet the
question was whether or not there were many of us who
could be called on to be character witnesses for Meg in a
court of law, to secure her custody of her baby.

Glimpsing the pattern of it, we were drunk with hilarity.
We were not accustomed to seeing ourselves through the
eyes of the friend of Chief Justice Taft, and he in turn
seeing us through the eyes of the majestic law. For a moment the room was in silence—Ray had gone in—because
we were so choked with the comedy of it, of us, that we
could not explode. Little rills of laughter sounded. Our
eyes were blind with tears. We clung to one another to keep
from collapsing.

Nobody thought of continuing the political discussion.

As a matter of fact, only one of us had come actually
drunk. Steve Simak. He was affected this way by official
functions. It was how he had gotten out of the draft. When
he received his Greetings to appear, he went on a binge and
arrived for the induction in time to fall on his face. They
ordered him to reappear in two weeks, but the same thing
occurred.

5

In the inner chamber, Ray easily passed the preliminary
questions. He was kind of blond, worked for the Light and
Power company, was properly married, and seemed kind of
sexless. His father was a Methodist minister. Duyckman

couldn't stand him. He preferred every one of the others, and it hurt his self-esteem in the law to which he had devoted his life that he might be compelled to work with such a witness.

The underlying reality—which the lawyer was quick to gather, although it was never forthrightly said—was that Ray did *not* approve of Meg, he did *not* think that she was a proper mother for the growing child. He thought that she was a wicked woman. This offended Duyckman's family loyalty, as well as his considered judgment of a remarkable person whom he had known since she was a baby.

Then Ray sprang his surprise: "It's no use anyway," he said. "I have to tell you that I won't stand up and swear in *their* court."

"What?" said the lawyer, taken aback. "You *won't* testify? Then what the devil are you wasting my time for?"

"I felt it was my duty as a friend to let you know my opinion."

"Of all the god-damned crust!" said the old man. "What the devil do you mean 'their' court?" he barked. "It's *my* court. I was admitted to that bar. I am an advocate before that bench. I will thank you, young man"—Ray was pushing forty—"to get in hell out of my offices." His offices became plural. He rose.

But as soon as he was on his feet, he was visited, as by a recollection in a psychoanalysis, with the thousands of hours of his life that he had spent in defending the civil liberties of protesters and purists like this washed-out fellow in front of him, mild in manner and grating with spite like a file. They conformed in every way to the degenerate polity of the country; they suddenly drew the line at some odd milestone of their own conceit. Yet they were individualists. They were stubborn. He sat down.

"Forgive me, Mr. Johnson," he said. "You have every right to your opinion, and I shall be glad to defend the right when the opinion gets you into trouble. But as you see—I am edgy—busy." He held out his hand. "Will you please send in the next?"

6

When Ray Johnson came out of the office, Steve Simak fell on his face.

There was one loud guffaw.

Yet our mirth remained restrained. Our situation was dismally hilarious. It was not easy to be practical, and there we were. Our mirth remained restrained because it was not our scene. This was as plain as the north light.

But the real world did not consist of scenes. And there was only one real world.

And there we were.

No one thought of continuing the political discussion; nor, for that matter, of picking up Steve who was flat on his face. Ray, who was offended by the old man's rudeness and not mollified by his apology, took his hat and topcoat from the wardrobe and walked out without a good-bye.

Even this caused no comment.

Out of the magnificent northern-light picture window— the building had been designed about seventy years ago for fashionable studios—stretched the panorama of the park of Olmsted and Vaux, northward to the rocky hill, the reservoir, the water tower. A great stroke of city planning, that had kept mid-Manhattan from becoming an endless slum. But it was hard for *us* to be practical, and our mirth remained restrained, although from time to time there was a rill of laughter. Our situation was dismally hilarious.

Since Ray had failed to say, "Next!" there was a pause. Connie, in her sensible way, was the first to size it up, and she knocked on the inner door and went in.

7

With Connie, the lawyer saw that he was dredging the bottom of the barrel, for she looked like a wide-eyed child. Yet she was a sophomore at the University, came from a good family, was an experienced baby-sitter, and had known Meg for fifteen months. Above all, she made sense and she conveyed that impression at once. Anyway, it was a pleasure to talk to her, so he drew her out and felt better.

But finally she asked, "How long would it be before a case like that could come to court?"

He was surprised by the question. "Why do you ask? It depends. We are really covered as soon as we file. I suppose I could get a formal hearing in four or five months."

"Oh, but then I'd be very fat," said Connie.

"Oh?"

"Yes, I'm pregnant," she said.

"Oh. Well, that's not a crime. It's even considered to be the reassuring run of things."

"Yes, but—I'm not—we won't have been married by that time. You see, Jason is still married to somebody else. The other side could make a point of that against me as a witness, couldn't they?"

"Yes, dear, they could," said Counselor Duyckman.

He bent his head and hastily pulled out his handkerchief. The tears of joy were rolling down his cheeks. When he raised his eyes to meet hers, he threw his head back and let out the first loud and free laughter that he had enjoyed since the last time they resumed testing the atom bombs. Connie had that effect on her older admirers.

She too saw that it was funny.

"What do you predict?" he said to Meg. "How much danger is there that—what's his name?"

"Amos?" said Connie.

"—Amos will put in a claim?"

"But I *told* maman," said Meg petulantly, "that he wouldn't turn up. He went away to Israel. He *said* he was going to. Why don't people believe that people often do what they say they are going?"

This was a long speech from Meg. One of the reasons, in her case, that people didn't take seriously what she meant was that she didn't say it.

"Why didn't you tell me he isn't in the country?"

"I don't know he's not," said Meg.

"That I can easily check," said the lawyer, and jotted down a memo for himself. "Until I have—"

"Let's forget the whole thing!" said Meg joyously, completing his sentence. She continually completed other people's sentences. It was a way she had of proving that she was paying attention and that she too could competently take part in grown-up thinking. She was joyous because she had felt all wrong about a lawsuit and appealing in their court and all.

She flew out to us and cried, "It's all settled! It's all settled! We can all go home!" Clapping her hands.

8

Harold let the two off at her house. The tired man judged that it would be cruel to leave her alone after the ordeal at the lawyer's, so he agreed to come up for a cup of tea. She said she had "things to show him."

Jason, who had been baby-sitting, working on his thesis again, left at once, just in case they wanted to be alone to make love.

She did have things to show him, along with the tea. As always, she was excited to be alone with him. She was confident—it was not a tense situation like last week's—that they would eventually make love, for after a while he always became amorous. She thought that he was funny, or anyway she kept laughing. She slipped off her underpants in the bathroom.

And she brought out a family photograph album. (It had occurred to her at Duyckman's.) Snapshots of herself as a child, as an adolescent; of her much older brother in a sailor suit; her brother at West Point; her father in front of the Museum of Natural History, of which he had been a trustee until his death; their sailboat; a trip through Britanny with two schoolmates from Swarthmore—how the devil did she come to go to Swarthmore?—the three of them at Westminster.

He was puzzled. What was it about? It was almost as if she were boasting of her connections! But this was absurd, considering the connections.

There was a photograph of the Mansion on Dunderberg, where Great-uncle Rodney was immured with twenty servants. Cousin Duyckman and the President of the United States. He was at a loss. In spite of himself, he felt rising both his peasant resentment and his rather royal, lawgiver disdain of these merchants and rentiers.

The album was boring. He was not only resistant but indifferent. He stopped saying, "Who's this?" and "What's this?" And she at once became speechless. Soon he was extremely uneasy. What *was* she trying to say by this extraordinary performance?

He grasped it. She was saying that her people *too* had once been important and useful, though they were no longer good for anything. "You see," she said, "Uncle Rodney is senile and lives in the mansion alone. They take up too much room and keep other things from happening." Her odd small-girl sentence seemed to him to be very beautiful, like good Gertrude Stein.

She was showing him the pictures of her life in order to prove—if he would pay attention to them—that she was not nothing at all.

And there swept over him the grief of all the lonely of the world, into whose arms came never, or too rarely, the friend or lover or parent who could soothe their ache. This went on for years. It was too bitter to weep for. "Poor kid," he murmured spontaneously, not for her, not meaning it especially of her.

"Why do you call me that?" she asked, protruding her lower lip. She was intensely curious to know what was in the grown-up's mind about herself.

There arose a curious noise from the streets, like the clamor of a thousand sick bullfrogs in a marsh: *Blah! blah!* barked the Mayor's sound truck. *You gotta register the primaries!*

9

He drew her toward the couch and sprawled on it, and pulled her down alongside. It was faintly clear even to himself that he became amorous in order to push aside the other feeling, which was intolerable. (Maybe it is wise to turn to life when faced by necessity.) For a moment she resisted her impulse, but then she pressed her face in his chest and clung hard to him with her arms, her belly against his knee. He kept his head aloof because he did not love her.

But it was comfortable and soon pleasurable to hold her gently, and he moved his knee suggestively. She rubbed against it with a certain fierceness. She raised her head from his chest and looked at him fiercely.

Inevitably, since the real situation was always the same, their lovemaking always took the same form. He moved her arm so that her hand—one would not say she—touched his erection. Not so much that he took a masculine initiative, as that he gave her permission to go ahead, and please him. He opened the top button of his pants, and she fiercely undid the rest and extricated his big penis from his clothes and after a few frantic caresses—also looking at it as if it were remarkable—she sucked on it greedily. He liked her greediness. (His wife was unusually squeamish.) . . . She buried her face in his belly to hide; then she looked up at him fiercely, from her black hair.

After awhile he pushed her over onto her back and, raising her skirt, began to fuck her. He knew that she had removed her underpants because she was confident that they were going to make love, and this pleased rather than displeased him. He liked to be used. But he had no wish to undress her. For his own comfort he stopped and took off his own shoes and pants, and resumed.

During this, not a word was said, not a term of endearment.

Her excitement was high and her orgasm was active and strong. But always she displayed despair and fierceness—she would suddenly open her eyes and look up at him fiercely, from her black hair—because he would go away, he was not hers to keep, the occasion was infrequent, she was afraid to alienate him by pursuing him. Her pleasure would be paid for by many hours of loneliness.

His own pleasure with her was moderate but it was

animal, and he napped a few minutes, holding her. Then he began to put on his pants and shoes and proposed cheerfully that they have another cup of tea. He drew greedily on his pipe, which he loved.

But to his surprise, she skipped about the room in a kind of childlike polka. It was always the same, and he was always surprised.

unable to cry out, help

1

"It's Terry," said his young voice on the phone, "do you remember me?" When I heard it, I realized that I had thought he was dead. As he had threatened, or as I thought he had threatened.

"Yes, Terry."

"May I come to see you? Right away? It's important."

I told him I'd be home for an hour. I did not intend to wait this time. Naturally he made no reference to having missed the other appointment. Terry was not one to apologize.

When he must have been at the corner, Lucy trotted to the door. When the doorbell rang, Lucy barked frantically. Visits to our home began in pandemonium. You could not hear, you could not be courteous, until she retreated under the sofa. And yet today when I opened, contrary to her usual way with strangers, which was to back up slowly and yap yap yap, she went to Terry and stood up on him, and lovingly began to lick his hand.

"She knew that you were coming," I said, puzzled.

He had reverted to the red Jimmy Dean and black levis. He was pretty in the doorway, though not so pretty and striking as he seemed to imagine. I could see he was in a panic, worse than at Columbus. His green eyes burned at me from the shadow, beseeching in despair. His way of coping with this was to leer at me insolently, his posture slouchy, and flaunting his pelvis in my face.

But he bent down and petted Lucy gently, because Lucy liked him.

2

In spite of myself, I could not like him. Simply, his self-centeredness was insufferably boring, even though it was obviously his way of not falling in ruins. His unripeness set my teeth on edge. He had no subject but the biography of Terry.

I took him into my little office, my daughter's bedroom, but she was away at college. And for half an hour he bored me again with his inaudible voice at three hundred words a minute. I didn't much bother to listen.

Sometimes he boasted that he had fine talents, sometimes that he was the biggest fuck-up in the world. It came to the same thing. Evidently he was a fuck-up, but I didn't much believe in his talents. Except that his mind was quick, too quick, and his mimicry amazing. Like the fretful suburban mother of a twelve-year-old who has been left back, he informed me that he had a high I.Q. and was "underachieving." When he told of his great successes, and subsequent failure, as a student at the Academy of Design, it was evident to me that he had no art in him. He might, if he were not so mixed up, have become a good illustrator for popular magazines, but he had never looked at a good painting, old or new. He had a wide reading of bad authors buffeted by the modern crisis, with whom he had successfully identified himself and amalgamated an odd vocabulary of which no part was authentic. Sometimes this was comic. He was fond of words like "imbroglio" and "germane." I was for a moment puzzled by "mank"—"a magazine illustrator mank"—for *manqué*. I think this one, like "nuance," came from Mailer.

And mixed in with this stream of retelling many times retold, was a generalized reproachfulness that meant that it was all my fault. It was all my fault, except that his abandoned body in the easy chair where I had set him, and his flippant fingers that sliced the air like scissors, indicated that I was anyway beneath contempt.

Finally I could bear no more and I interrupted him. "I can't hear you," I said. "I haven't heard anything for twenty minutes."

"Yes, you have!" he insisted, loud enough.

"Maybe. An occasional word like 'imbroglio.'"

He said another sentence too much trouble to make

out. He was uneasy that he might not really know the meaning of "imbroglio."

"Didn't hear that either," I offered.

"Then why don't you try to listen?" he said insolently.

At this, I suppose, I should have slapped his face and let him flash his knife or try his karate—he was frail, but likely to go berserk—but instead I said, "Why bother? Everything you have said so far is boring."

He was not boring, and I did not want to cut the visit short. But what did I see in such a fool? He was foolish so that one was embarrassed for him. I was drawn to him. The attraction was not sexual, for he did not have any animal vitality either. Yet it was as if physical. I was drawn to him as, in the old novels, people instinctively embrace their own flesh and blood. He was my problem.

And my little spaniel's behavior was remarkable. She went to him and stood up on him and kissed his face, and she came to me and leaped up in my lap and kissed my face.

3

Abashed by my harshness, he did speak a little louder and thereby came to say something about present facts. For an instant he actually looked at me with his shifty green eyes. I hoped that he would now explain his panic, that was real. But he couldn't; the reality did not cohere. He was still in the nightmare.

I tried to piece it together. When he was expelled from Columbus, he had hitch-hiked home through the night to Akron. (He seemed to have forgotten about attending the last session of the Conference. He had blotted it out. His sober mood of then did not fit with his red-jacket mania.) In Akron he had—his language now was—to "consummate" the "strategy" of "seducing this chick." The "bit" was to feed her pot. They then stole her father's car. There were police on their trail. But she "happened" to be driving, so he got off. The "nuance" was that he had got sick to the stomach and the sex had been a fiasco.

He told all this in a chaos of pride and terror, racing through the night. But alas, the fact that it had a relation to reality and that to him it was grippingly alive did not make it any the less boring, for the reality itself was trivial. It had no lust; it had no destination; it came to the fact that he could put his foot down on the gas pedal and be afraid that he was driving too fast. I stopped him again.

"Terry," I said, "shut up. Try to remember something for me."

He looked up at me obediently.

"It was Thursday evening that you were expelled—" We were now at Saturday.

"I *wasn't* expelled," he said firmly. "They just suspended me until—"

"Do you remember that you attended the Conference on Thursday night, when all fifteen of us were on the dais?"

"Yes," he said dully. He saw that I thought he had completely flipped. He himself was afraid that he had completely flipped. "I asked a germane question," he said, "you and Green said that it was a germane question." He hesitated. "I don't remember what it was."

"You made an appointment with me for yesterday morning at the bookstore. Why didn't you keep it?"

He flared in anger, caught with the goods. Then he stared at me glassily. "Did I?" he lied.

"You're lying, Terry. Never lie to me. You're lying now when you say you don't remember. You were lying then when you made the appointment."

"No, I wasn't lying then," he said flippantly. "It was a dialectical promise." (Again something of Mailer's.)

This time I did slap him. But not for real. It was the kind of slap that one gives to a drunk to get him to come home, or to a stupid belle who has decided to make an impression by swooning. For me it did nothing at all.

I did not say what I should, for my own peace, have said: "Who do you think you are? You have insulted me by making me a dialectical promise. You do not recognize *my* existence as a person. Now get out of my house."

Naturally he did not understand my flaring up. If anything, he was pleased that he had got a rise out of me.

74

I had a job with the youth of America, that I was failing and would no doubt continue to fail, while our civilization was drifting toward the explosion that made this job
ludicrous, and the only job relevant. I was surely the wrong
person for it, but for various reasons I cared. Anyway, they
sought me out; I had no choice.

Here he was. This boy had lost touch with the Western
tradition. Beginning somewhere in the first half of the
twentieth century he could no longer be taught it. He tried,
but he was not going to learn it in college. The colleges do
not even bother to teach it.

Maybe it is a good riddance, for our tradition has badly
disgraced itself, it has come to deserve little loyalty. But
what will he do then? For the fact is that, although he has
lost the thread of what it means, he still has had to grow up
here, into the institutions and among the spectacular junk
that we in the West have engendered. We no longer have a
city, but he certainly has had an urban environment. Yes,
he has! a chaos, sometimes bland, sometimes horrible, never
inspired on by justice, art, or our peculiar Western virtue
of disinterested scholarship.

Listening to Terry, I could hear that he had never
studied a subject, never lost himself in a stroke of art or
discovery, never acted like a citizen. He did not even aspire
to such things, as if he recognized that they existed. This
was what made him boring. There was nothing but the
biography of Terry.

But there was something worse than his emptiness. He
was not empty but crammed. It was that he regarded the
detritus of our culture, the world of TV or Hollywood or
even the advertising, as if that were the normal lively world.
He did not have enough common sense, or confidence in
himself, to look directly at the street. If a scene was on the
TV and had that official warrant and interpretation, he had
the courage to think that it was real; otherwise he doubted it.

But then when, inevitably, he became nauseated and
disillusioned with such an unsatisfactory reality, he pathetically began to assume that there was a secret meta-

physical truth in the disillusioned French and Italian movies, the stereotypes of Harlem and hipsters, the ideology of hasheesh. He desperately wanted these too to be on TV, in order to make sure!

He was in a dilemma. He did not know whether the phony world of the conventional mass media was real, or the reactive world of the offbeat mass media. He decided that the Way must lie in the dialectical interplay between these two figments, each of which was trivial, and both taken together adding up to less than nothing.

I was wrong to be angry when he lied or was irresponsible to the existence of anything, including me. By what standard of existence should he judge? He had so little reality to be truthful to, and so little self of his own to *be* responsible.

I had the impression that, wherever he was, he was no longer there but continually on his way to the next appointment, for which he would also be irresponsibly late. He was worst when he tried to be frank; then he was not there at all.

Yet I hated liars. They robbed me of *my* space and time.

5

"Well?" I said coldly. "What should *I* do about it?"

He looked at me blankly.

"Don't play dumb," I said. "You rang me up. You've come to my house. You must have had some reason."

He flinched at my tone. "You know," he faltered.

"I know? I don't feel like guessing."

He swallowed. "I thought—I thought at the Conference, when you—that you—that if I needed any help—you know —I mean—"

"Oh, thanks," I cut him short. "That's another remark in the biography of Terry. Chapter XV, *Thoughts of Terry at the Conference.*"

There was a pause.

"I don't dig, you know," he said at last. "I was trying to tell you. I mean."

76

He was now going to say "you know" "I mean" compulsively in every sentence, because he did not mean, and someone ought to know.

"You keep on telling me about yourself. But what the hell should *I* do?"

"I was—you know—I was trying to tell you!"

"No, you weren't. Repeat the sentence and listen to it."

"What sentence?"

"The one about Terry at the Conference."

He was sincerely puzzled. There was a trace of perplexity on his usually thoughtless brow. "Should I repeat it? I thought—at the Conference I thought—that—"

"You see? *I* thought, if *I* needed help—"

"But I do need help!" he implored me. "You know what I mean."

"Another sentence in your autobiography!"

6

Suddenly he was aware of the form of the sentence. "Oh! you mean—I see what you mean. *I* thought, *I* need. Yes, it is a sentence about me." And he smiled, beautifully. His entire face was transformed. I had the feeling that he had not been aware of any simple reality in months, maybe years. Like everyone else, he was delighted to learn something. But he was very hard to teach.

His eyes clouded. "How else could I say it?" he asked me, dully.

"There!" I said. "You just did ask me something! How to ask. But I won't tell you. Find it out yourself."

He fell silent. It was like pulling teeth. I was bored to death with him, and I was on the verge of telling him to go home. "Well?" I said with that feeling, which conveyed.

"What the hell do you want out of me?" he said surlily. In a pinch he would get himself thrown out, before I dismissed him.

"What do *I* want out of *you?* That's great. Jesus, Terry,"

I taunted him, "you must want *something* of me, otherwise you wouldn't have come all this way. Why don't you speak up and tell me all about it?"

"*I told you!*" he nearly screamed. His voice was normally loud. "I want you to help me out!"

"Another sentence in your autobiography! Terry wants! Terry wants! Terry wants a cracker! Terry wants a cracker!"

7

He began to fall to pieces before my eyes. He truly no longer knew how to speak to anybody as if the other person existed independently, not according to Terry's ground rules. He did not know how to ask a question. He did not know how to make a demand. He could not tell you something that *you* might really want to know. It was too risky. Maybe the other one, I, would not know the answer or would refuse the demand. (And in fact, maybe I would refuse!) Maybe he no longer knew a truth about himself to tell.

He broke into an icy sweat. His flesh was mottled white. He looked at me with eyes blazing like jewels. His mouth fell open. When it became evident to him—but I say it to my shame, he was wrong—that he was going to have to talk directly to me or not at all, and to treat me as somebody existing in time and space, his speech deserted him altogether. He began to utter meaningless sounds like a cretin. One felt that he still wanted to say "I! I!" but all he could get out was "Uh . . . uh . . ." Then he began to stammer, "W-w-w-w- . . . h-h-h-h-" and he began to be asphyxiated.

Next moment he had recovered with aplomb, and what little color he had flowed back into his cheeks. "I dig!" he said excitedly, "the bit would be to say 'Help me.' Is that it? 'Will you help me? I need help.' Is that what you want me to say?" He looked at me like a bright boy for approval.

I was astounded. What had happened? Surely he didn't expect to get away with indirect discourse? But of course that was how he existed, in indirect discourse. Playing the role that I expected of him, in indirect discourse.

He was now a thousand miles from saying, "Help me." And all of him was shouting out, "Help! Help me!" and, "Tell me what I mean."

8

He was not shrewder than I, but I was not shrewd enough. I did not think, when I was gazing candidly at his suffocating face, that he could see my face, and that a shadow of distress had passed across it. As soon as he saw this, his spirits rose. He saw I was a coward, no true surgeon. I was gentle enough and precise, but not finally firm. Maybe he would get off! He would please me. He would rescue *me*. There was sweat of relief on his face.

But the case was different than he thought. If I let him off—I did not know if I would, I did not know my own nature—it would not be because of pity but simple decency. It was that I was not going to be responsible for Terry, not then, and never, never, never. Because I didn't like him, though I came to love him dearly. I didn't trust him and so I would not let go with him. Not even to take him through his asphyxiation and make him breathe, as you slap a baby hard to make him breathe.

I was kindly, and we had gone far enough. I was not willing to humiliate him by forcing him to cry out *Help!* to one who, when the emergency arose, might not come across. It is better to drown in silence than to drown shouting to someone watching you from the shore.

Instead, following the impulse I did have—for again, as with Meg, I cowered into sexuality—I crossed over to him, took him by the hands and drew him to his feet—he rose wondering—and tightly embraced him. His body stiffened. I kissed him several times warmly and pressed my lips into his neck. He shivered with excitement and threw back his head and faintly cried out. He had a delicious smell. With high excitement Lucy, my little black spaniel, leaped up on us, as she did when there was any embracing, trying to get between, to be included, nipping at our ankles and our flies. Yet I was not going to topple him onto the couch, lie on him and hold him close and kiss his delicious neck until I would come off. My wife was in the other room. I was not willing to give myself to a moment of simple orgasm with him anymore than I was willing to risk being responsible for him. Because he was a liar.

Nevertheless, it was a relief to me to have expressed my sudden desire, and I sat down flushed, breathing deeply, and embarrassed. "Shut, Lucy!" I said. "Down, Lucy!"

9

He was leering and his mind was racing an obvious path. In big type and as easy to read as *Dick and Jane*, he was rapidly conceiving and even sketchily rehearsing his hipster strategy. Since I was queer for him, and he trusted me, he could use the opportunity to explore a new scene, which he had up to now been timid to venture. Besides, he could exploit me. There would be trips in airplanes and the company of Deans. He was already shining as my *protégé* —he had the word somewhat confused with "prodigy"— and now they could not suspend him. I would launch him in the world of TV. And because I was by definition to be disdained, he could escape from his fear and awe of me.

Busy with these plans, he was unaware that his fingers were trembling and that a tide of almost normal rosiness was creeping to the roots of his hair.

At this, he became aware that I had mussed up his hair-do. Again to my amazement, he became genuinely upset and angry. Coldly, without a word, he went to look at himself in the mirror on the wall, whipped his comb out of his back pocket, and—was I seeing things?—he proceeded, for fully five minutes, to primp and repair the damage in the mirror, replacing each strand in a way that, so far as I could perceive, did not make any difference whatever. I did not know whether to laugh or cry.

When he sat down again, his manner was friendly and confidential. He made a thing of petting the dog and saying, "Lucy." Unfortunately for his interpretation of the situation, he kept batting his eyelashes without knowing it. And he said, "Well?"

This time it was I who looked and said nothing.

"*Will* you help me?" Now that he had worked out the scheme of our relation according to his ground rules, it was easy for him to say, "Will you help me?" He could even have loudly shouted, *Help! Help!*

I weighed it. I looked at him. Our eyes met. I looked awhile into his eyes that had no moral courage. Whatever he saw in my eyes, his eyelashes ceased to bat.

I shook my head and said, "No."

"No?" His voice was weird. Was that what I had said?

"No, Terry, I won't. I'd like to fuck you. You see I think you're attractive. And I hope we get to be friends. But I am unwilling to be responsible for you because I don't like you."

He was staring at me like one who has been betrayed. Tears slowly welled into his eyes. They were not tears of hurt feelings, for he was on the other side of humiliation. Having tricked himself—I did not trick him—he had authentically asked me his question and done me the honor of treating with me as existing. And with horror I saw that I *had* betrayed him. Tears slowly rolled down his cheeks. I was to betray Terry at other times, but it would never be any different than this first time.

It was hard to take seriously that this sneaky child was twenty years old.

These youth had to grow up on something. I had influence among them because, although I paid attention to them, I had a life of my own. I was not interested in being a leader of any one toward anything. It was already beyond my powers, or will, to be a father for my own children. I did take these youth seriously. But I did not take seriously, although I saw it with my own eyes and knew the causes with my own intellect, that some of these youth were desperate.

I was in distress at what I had done, though I would not have done otherwise. Sorry, I reached for the phone and called Arabelle, and set up an appointment for him at the beginning of the week. She bent my ear off with questions, but I said only, "You'll see, you'll see. He's in my office now."

"All right, so long, good-bye," said Arabelle. She was a Berliner.

"Here is a woman for you," I said to him, "who is the best psychotherapist in New York City. She'll help you. Can she bend my ear off! Do you have any place to live, Terry?" I asked.

He explained, in a flat but audible voice—he had stopped weeping—that when he came to New York he rented a room in midtown, for twenty-five dollars a week, and lived there alone. I could picture him in that room. There he was.

I phoned Harold and told him to put Terry up for a week and to help him find something in Vanderzee, with a kitchen.

11

Matter-of-factly I mussed up his hair-do, as if forbidding him ever to make it up again, and I put my hands on his shoulders and kissed him once on the forehead. "I love you, Terry," I said, "but I won't be here anyway. My wife and I and Hugh—he's my boy—are going on a trip. Maybe all summer." The dog came leaping and I petted her. "Yes, Lucy, yes—you're going too. We won't be back till September."

"Where are you going?" he asked with, to my surprise, unfeigned interest. I did not realize how important I was to him, and that all the details were important.

"Just away. From here. From you. From the Conference on delinquency at Columbus, and from the Department of Community Planning in Berkeley. From quarreling. From the World-Wide General Strike for Peace. We'll just go driving north. From the White House Conference on Rural Redevelopment. From the interpersonal relations that oc-

cur in Vanderzee. From Harold's little junkies in Riverside
Hospital. Among the Laurentians! Terry, it's amazing how
a person who is so essential for the life of the Americans
can vanish for three months in the summer, and everything
goes on just as it did before. I think we're going to drive
north. Also up the Saguenay; we've looked at the map.
Yes, Lucy! You're going too. North! Away from my monthly
commentary on WLSR, the Listener-Supported Radio. Away
from the Fathers' Club at Junior High School 6. From
quarreling—Terry! Help me! Lucy!" And I began to cry,
silently, not bawling, but as if I could never stop, for my
weariness; because it was peaceful to lay my hands on
Terry's shoulders. "Yes, you do help anyway," I said.

I did not know that meanwhile, while I was complaining, there was forming in Terry's soul, as happens with
generous young fellows befitting their age, a quixotic and
quite impossible resolution, that somehow he was going
to make me sometimes happy. He set his mind on this. I
was his Project.

part two

part two

eagle's bridge

1

They stopped the car by the bridge and went down to the riverbank to eat lunch. The rapid stream swept onward past its dark pool. On the map the place was Eagle's Bridge.

Across the river stood a white substantial house. A barn-red general store was across the road from their car.

Gladly the little black dog leaped out the car window even before they stopped, and waited for them, looking back, and preceded them down the steep path that was obscured by flowering bushes. When they came, she was lapping the water.

Suddenly in the dark pool, under the bridge, the man saw a great dark bass looking out at them. It must have been thirty inches long. Excitedly he called out to the boy —the fish turned and vanished in the depths—"Hughie, here is a fish this big! I think it was a bass." Hugh came, but there was no longer a fish to be seen.

"Why don't you go get your line and fish him?" said his mother.

The father, the mother, and son were pleasantly wasting the last week of their summer driving across mountains and lakes of the Northeast, and they might as well loiter an hour here as elsewhere. Eagerly Hugh climbed up through the flowering bushes to get his rod from the car, while the little black dog followed him halfway up, but then ran back to the others on the shore, for her business in life was to shepherd them together, hastening nearsightedly to each one and leaping on him, doubling back to make sure. She was always bewildered. They stopped the car so often that she could not judge if they were now going to get in again and drive off; but she had to be in the car first, as if to make sure that she was not left behind.

But Hugh returned and began to fish with a red- and silver-striped spoon for the dark master of the pool under Eagle's Bridge. It would have given him quiet satisfaction

—that's how he was—to catch the great fish that his father had seen, and his father would have been proud of him. "Maybe I ought to use a worm," he said judiciously. His father thought so too, and began to scratch with a stick for some worms, but the soil was wet and sandy.

Polly, however, climbed up the steep path through the flowering bushes. In her practical way she was going to get a tablespoon from the car and dig up above where worms were likely.

There was a pause of silence on the bank of the river sweeping under Eagle's Bridge, and one could hear the gentle waters and the breeze in the leaves of the willows. Hugh was fishing in the pool where somewhere in the submerged rocks was lurking that great fish, while the red-and silver-striped lure flicked on the surface.

Then Polly's voice called out from above, "Please come up here at once." It was the deep and strained voice that she had only when something was very wrong and must be attended to. She had used it when the house was on fire. The husband did not hesitate but climbed up the steep path through the bushes with foreboding. He could not imagine how she could be hurt—her voice did not sound like that. Was it the car on fire? It was an old and abused car.

When he emerged, he saw her seated on the concrete foundation of the iron bridge, holding in her lap their little black dog Lucy. Blood was slowly dripping out of the dog's mouth onto Polly's white-and-black print skirt. Polly's face was set in despair. The dog's head did not sit right; her eyes were closed and she was dying. Beyond, through the bridge, could be seen the black car that had hit her. It had stopped at the other end, and the driver was walking back across.

"Her heart is still beating," said Polly.

"What shall we do?"

It was their little Lucy with her beautiful glossy coat that had, on this trip, become more full and glowing every day. The man reached out his hand to touch her fur.

"Don't touch her!" said Polly unaccountably.

"Why shouldn't I touch her?" he cried.

The tears welled hot in his eyes. He turned away to look down from the bridge. "Oh, Christ," he said, "how are we going to tell Hughie? . . . She loved me so."

She loved each of them in a different way, as dogs do. When he came home she jumped for joy and bounded from room to room yipping and came back, and could not stop, trembling and frantically wagging her tail, until he bent down and let her kiss his face.

Hugh was below, happily fishing the pool. She was his first dog.

Polly sat with despair on her face, and her heart was bleak. As if peacefully, the little black dog lay in the woman's lap, in her arms. The man touched her and she was still warm. Her eyes were closed. The blood ceased dripping from her mouth.

"I crossed the road to dig," said Polly, "I didn't think she followed me up—" They had always been extremely careful with the dog—just for this—shouting at her, grabbing her by the collar, putting the leash on; for she was always impetuously leaping and bounding.

2

The driver came up to them. He was white-haired and had a lined, rather hard face and frightened eyes. "Whose dog is it?" he asked.

"It was our dog," said Polly.

"I stopped right away," said the driver. "We have a law in this state—"

"It's all right, mister," said the husband, "there's nothing to do about it now."

"I stopped right away," he said.

"It's all right, mister," he said harshly. "You just go on your way."

The driver hesitated.

"You just go away," he said.

He went, but one did not notice him going. Probably the dog had leaped out from behind their parked car.

"I heard a thud," said Polly. "I knew right away that something—"

"Let's bury the dog," he said. He hesitated. "All right. I'll go down and tell him." And he directly went down the steep path, pushing through the flowering bushes, with the definite steps with which one does a fatherly duty. The car had swiped the dog on the side of the head and she must have felt no pain at all. It was not as if her back had been broken and she had screamed—so the man tortured himself on his way down.

The boy was out on a little point of land around a copse of bushes trying to disengage his line that was caught in the rocks in the depths.

"Hugh, come here at once. I have to tell you something."

She had always been a happy little dog. And she looked so sweet there, dead in Polly's lap. She had really loved only three things: them and food and to sally forth in the world triumphantly barking, holding her feathers high. Of these she had had plenty.

"My line is stuck," said Hugh.

"Break it off."

3

The boy came edging around the copse of bushes with his rod, trying to keep his shoes dry. His father told him that Lucy had been hit by a car and was dead.

"Do you want to come up and see her?"

"No! No!" He turned away and sat in the bushes, getting his shoes wet, and began to bawl.

"She—She looks all right—" his father began to explain, but left him and went back up the path.

"He won't come," he said to his wife.

He went across to the general store to buy a shovel, and they began to look to see if they had one in stock. "My dog just got hit," he said, "and I want to bury her. Can you lend me a shovel?" he said.

"Take the shovel outside by the barrel," said the storekeeper.

"Where shall we—" said Polly, when he came across to her with the shovel.

"Down by the river," he said. "You'll have to come down with the dog. Can you get down the path carrying the dog, or shall I—"

"No, I will," she said.

He began to have strong flash-memories of the dog—leaping, always leaping, high up in the air to catch her ball.

The boy was sobbing, hidden in the bushes, in the sullen and withdrawing way that he sometimes had.

It was hard to dig in the stony sand. He had picked a spot above the usual flood line, in a little clearing behind the copse of bushes where the boy was sitting with his feet in the water. But of course the spring torrent would flood the grave out.

When Lucy would get the ball, she trotted off with it triumphantly and would try to keep it away from them, even while she came back, wanting them to get it and bounce it again. She was bewildered, torn between the twin desires of having the ball in her own possession and playing catch with her people. Finally she would come to terms with love and lay the ball at their feet. But sometimes she would trot spiritedly with it in big circles, triumphantly waving her plume. They thought she was like a circus dog.

"Dig it deep," said Polly. She was there, carrying the body of the dog, whose eyelids now had fallen half open. Her black-and-white print skirt was spotted and blotted with blood. He took off his shirt and cut away into the stony sand.

Then there was a gray hole and its heap of stony dirt, and the dog was lying in the hole drawn up in a fetal position, as in those uncovered graves of primitives, of the little children of primitives. The dog's head did not sit quite right; her eyes had the glazed look of a dead dog. But her coat was burnished like black fire, and the auburn in it was shining through. They had never seen it so beautiful. The fur was still alive. In that gritty hole she lay like a glowing star. "Shall I make the boy come?" said the father. Polly looked at him with a face of despair.

"Come, Hugh," said the father firmly, "bury your dog."

To the father's relief, the boy let himself be taken by the hand. He took the shovel.

4

While the boy was shoveling the dirt, the father had the thought to get some rocks to pile on the grave. He pulled and tugged in vain at a big stone rooted in the sand, but he collected a few stones big as a football and big as a fist. He wondered about his grief. Perhaps it was two things: first, of course, the pathetic truth that this dog had been the only thing in the world that simply loved him and showed her joy when he came. But secondly—and to this they would all have agreed—it was that she had such a lovely spirit, whether human or not, leaping and eager, indefatigable, wanting to come along and be included, obviously joyful when the least occasion offered (and there were many); and also bewildered—that was an important part of it—perhaps even a little stupid, for she was only a dog. O our little Lucy!—he was surprised by tears as he bent over to tug at a stone by the riverbank—who had been so animated and happy and persistent to get close and in-between and be included, whose heart was nothing but love. At first she had not been the kind of dog he preferred; but she had won everybody by the spirit in her.

It was happening terribly swiftly, thought Polly. Hit and dead and buried by the river, and off to drive away. One did not have a chance to take it in.

Very thoroughly, as if it were a duty that he willingly took on himself, Hugh was filling up the hole with the big shovel. And now the boy and his mother were placing the stones on the little grave.

Was the great dark fish looking out at them from his pool? Or was he simply lurking, in his meditation, in the depths among the rocks. That dark fish, he flashed in an image, like a spirit of death. And if only they had not seen him, and had not had the thought to fish for him when they stopped for a rural lunch! And Polly said: "I wasn't thinking about the dog at all when I crossed the road. We were always so extremely careful."

There they were. Standing. It is a little round grave piled with a few stones. Down under the right of the bridge just off Route 22, until the spring torrent washes it away.

"She was always a happy little dog," he said, to say something.

"Yes, because we were always very good to her," said Polly. Especially she.

"Let's get away from here," said the boy. He did not want to talk.

The man climbed up to take the shovel back to the store, leaving the woman to collect the gear, while the boy wound up his broken line. They were in bleak silence. Their party was empty of its spirit, and they did not want to do anything except drive the two hundred miles home as quickly as possible. Their car was not going to be crowded anymore—it was without its little pest who took up more than her share of the room and kept snuggling into the front seat, annoying the driver.

"It was too sudden," said Polly. "One moment she was there, and the next moment she is not." It was too quick, the way she died and they buried her and were driving away in the car without her. They did not have a chance to take it in.

For a couple of months they had come on a long and somewhat hazardous voyage, over high mountains and some bad roads. It was as if they had to offer some sacrifice. And so they stopped at Eagle's Bridge, and the man saw that cursed death looking at them from his pool.

"I'll drive," said Polly stolidly, still wearing her face of despair, as if she thought that he, if he drove, would be desperate and reckless. He gave her the keys.

in a poolroom

1

It was typical. Having again and again thrown it away and put himself impossibly behind, Terry was now going to run out the game after all. With twitching fingers he finally took the butt from the corner of his mouth and laid it on the rail, and with elegant address he aimed the five-ball for the long diagonal that he was not going to miss. Moment by moment, the demonic power kept pouring into him, with which he made his brilliant saves. These were the lurid and orgastic moments for which, like an addict, he plunged into the seedy and to him sinister storefront on Eighth Street, whose window was painted black. He shone like Lucifer in his pride.

The door opened and he was found out. It was Jason. The family had penetrated his underworld! Violently his twitching fingers began to tremble. He goofed it. With a snort the hood, who had been about to lose the game, grabbed his stick to make short work.

Terry saw that there was not even a men's room to hide in. He looked about him wildly. His face was like white paper. There was nothing to do but be cool and face it out, but it was hard to be cool when interrupted at the epileptic moment. Despite himself, as Jason approached, his eyes became blazingly evasive. He was in a state of sin, burning up like a piece of paper, the invisible ink of his double life appearing.

"So I shows my aces full an reaches for de chips!" croaked a voice in the silence, "de man produces four sevens!" It croaked with relish, with enthusiasm, the high point of a human career.

"Play pool, punk," said the hood. In his greed, he had also bitched it, though it was now a set up. He stank. Between Terry's deprivation of Grace and his opponent's general inepitude, it was the worst pool ever shot in Vanderzee.

"Hiya," said Jason to Terry, and proceeded on back to the bookie who was sitting in a swivel chair with his feet up on the billiards table. Nobody played billiards anymore.

Harold had not yet come in, on his way home from work. Jason passed the time by cheerfully ribbing Dominic about last night—the bookie owed him fourteen bucks. But what burned Dominic up was not that Jason won but that he waited for Harold's tips and won, while Harold never bet with him but went to the track. (And at the track, after the long brooding drive, Harold hysterically second-guessed his own choices and lost and lost.)

Terry's situation was infernal, like something existentialist. He wanted to cut and run but he could not manage to lose the game! His opponent wouldn't let him. But his hands were shaking so violently that he couldn't win it either.

Harold came in. "Hiya," he said to Terry, and proceeded on back to Dominic, who brought his feet down from the billiards table and his notebook out of his pocket. As always, Harold had the program well marked up. He did it during lunch hour, withdrawing from the other men because they kept talking about women and he was afraid to admit that he was queer for Puerto Rican hustlers. They thought that he was queer for trotting horses. Yet he was a beautiful handicapper, as he was a beautiful inspector of radio tubes, and he didn't win. He was loving and couldn't keep a hard-on.

Slowly Terry had become pink with indignation. What right did they have to follow him off the street? to ferret into his secret life where he was so elegant, and competent, and damned? Viciously he made a brilliant shot to spite all squares. It flashed like a jewel in a coal mine. The flat that he had rented two flights under Harold had a kitchen stove. Was he therefore supposed to buy butter and fry eggs, and bake a date-nut loaf in a coffee can in the oven? Viciously he ran out the game.

He had not noticed the door open again.

"So she walks outta de house and leaves me wid four kids!" the voice in the silence croaked triumphantly.

"Hi!" This time it was Connie. And she was standing there. Five months pregnant and a little filled out. And there he was, in a poolroom, with a stick in his hand, looking up. The cigarette on the rail had burned another dirty

scar in the varnish. She stood alongside the pool table looking at him with her wide-apart gaze.

Connie had come to pick up five dollars from Jason's
winnings in order to get supper.

Terry had told her about his own woman, but he felt
that Connie doubted that any such woman existed. *"She
knows I come here!"* he wanted to protest, calling on an
intercessor saint. But this did not help, for it cast also that
into confusion.

"It's yourn, you mother," said the hood, throwing a
buck on the baize like so much trash. On Eighth Street
the white boys swore like the black boys.

Coolly Terry folded the bill and put it in the pocket of
his levis. He put a protective arm around Connie in this
dangerous environment and walked her back to where her
husband and Harold were talking to the man in the swivel
chair. He tried to steel himself, but somehow he couldn't
think of the bit. There was something wrong about those
closing shots of his, that had been touched by wrath instead of only fright and flair. Connie was warmly pressing
the hand that he held around her, almost touching her
breast, and he couldn't think of the bit.

"You're just stupid," Jason said to Harold, deeply concerned for him. "You say the colt will breeze and he breezes.
Where are you? What's the matter with you, Harold, anyway?"—and he looked at him with an unconcealed affection
that transformed the town of Vanderzee into a human
habitation, with a badly kept up green and a bandstand.
Then Terry was amazed, for he had taken Jason to be only
a Yale graduate often stupefied on beer.

"No—no—" said Harold stubbornly, "Silver Dollar was
a lock, but he was boxed in the back stretch and Richards
couldn't get him off the rail. He—" He could not endure
the pressure of Jason's concern.

"*Come* and have supper with us, Harold," said Connie,
and she happily stretched out the five-dollar bill in the air
before them. She refused to accept his desolation; she decided, if the baby was a boy, to name it Harold. This was
bound to fluster and delight him. "You too, Terry."

She had included him. "Connie and I will shop!" he

blinked once—"I'll buy a pie!" he cried, folding her arm under his. His happy voice rang strangely in the seedy old pool parlor that heard mostly whispered or surly voices. And he *would* buy the biggest pie in the store, amusing everybody with his generous impulse, and then eat three-quarters of it himself. He did not know it, but he had fallen in love with these people. He would know it instantly when he found a writer to tell him what it was all about, that there was such a thing as community.

But though he loved Connie, he did not like shopping, and he was miffed when he saw that the two men were going to loiter behind and shoot a game of pool. Without *him*. Yet to his surprise—when he carefully thought about it later—he did not change his mind and send her shopping alone, nor even hang around for half an hour to watch, till she went alone. He actually stuck to the proposal he had made a minute ago, though it did not promise, a minute after, immediate satisfaction.

money-matters

1

I saw, I kept seeing, the dog, leaping for her ball, hounding us from room to room, always in the chair where one was about to sit down. And sometimes I saw in a flash her black body curled up in the circular grave.

These images were grievous, but there was also something uncanny. Her spirit was present in the little room. Not hovering there, but pervasive, making the atmosphere luminous, and closer to me, of course, than when she had been alive. I could not see the spirit, yet it seemed to be with my senses that I knew her. She *was* alive. And she was not a dog, but her own lovely spirit, one of the loveliest I have ever known, whether of a human being or a dog.

I wished that that spirit would go away, for what could I do with it? It haunted me but it was not practicable.

I turned to the bills that had accumulated on the desk, and looked with apprehension into my summer-ravaged bankbook.

2

Worry them as I would, our finances were not bad. (I was prudent to the point of stinginess. I hated to part with a penny.) We had more than seven thousand dollars. We could subsist for two years on that, even if I made nothing! Granting of course that there were no other incidents or accidents, even though I lived in frequent fear of disaster because of either my vices or my virtues, hard to know. In reality my wife had a job that interested her—I thought —and paid a hundred dollars a week, but I did not take that into account, since in my need not to depend on anybody I mentally took care of everything. My daughter, God bless her, was battening in college on an immense scholarship. Nobody ever gave me anything like that when I was young! Nobody ever gave me anything until I didn't need it.

The reality was that, although I had no job and made almost no effort to make money, I made more than we spent, for we spent little. As I explained on the scholarship application form, our car was twelve years old, it cost me $125. Yet it was a good one. When I bought it, I took Jason along to inspect it, and he used to work in a garage.

Despite myself I was making money. As the colloquia and the colleges and the veterans' hospitals and the national foundations kept calling on me for my opinion, advice, criticism—I never quite knew what they expected from me, but I went—plenty of checks were privily handed to me as I was driven back to the plane. I was living on honoraria, given clandestinely as if no such thing as money existed. Sometimes there was no pay at all, and I went—I was stingy with money, but spendthrift with my time and effort and attentiveness. Other times I was paid very well. There were floods of Soft Money in the country, from tax-dodge foundations, government subsidies, the perquisites of being a personality. Some of it trickled to me. I was a personality.

In the preliminary correspondence, they sometimes asked me what my fee was. I used to be embarrassed by this, and a little offended. I was not a professional lecturer. And having no standard, how would I know? So I wrote back $50 and fare, since that would buy food for my family for a week. After a while I wrote back, arbitrarily, $300 and fare, explaining, however, that "Of course I don't know your resources, and if you can't manage that sum I will come anyway. It's an interesting topic and I should like to meet Professor etc., etc." Yet when I peeked at the check on the plane, sometimes it went as high as $600. Now, that's a lot of money for an hour speech at a Convocation: $600 paid seven and a half months' rent. In one day. That gave many free days. (In fact I had no free days.)

3

By and large they were paying me as a court jester, like the Fool in *Lear,* to recall the sweet nature of things as they continued on their course just as before. Nobody likes to be used this way, but I had no alternative. It would be churlish not to speak up if they asked my opinion and then gripe that I was not used. And the kind of Americans who did ask my opinion were uniformly benevolent, good-humored, confused. By paying me well, according to their absurdly inflated standard, they legitimized opposition, as they ruthlessly went their way.

Well, I made the opposition as irksome as I could. I never tried purposely to bug them, but I had a kind of genius for embarrassing the Commissioner of Education who had just pompously introduced me on the platform, and attacking the beer ad of the sponsor of the TV interview. I was often quick to suggest that the main principle of the organization, my host, was invalid, and that its wisest first course might be to close up shop.

But since the speech was worth $500, it must be solid.

I noticed that my indifference to reward gave me a strange power. I did not want money from them, I did not want a job, I did not want *anything,* except, a simple thing, for them to make me a world that I could be proud to live in, and for my young to grow up in as men and women. This they did not grant me, but they gave me $700 for asking.

4

For my young to grow up in as men—I idly wondered whatever had become of Terry. I presumed that he had gone home to Akron.

It was horrible—I felt it again—how the premises of my life made it so hard for me to enjoy a simple satisfaction when it offered, when it offered. But instead we were whirled from each other always further away. Maybe it was so for everybody. The difficulties of life, as Kafka said, are mathematical.

5

And I thought of all the people who did not have, like me, the troubles of the rich, who had not "made" it, as I had made it by years of prudence, by sticking to my guns, perhaps by special talents. They were not getting any of the Soft Money, that was spilling into my hands from the foundations, and splashing from them back onto the ground in taxes for the missiles and the bombs.

In Vanderzee my friends were getting, if they were getting, the hard money of the basic economy. Roger did it on the primitive level. Since he was too intransigent to work, or to be able to work, for the corporations, he made his few dollars by painting walls and doing careful carpentry. But he persisted in ruining himself by estimating his jobs too low, and then, resentfully, insisting on sticking to his bad guesses. He netted about forty cents an hour.

Harold made a living wage in the radio factory, but he was always in debt because of the horses. Naturally. He had to come off somehow.

Jason struggled along—his beer and his peep show did not cost him much—on $3,000 as a Preceptor, a new academic dignity that the University had instituted, while its markup was 400 percent for something called Educational Administration.

Soren, our mind-wandering poet, did not understand money. He sometimes forgot to eat until we forcibly called his attention to it. Then he would dutifully wash dishes for a week at eighty cents an hour.

It was hard in our city to be decently poor. It was not impossible, but it was very hard. Mostly, you were either in the system or out altogether. Most Negroes and Puerto Ricans were out altogether; they were dropouts. Some of our friends were too busy to make money; they contracted out.

To exist in decent poverty a man had to meet strict requirements. He had to have a refined taste for the highest things, which alone do not cost money. He had to be doing something so worthwhile that he did not need extrinsic rewards. He had to choose his vices very carefully and healthfully. His wife had to respect their way of life so highly that she did not need to keep up with the Joneses. They had to be able, in a pinch, to live on bread and water.

People like that had to be prudent, and not miss small opportunities.

6

These requirements were far too strict for our young friends. In the nature of the case, most young people who, because of independent spirit and good sense, are restive in the usual jobs and cannot agree to the usual prejudices, are terrible fuck-ups. And when they slip, they do not have enough social support to bolster them up. With them it goes hard.

I had to be their banker, an odd role for a stingy person; I don't know whether I played it well or badly. I would pick up the restaurant check or pay for the gas, but I was unwilling to support any one or any vice. I refused to lend money and increase their obligations, though I would go through the pretense of lending sums up to $50 which I could afford to forget. Luckily Polly was less scrupulous and would lend a couple of hundred from our joint account without exacting a means test or asking for a certificate of purity. Of course, in an emergency I too was good for a few hundred dollars, when somebody was ill or had to be bailed out. (They always paid me back, four or five years later.)

I should have liked to employ some of my friends, paying them for real work that I needed, but I never needed any work done that I could not do better myself. I spent a lot of time proposing and recommending my friends for small useful jobs, and then I was furious when, often, they failed to appear. I was a nag.

It was deeply painful to me, especially when I was amorous, to see a friend working long hours at a bad job when I could easily have given him the salary to spend the day with me as we both wished. But my Puritan soul forbade.

And again I thought of Terry, primping for long minutes before the mirror. A kid like that would never wash his own underwear and socks! He didn't know how to be poor. I could see the laundry piled high in the corner. There was a lot of underwear, socks, shirts, and jeans, bought for him by that mother who had bought the chocolate velvet jumper, or on Daddy's credit card. Finally, on a red-letter day, the heap would go to the hand laundry, and the bill would be astronomical.

Often these kids aspired to be writers—I didn't know about Terry. Very little would be written, but they would periodically trade in the typewriter that they did not use for a new and superior model that they did not use.

There were others—not Terry—who wore their socks and underwear until they stank and were too shameful to present even at the laundry. I often came on these articles left in the back of dresser drawers in hotel rooms.

And then here was the one—Terry for sure!—who ate malted milks and cheeseburgers, cokes and pie à la mode, the food that gives quick sugar for a kind of energy, that does not have to be chewed, that can be swallowed whole.

What had happened to Terry? I had a flash of him, standing in the doorway.

I had a flash of Lucy standing up on him, in his red jacket in the doorway. Hounding us from room to room! Leaping for her ball!

I saw in a flash her black body curled up in the circular grave, like an emblem.

And then it recommenced as before. Her spirit was pervasive in the room and made it luminous. Closer to me, of course, than when she had been alive. And even though that spirit was one of the loveliest that I had ever known, whether of a human being or a dog, I wished that it would go away, for what could I do with that?

I walked out of the house to escape.

the community in vanderzee

1

Eyes closed, the little fellow was slowly typing at the table with all ten fingers. The record player was deafening. Quietly and calmly, according to his standards, Terry was washing his dirty underwear and socks. It was a new experience, thanks to Connie, but he had worked out a high style of his own from the television commericals. He lived down two flights, but he was up at Harold's because Harold had the superdetergent. He was also giving Ramón the morning lesson in typewriting.

"*Maricón!*" Ramón opened his eyes and saw his mistakes. His ritual outcry was swallowed by the tribal jazz. The scene was like the photograph in the *Times* of the business college in Central Africa, where the blacks are wearing collars and ties as they peck at the adding machines.

Carefully drying his hands, Terry gave his critical appraisal. He believed in a thorough grounding in the fundamentals. To be sure, Ramón could not read, but he was fast learning a-s-d-f-g and h-j-k-l-semicolon. And incidentally, by playing with the machine, he *was* learning to read. Terry had also tried to get him to do the breakfast dishes to make Harold happy, but Ramón and Harold were not speaking to each other this week.

Since his hands were dry, Terry put on another record and automatically turned it a twist louder.

Ramón put a new page in the roller. He liked using a new white sheet for every try. It was not cheapskate.

The sunlight poured into the bleak kitchen. The young pair, like brothers, happy with their obsessional tasks that kept them from tearing each other to pieces, shone in the beauty of life. There was a touching beauty in Terry's fair awkwardness when he was content and his childlike abandon broke through his compulsions. He held the laundry stiffly but not disdainfully away. He wrung out his blue jeans with all his might.

His kitten, Megaton, had followed him upstairs, the son of Soren's Atomic Fission, and he sat on the refrigerator in the sun, planning his next move. In an intelligent arc he leaped onto Terry's shoulder and sank his claws in good, and poised there, langorously waving the top of his upright tail. Terry's yelp was also swallowed up in the jazz.

Angrily the neighbor below thumped on her ceiling with a broomstick.

2

Meg stood frozen outside the frosted-glass door, and did not knock. She was pinkly visible from within, but they did not happen to look.

Her face was contorted with jealousy because she was excluded from the ongoing life. (The baby was at Connie's.)

She was eavesdropping, to find out exactly what they—the boys, the grown-ups—were doing.

It was her vice. It gave her knowledge and the feeling of power. But then she was all the more guilty and afraid to knock.

Nor was it easy to interpret what was going on. What was that yelp? She turned pale. Who had cried out? What were they doing?

She put her ear to the glass, trembling because she knew that she could be seen.

When the neighbor knocked on the ceiling, Meg thought that a terrible struggle was going on. She decided to enter.

Inside they could have seen the doorknob turn.

But at this instant, her friend from New York came bounding up the stairs, enraged at the noise that he had heard halfway down the block, and assuming it was the Puerto Rican gang. He surprised Meg with her ear to the door—nobody expected him anyway—and she let out a cry of dismay and fled past him downstairs and out the building. She was convinced that he had come to Vanderzee to see Terry. Her breast was clenched with jealousy.

But he did not know that Terry was there. And indeed,

he had first called on Meg, because she lived near the terminal. She was eavesdropping! He was surprised at that. When she bolted past him, he was at a loss.

The neighbor below shouted up stridently.

Firmly he walked in and turned the player off with a click. "Are you boys out of your minds?" he demanded. "Can you afford to have the cops up here?" The silence fell like heavy snow. The woman below gave one last thump.

"Why you no knock?" said Ramón angrily.

3

He turned, and it was Terry.

The young man flushed with welcome to see him.

He was startled that it was Terry. His anger was crossed by a pleasing remorse, to see Terry washing his underwear. He had misjudged him. He had misjudged him in this. Perhaps he was misjudging him in everything. Perhaps, to his relief, he was misjudging everything in the world. For it was impossible for a man who had so many strong articulated opinions not to doubt more and more that he might be in the wrong 100 percent. But unfortunately the world kept confirming his predictions. So Terry had not gone back to Akron!

Smiling at one another, they spontaneously stepped forward and put their arms around each other and kissed. They were lovers. They drew back their faces to look into each other's pleased eyes that, this close, were without duplicity or reserve. The older man took off his eyeglasses that annoyed him, and he held them in his hand as they clutched each other again, beginning to feel the warmth of their bodies. Terry smelled delicious, but soapy.

There was not much sexuality in the surprising embrace. The older man was not cowering into sexuality. If it would arise, he knew, that would be all right. Anything would be all right. Rather, this close, they felt with each other ordinary peace, as if they were safe inside the panic, worry, and weariness that they experienced everywhere else. Like in the calm center of the hurricane. They were quite aware of Ramón's presence, but that too was all right.

"Why you no *knock?*" repeated Ramón plaintively. He did not like it how everybody walked in and out, and now this one turned off the jazz. He was puzzled to see them kissing each other. With their mouths! He knew as an article of faith that Terry was not queer and had a woman. He had learned to respect the funny older man as one of those *macho* men who beat their wives and did exactly what they pleased, and besides he was a celebrity, he had seen his picture in the papers. Anyway, queers did not kiss; they never used their mouths above the waist. Then—what *were* they doing? What did it mean?

They paid no attention to Ramón at all.

"Is this where you live?" he frowned, beginning to run Terry's life. He might have known that Harold would take in another waif without rent.

"No," said Terry, "but Harold has the SPLURGE."

"The what?" He did not watch television. He was puritanic about it, like about drugs, even aspirin.

On the sink the big economy-size package was orange and yellow and had a picture of a billowing white bed-sheet tended by the head and shoulders of a trim nurse with long bloody fingernails.

"Yes, puss, miaouuuw," he said, nudging the cat with his toe. "What's this cat's name?"

"Megaton," said Terry. "We're two flights down."

Wrong again; Terry was not sponging. He noticed, sharply, his own propensity to leap to bad interpretations. With a pang of sadness he realized that Meg had cried out and brushed past him because she had known, when he had not, that he had come to Vanderzee to see Terry. To look for Terry.

"In the community," said Terry proudly, with a mystical light in his eyes, "we just walk in and take what we need. The doors are always open!"

"In the *what?*"

"In the community."

"What community?" Where in hell had he picked up *that* word?

Terry consulted his watch in a panic. "I'm late for the appointment with Roger!" As ever—there was no change—he was continually on his way to the next appointment, where he would also be late.

Yet there was a profound change. His eyes were distraught but they weren't shifty. The next appointment was not a secret. It also was in the community, public and available to anybody. He needed to get going, but he did not need to go away. Come along.

4

With excruciatingly deliberate dispatch, Terry collected the twists of laundry to take them downstairs.

"Hasta la vista, Ramón," said the other, putting his glasses back on. It was the first acknowledgment that he had given of Ramón's existence, as if he saw him for the first time when they left.

Downstairs, behind Terry's closed door, they clasped each other again, holding the laundry.

They had erections. More than once the young fellow had masturbated to the fantasy of this scene while, all summer, his friend was touring with his family where the jaggy pines were silhouetted against the white sky. A twist of laundry fell to the floor and got dirty.

They made a thing of hastily, abstinently, hanging up the wash.

The tired man decided, with a wrench, not to make love. Not now, not in a hurry. Especially with a person like Terry, always late and always panicky about being late. And he knew—they both knew—that for persons like themselves the important thing was not the sex but their trust and their acceptance. Yet sexual pleasure too was very good, and he felt an unpleasure because it was himself who was thwarting himself. But Terry, for a quarter of an hour, had been entirely at peace and happy. Not evasive.

He watched him out the corner of his eye. The boy was not making nice.

But Terry had to comb his hair, and his friend was annoyed at the waste of time.

5

As he looked at himself in the mirror and arranged a wisp, Terry suddenly smirked and became hip. He had thought of the bit.

Joanna was coming in the afternoon to "look at" the community, and she could not possibly like what she would see. It was too crude for her Westchester taste. She would curl her lip. It was too square for her hip adventurousness. She would get jumpy and want to leave. But now he had solved the problem! He had an important person to show her.

He dismissed the idea; it was temporarily irrelevant. His smirk flew across the mirror, and vanished. But it worked in his unconsciousness, to complicate his life, to erode his innocence, gradually to spoil his day.

"If you have enough underwear and shirts to last you through a week," was the older man's wise advice as he drew him away from the mirror, "why don't you use the laundromat? Costs a quarter."

They squeezed hands, and opened the door.

Meg was on the landing.

He knew that she had been eavesdropping again.

She proceeded past them without a word, on her way upstairs to Harold's, to talk to Ramón.

The look on her face was close to hatred. One had to dismiss it from mind, just to live on awhile.

6

Terry's gambit was now so idiotic that one could not even be annoyed. He had to turn up Hamilton Avenue, in the opposite direction from Roger's, in order to buy Roger a book, a certain book, that he had seen in the shop.

"But you said that we were late."

"Yes, but Roger never read Purdy."

"Then let's go to Roger's first. Then we can all go together."

"No, that's no good." He was afraid to visit Roger empty-handed, without a subject of conversation that he was sure about.

"O.K., O.K." It was not worth wondering what it was about. For, looking at him sidewise as they walked along, he saw that Terry could not change any plan, or support any unstructured facts of life, but only elaborate the structure further. It was evident by his gait. His toes pointed out too far; his heels, though not strutting like a hoodlum's, did not give enough contact with the ground. His ass was pinched tight. Poor kid. Presumably Arabelle would get around to this department after she stopped being mesmerized by his gabble.

The shop did not have the book. It was at the other shop at the far end of Hamilton, on the corner of—with splendid impartiality—Burr. Undaunted, Terry's plan was now to walk to Burr and take the bus back, which would be just as fast, if a bus came.

By the time they knocked at Roger's, with the book, there was no answer. This did not necessarily mean that Roger was out, for he would open or not depending on his mood. But he ordinarily gave one the score by making some kind of sound. There was no sound.

"I'll leave the book," said Terry, "then he'll know we came. Next we have to go to Jason's. I said I'd look over his new poems," he said importantly.

His friend looked at him, full in the face, with curiosity. *What* was he doing? And the answer was poignant. He was shepherding them together, so that, in his need, he could rely on them one and all.

7

The poor beaten kid! He had survived the terrible moment at the last session of the Conference at Columbus, when it seemed that for him—and not only for him—there was in our society No Exit. When he had asked his germane question, and fifteen experts on the dais did not know an answer for him. But with ingenuity he had hit on a painfully American answer, *Do It Yourself.* If there is no community for you, young man, young man, make it yourself.

To be sure, our friends in Vanderzee, unlike the usual dissident community, happened to be lucky material to work with, though we had our vices and neuroses (sometimes fit to be tied). Like other dissidents, we were without many of the American daydreams and nightmares and got some real satisfactions by avoiding many unnecessary difficulties, like neckties, racial prejudices, Puritan morality, an excessive regard for private property, as if life weren't hard enough. Nevertheless, unlike many dissidents, we were not isolated or outcaste. Most of us made a living, some of us had families, we mixed in the universities, we took part in politics. We were open to a lot of world, indeed to the ordinary world.

And we had a peculiar style, that combined, perhaps confused, psychotherapy and the life of every day and night. We often stopped and took a breath and got off the escalator. We did not one-up or conceal our misery from ourselves by winning victories. Even in violent rivalries, we tried to become aware who we were and what we were doing. It was not taken amiss if somebody called attention to what we were doing, though we might look with baleful eyes at the truths that we could not alter. For a young fellow like Terry, who was pitilessly self-demanding and self-accusing, and therefore always proving something and lying to himself, it was like a dash of cold water to come among persons to whom his gambits were utterly indifferent. With whom he could not compete because there was no contest. To his credit, he saw that *this* was not a gambit, and he soon became less tiresome.

Our unrebellious lawlessness seemed to relieve him of much of the guilt that he walked around with as a middle-class boy with a yen for low haunts and criminal characters. He was pleased, rather than feeling exposed, when he discovered that Harold knew in a business way the pimps and pushers of Times Square whom he himself guiltily cultivated. Our friends made even the infernal poolroom legitimate by going there to bet with the bookie.

Three nights a week he went to New York to work—he made $40 as a TV monitor. When he had the resolution, he headed straight home by the 1:15 train. But maybe once a week he succumbed to the all-night movie, to masturbate, and then he ended up sitting till dawn in the Astoria Cafeteria, with Jeff or Tony or other pimps. It was an ancient pattern. Since age thirteen he used to steal out of a genteel home, into whatever sinks of degradation he could find. His family moved, but year by year, in various cities, he could always sniff out the operators, adroitly ward off their sexual designs, and share their discourse. Feeling himself in the center of things where history is made, in all innocence he led them on, he teased them. Naturally, as he grew older his interest waned, but he did not know any other alternative of corruption. Mailer's treatise on the White Negro proved to be a find, since he now learned to regard himself as a White Negro. Even so, he often yawned and yearned for his bed.

From Times Square, he invited rough Jeff and tiny Tony to visit him in Vanderzee. They came—it would be a gas—but to his amusement they were terrified by the daylight, and huffily withdrew into offended dignity. They thought that our rather functional disregard for the law was immoral, and that our radical politics was un-American and should be reported to the FBI.

It was the honeymoon of Terry's psychotherapy. Arabelle was charmed by him and alarmed for him. She had never before known an American youth. She cut the fee to $5, which was what he could afford, though he put on airs that money was indifferent.

9

They walked along from Roger's to Jason's. It was half-way before the mystery of the word "community" was solved, though his older friend kept listening for the clue. Terry had picked it up from Goodman, the anarchist writer, whom he had newly added to the pantheon alongside Nathanael West and Mailer. Every time he underwent a crisis, Terry stumbled upon an ideology that helped him to live on. It was one of his more tiresome boasts that he gravitated to important authors; but it was true. He needed them.

"Goodman is it? Hm, Goodman." At once his friend became jealous. It was unfair, but he couldn't help it. It was hard for him to bear in mind how much they needed fathers, how confused they were, and that they had more to lose if we went down, because they had not lived. Now, hearing Terry refer a couple of times to the peasant anarchist who tried to offer a way out, however chimeric, he became spitefully critical. "Community is it? What the hell does he mean by community?"

"Goodman," said Terry, "defines 'community' as people using one another as resources."

"Does he?" They walked along. "That sounds useful, but—People are more likely to get one another into trouble than to help one another out of it. I don't know Goodman's work," the tired man said, "but my impression—my impression is that he expects people to do the simple things that are exactly what they can't do. Is that realistic?"

But Terry took it personally. "Don't give up on me!" he implored. "Please don't give up on me." He took everything personally.

"Don't mind me, I'm just jealous because I love you."

10

With a cry Connie flew into her Dutch uncle's arms, to welcome the traveler back, for she too liked to have all her extended family around her.

He held her away to look at her. (He noticed that Roger was there.) She was rosy and beginning to look pregnant, which artfully she dressed not to conceal. What trick did she have, with her eyes and her smile, to make him feel that he too looked young? Gravely, as was his manner with Connie, he kissed her on the forehead. Terry—

It was uncanny. Terry, like the dog, could not tolerate being left out. He was enfolding them both, trying to kiss him and trying to kiss Connie at the same time. Flustered by so much affection, the old man disengaged himself. And suddenly the spirit of Lucy was pervasive in the room, making it luminous. It was uncanny.

In a flash he saw her leaping for her ball, and bounding in the direction of one and bounding in the direction of the other, to shepherd them together, and also to keep the ball for herself. Bewildered.

No one had seen her bound out from behind the parked car into the path of the other car. She was bewildered.

She used to be roused to frenzy by the sight, or maybe it was the smell, of affection, and she leaped at your genitals and wanted to be included. Her presence was too close in the room.

But as he stood there, disengaged from them, he sensed that spirit fade into the light of common day. It was only Terry, shepherding together his community. Bewildered. Trying to kiss them both at the same time. It was a big, pretty, shabby room, and he noticed that Roger was there, and Jason was coming with a can of beer and asking if they wanted a can of beer. Jason said, "Oh, it's you. When did you get back?"

"I left the Purdy book outside your door," Terry said.

"Thanks," said Roger. "I'll read a chapter and throw it away."

"But maybe you'll like it," protested Terry.

"No, I won't. They don't write them anymore that I'll read." Roger liked Genêt. He respected Goodman but thought that his books had no juice of life. He, personally, was not one to keep his door unlocked.

A last time! in a flash! he saw her body curled up in the circular grave. Like an emblem.

Jason read his poems artlessly, for the prose sense and not the sound. His style was changing rapidly. The theme was the same, dismay about Jason, but the location was more frequently the streets of Vanderzee. With a certain awkwardness he remained loyal to the meters and syntax of the traditional poetry that moved him and from which he made a therefore honest living at the University, but the Yale Man was fast becoming a local:

> "Where Burr meets Eighth, I hated the corner
> just because every day I turn in there
> rotating in my little world.
> Today I'll go as far as Ninth and turn
> toward home in this heavy rain—"

The iambs and anapests had a brisk pedestrian gait as, turning up the unusual street, the poet saw, to his embarrassment, a beaten old Puerto Rican whore, or maybe she was just a grandmother, squatting in a doorway pulling up her skirt to attract him. He's embarrassed because she is so much in need that he doesn't know how decently to pass her by. But when he comes closer, it proves to be after all a tattered broken umbrella blowing in the wind; and now he is doubly embarrassed that such was his fantastic wish.

This was pretty good, but the bother was that the story came back only to Jason. To be sure with a true interpretation; but what has poetry to do with true interpretations? Why didn't that pedestrian, instead of becoming doubly embarrassed, pick *up* that broken umbrella and hold it over his head against the rain? Since that's what the world had to offer. Why did it have to be a "little world"? Jason had yet to learn that, little or big, it's all the world that there can be. But he was still too ashamed to affirm it.

Roger, sitting in his bearish detachment, liked Jason's poetry because it was so pathetically honest. He shrewdly compared it to the Zenny exercises that the pothead cronies read at one another, seeming to form such an integrated clique, as they kept digging one another and stylishly spouting a *lingua franca* contrived of Laforgue, Rimbaud,

Cummings, Apollinaire, Carlos Williams, and etcetera; and in fact each one was soliloquizing in uniform. But Jason was doggedly, doggishly, trotting the street and looking for other dogs.

12

And what must Jason do to be our community poet? His poem must lash out at Roger who is sitting there appreciatively appraising him, and what right does he have to appraise him, rather than being moved? It must grab Terry by the shirtfront, when Terry is rudely and noisily going into the kitchen to get something to eat from the icebox.

Jason did not yet see, he did not want to see, that it was not a "Puerto Rican whore," whatever that meant to him, who was squatting in the doorway pulling up her skirt; it was lustful lonely Meg, the scion of the patroons. But of course if you say that in a poem, something has to follow from it in your behavior. Nor are your friends going to love you.

13

Terry's rudeness was painful. He could not get out of his skin enough to pay attention to the reading and understand it. And his anxiety began to mount again, he didn't know why. He clattered into the kitchen to comfort himself with a sandwich. He slammed the refrigerator door.

The others, except Jason who was trying to read his poems, took all this simply. Terry was impossible, and it was impossible not to put up with him. With her wide eyes Connie looked at Terry and at Jason, and at Terry stuffing the big sandwich into his big mouth and at Jason becoming angry.

"Shit!" said Terry looking at his watch. He was late again. "Oh, shit!" He crammed the crust of the sandwich into his mouth.

"Now what?"

"I'm late for Joanna. She came at four." It was a quarter to five. "And she was coming to look at—to see—"

He was overcome with confusion. He could hardly say that she was coming to look at you people, to see for herself how you people live. Whenever it came down to the actuality, his hipster rehearsal didn't work out. He said, "She is coming to be introduced to the community."

"Who is Joanna?" said his friend.

"What community?" said Roger.

"Oh, I'm so glad she's coming at last!" said Connie, clapping her hands.

"Why in hell did you ask to hear my poems," cried Jason, "if you don't listen to them, you arrogant little snot?"

Terry looked at his friend in disappointment. "Joanna —I *told* you about Joanna."

The intonation of this "I *told* you" recalled the visit that took place three months before. "Oh, she's the one you kept calling 'this chick.' You never bothered to give her a name."

"It's the first time she's been willing to come out here and see for herself."

So he had made the insulting remark anyway. She was a tourist. It was hardly an ingratiating introduction for the young woman. Yet the others were perfectly willing to accept her in spite of him, that is, because of him.

"Oh, she is coming to see for herself. Then why don't you just trot off to Joanna and bring her back? Here she can see the poet in his lair. Meantime we can continue Jason's reading."

"*Don't cop out on me!*" cried Terry, clutching him by the arm. "It will be easier if she meets *you* first." This was beyond anything. He threw himself on the mercy of everyone, and everyone tried to come across. But sometimes, the way he set it up, one couldn't.

"Let's go," said his friend quietly. He was angry.

—Yet again, on the stairway, they spontaneously fell into each other's embrace, bellies close, lips locked, not without sexual feeling, but mostly trying, with their whole bodies, to find the peace that kept slipping away from them.

They were in a hurry. One was lying, the other knew it. Their minds clouded over and they faltered. If they had not separated they would have fallen down the stairs.

14

She was waiting on Terry's stoop, improving the shining hour with a paperback, but tapping her foot. Joanna was good-looking, almost beautiful—to the old man's relief, for she might have been anything. But her mouth was tight. It must be like her mother's.

Terry kissed her. He made a thing of it.

Her voice was puzzling. It was childish, of about age twelve, but also hard, as if her mother were an intelligent clubwoman without either common sense or heart. But besides—this was alarming—her tone and diction occasionally became jazzy, throwaway, throwing herself away, throwing away one of Terry's hipster phrases, which she understood more organically than he did, though she had learned them from him.

The book was J. S. Mill on *Representative Government*. Her parents had allowed her to switch from Wellesley to the University, and she was getting in some of her studying before the term began. She was afraid of the famous school, but very ambitious to succeed in it. Naturally her parents did not know that Terry had left Columbus and was in New York and would maybe go to the University himself. She lied to them about everything.

She was timid and embarrassed at meeting the prestigious older man, about whom Terry had boasted too much. Terry could not have calculated worse. She was annoyed because Terry had again sprung a surprise on her. But of course that was also what made Terry exciting. She too much needed something exciting.

Proprietorially, as if all his plans were working out, Terry put one arm around his girl's waist and the other around his man's waist, to march them upstairs.

Infuriatingly, the Mayor's sound truck passed and barked *Blah blah blah blah blah in Vanderzee.*

No, the man had to get back to New York. He could not possibly go upstairs, not even for a moment. Of course he would come back tomorrow, if he could manage it—if it was convenient—his family—not too early—maybe for a noon breakfast.

Was this what the day came to? he thought bitterly, to be used as a decoy, a celebrity? He liked being used, but he didn't like being exploited. Had the whole day been, unconsciously but deliberately, for this? That mind quick as light, too smart for his own good.

"But you had time to hear the poems!" said Terry with hot eyes, that were opaque.

"Tomorrow at noon in time for brunch!" said Joanna brightly.

"Please, Terry, don't ever ask me for a favor. You know I'm more than likely to refuse it." The tumultuous storm on his brow made it clear that the day was darkened.

Terry leered, but his eyes were so full of self-loathing that one feared he might do himself an injury.

His lover winced, and dutifully quickly surveyed Joanna, so that he could afterward discuss her as a friend. He could see that the young woman was besieged by too many forces and was desperately charting a course. She was too jazzy. He feared, for Terry, that she was not going to like the Community that had too many real troubles to want any excitement. He was sorry for her because Terry was not to be trusted.

She would take Harold's sex with Ramón the wrong way. Yet it *was* senseless, in the present, in the future. She would certainly take Meg the wrong way! She would even take Terry's domesticity the wrong way, not recognizing it for occupational therapy. She could not be expected to admit to herself how disturbed her young man was. He was not a good partner for kicks.

She would, indeed, take everything about their community the wrong way. (A community, was it?) And probably she would be, in terms of practical consequences, right. What put her off might be, considering the circumstances, quite simple and sane, and nevertheless it would come to grief.

He would have a problem to keep her from taking himself the wrong way. How *should* he be taken? Was he really going to endure this impossible youth? One thing was for sure: Terry would not be frank with her.

These impossible youth—there she was—disaffected, they had the courage to launch on their own, and that made sense. The truth had to be a project—one could not know beforehand—an enterprise into the future that either worked out or not and was, thus, either pragmatically true or false. But they simply didn't have enough feel of themselves to sail by dead reckoning. They went by abstractions, stereotypes out of their authors. And maybe, in terms of practical consequences, those authors were also right: that during the Cold War it was best to be hip or crazy. But God, how boring that was!

He was disappointed that he hadn't had a chance to fuck the young fellow. It would have been a pleasant way to end a restful day.

16

On the way to the station, he again stopped at Meg's, to ask point-blank what was eating *her* up. Of course, he thought he knew what was eating her up, but his style of life was to smoke everything out into the open, except what he overlooked or concealed from himself.

He was more and more shocked that she was an eavesdropper. It wasn't nice. Yet it added up. It was all of a piece with her speechlessness. Everything was always all of a piece.

She wasn't there, and that was a relief.

ramón

1

As soon as the two had gone, leaving Ramón with the now bleak typewriting lesson, Pedro opened the door from the front bedroom. "Who was here?" he asked in English.

"*El viejo*—the old faggot," said Ramón morosely.

"Don't talk like this!" said Pedro, and automatically cuffed him. "If I hear you talk again—you know what. Show some respect. Harold makes you a home. *Venga!*" he called to the girl.

Linda came out of the bedroom. She was a dumpy, bosomy little thing, not more than fourteen but made up like almost eighteen. But her bright yellow hair was unfortunately discolored with black. She had run away from the reformatory only two days ago and had not yet had time to renew it. Yet today Linda was gay, pleased with herself, for Pedro was the big shot! and she could twist him around her finger.

She turned the record player on and up full blast, because the silence made her icky, it was like being in the grave. Pedro turned it off and punched her in the face and knocked her against the wall. How did she dare? She had asserted herself. He had enjoyed himself with her, but she was a whore. She could not satisfy him. Nothing could satisfy him. (He was off heroin.) "You"—he turned menacingly on Ramón, "how you are with Harold—*talk* to him today. From me!" Ramón edged behind the table.

He signaled to Linda, and she meekly followed him out the door.

When the door closed, Ramón thumbed his nose at it.

Yet it was not because Pedro was brutal that the gang was in awe of him. On the contrary, it was because he was intelligent and often just and compassionate. He protected them from the abyss that each one felt of his own viciousness and need to wreak ruin. Without him, they egged one another on. Pedro would ruin only himself.

He was always more passionately devoted to Harold,

although disappointed that he was not a robber. Harold provided him a kind of Youth House where he could bring his tail and even look—as if it were the lounge of a club—into the *New York Times,* Pedro's paper. And this Harold did for nothing, for nothing. Pedro had taken it for granted that something would be demanded of him in return; but soon, being himself unsuspicious and generous, he allowed himself to take Harold at face value, and he saw with compassion how suffering that value was. He was appalled at how cruel Ramón was to him. If he saw more of it, he was going to twist his arm and break it, teach him a lesson.

2

But Ramón's resentment, the long silences, the studied rudeness when he knew it would sting, were not his own to control. He was crazy jealous of Harold and Meg. He did not know for sure if they had sexual relations. He would have flamed with spiteful joy if he knew that Harold lost his erection with Meg too. Instead he had no appetite, because of his morose fantasies of them. Naturally he could not tell this to Pedro, who would have respected it.

Unlike with his sister-in-law, there was no peephole through which to see Meg naked.

What he saw was Harold sometimes going to Meg's apartment, when there was no one else there but the baby. Another time they drove away for the whole afternoon in the car. That time the gang drank up the beer in the refrigerator and left the place littered with the cans. When Harold came back, Ramón wouldn't pick up the cans. Harold slammed him, and he ran away for two days.

There was no longer any sex, but instead a contest of wills, between the fifteen-year-old boy and the thirty-five-year-old man. It was embarrassing for the rest of us to watch it. And yet, to Harold, this contest, of warm resentment edging on hatred, seemed better than the empty self-reliance in which he usually existed when alone. But he was hurt when Ramón refused to talk to him.

Meg walked in, sweeping upstairs from the scene that she had not witnessed below. Ramón let her too feel his spiteful silence awhile, while he pretended to be touch-typing.

"Why you no knock?" he said crossly, not opening his eyes.

She took this to mean that he and Terry too had reason not to be walked in on. But since she saw that he was showing off for her, she asked, "What are you doing, Ramón?"

"Typing!" he said, and proudly ripped out the page. "See, no eyes!" He was fatally in love with her, not as his sister-in-law but as mama herself.

"Can you read it?" she said admiringly.

"*Sí! sí!* 'A—S—D—F—G. H—J—K—L—semicolon.' "

Meg too was teaching Ramón to read. Everybody was teaching Ramón to read. By their combined efforts they were bound to prevail over his will to be stupid.

She took the morning paper out of her bag. She used the headlines of the *New York Daily Mirror* as a text that was likely to interest him, though not providing much food for thought.

She had invented the method at the Remedial Reading Coffee-House, to which she patricianly gave an afternoon a week. With the hulking Negro fourteen-year-olds or even the little Indian ten-year-olds who came in reeking of the model-airplane glue they had been sniffing, it was absurd to read from *Dick and Jane*, "Run, Spot, run!" They did not understand the pictures with the lawn mowers and the watering cans. One of the male teachers had mimeographed a primer of basic pornography, but Meg objected to this that it was not in printed type. She found virtue, however, in SPOUSE STABS BLONDE IN NEST and ALL-OUT PROBE IN 6-DEATH FIRE.

But the headlines were so allusive that it was often hard for Meg to decipher their prose sense. WE FOTO BASES was Cold War politics. STIX NIX PIX FIX meant that provincial movie theaters had rejected the effort of the big companies to foist block-booking on them. But what was CHISOX? CHISOX RIOT ON BAGS.

Ramón laughed at her and told her. She had a great merit of a teacher, an ignorance that gave the pupil a chance. Also, she blushed when he teased her; she gave him the satisfaction of knowledge. He had a lot of baseball lore and seemed to be especially interested in the prospective trades and buying and selling. "These days pitchers are hard to get," he explained. "Without Pascual, Minnesota might as well quit. The Mets would give $500,000 for Willy Mays, but without Willy Mays the Gi'nts might as well quit." He pronounced Giants to rime with pints. "Mickey was some ballplayer," he said, "one of the all-time greats, but his legs was bad." He had learned all this verbatim in the candy store on Third Street that pushed pot.

Artfully she tried to draw him out about Terry.

He clammed up. An instinct made him protect the secrets of all the men, whoever they might be, against the prying female. The members of the gang did not gossip. They protected each one's privacy of shame at the same time as their conversation consisted entirely of putting one another down and boasting.

Meg was trying to find out what Terry "really" did and felt, as if that itself were something definite and a kind of fact that could be known. But even if he knew it, Ramón could not have said it. For Ramón and his friends at no moment, except in rare explosions of blind rage, could say anything that put them in danger of communication, of being understood, of becoming real to one another. They might incidentally drop information about something that had actually happened, including even a terrible crime that they had just committed, like stomping an old man, but this meant simply that the happening had not happened to *them*. They were not engaged in the act that they had apparently performed; it was just in passing by that they had stomped the old creep. If they really did something, they clammed up. Each one was hermetically isolated with his own inexpressible feelings.

Their conversation consisted of slapping one another, or cringing from slaps, putting one another down by ridicule, affirming oneself by boasting, and parroting grown-up lore heard in the candy store on Third Street to prove that oneself was a man of the world. But if something serious occurred, like a boy's killing himself with an overdose of heroin or another boy's being sent away to jail for five years, it would never be mentioned.

But this invulnerability was powerfully shaken by the community in Vanderzee. Often Roger or Jason or Terry or Harold or the older man from New York or even Soren would, out of ordinary concern, "for nothing," want to know what the case *was,* and he might persist, paying attention and questioning, until he found out and came across with help, calling a doctor, providing bail. Such moments of contact were unbearably painful for these youths and were blotted out of existence. Ramón did not remember the conversation in the car on the ride from the airport.

Those who paid attention to these young tended to have what society judged to be anarchic ideas and vicious motives, though both the ideas and the motives were usually tame and harmless. Society, like themselves, paid no attention to these young at all.

4

She was wearing a sleeveless dress, and he was inflamed by the sight of her armpits when she lifted her arms.

"Somebody put a butt on the floor!" he said indignantly, and crossed the room to pick it up so that he could see up an inch under her skirt. "It was Linda! She don't know how to behave." Meg had, as usual, taken her shoes off—her bare feet were always dirty—but of course it was not her bare legs that counted, but the revelation of what was concealed.

He was beside himself with lust. His half-developed penis was stiff, quivering, and wet.

She was not like his sister-in-law *or* his mama. She was "available." Like a whore she went behind a closed door with Harold. Terry took her in his arms.

One day long long ago—two months ago—he saw her nursing the baby.

"Are you sick, Ramón?" she said. With a cry he flung

125

himself across the room at her, and knelt between her bare legs, frantically nibbling the flesh of her thighs, overwhelmed by the smell of her underpants. At once he ejaculated and lay whining, clutching onto her bottom with both hands.

Meg caressed his hair.

She was confused by the impulsive advances of the kids. They occurred frequently at the Coffee-House, when she unselfconsciously touched them.

She generally managed adequately simply by letting them be and do.

She liked Ramón like a funny child—she found many things funny—and she idly stroked his hair and his neck. He sprawled there, gasping.

Soon, he would be emboldened. As he would put it, "She lets me get away with everything." And he would insist, demand, to have her with his pint-size penis in high grown-up style. She would be confused about this too. She did not have the ability to say No when, indeed, it made no difference to her. She wondered that their need was so intense.

Ramón got to his feet and became conscious of the wet stain on his jeans, and Harold returned from work.

"Why you no knock?" cried the boy in anguish. They walked in and out like on the street.

"Meg!" said Harold.

Neither one paid any attention to the boy. Nervously tired, Harold was delighted that Meg was there. With her he came to life, gracious, helpful, attentive. He was in love with her, and it made him gracious, helpful, attentive, inhibited, impotent. He was a fine escort up to the point of his anxiety and gloom.

He made Meg uneasy. She allowed herself to be involved in a continually deeper and more abortive love affair with him because it was important for him.

"Why you no stay with your baby!" screamed little Ramón. "You leave it all day with Connie. I watch!" he screamed. "She come here and leave the baby there!" he screamed at Harold. "Bad mother!" And he began to beat her with both fists on her shoulders and breast, like a five-year-old in a tantrum. But he was fifteen years old; his blows hurt.

Harold grabbed him by the neck in an iron grip, but having grabbed him he did not know what to do with him. Meg was hurt and speechless with humiliation.

Immobilized, the boy was miserably ashamed that they could see the stain of his ejaculation on the leg of his pants.

Terry pushed open the door and followed Joanna in. He had brought her upstairs to meet the community.

With amusement, he at once noticed the stain on Ramón's pants. Except that he knew it couldn't be, it looked as if Papa had caught Junior jerking off. Meg and Joanna did not notice the stain, and perhaps wouldn't have known what it was. Harold wouldn't have noticed it in a hundred years. By then it would be dry.

"Why you no knock?" whimpered Ramón, in defeat. With a jerk he broke from Harold's grip and bolted out the door and could be heard bounding downstairs and into the streets.

5

Harold closed the door sadly. He wanted to ask, "What is the matter with him?" But he had to be at home to his un-expected guests, whom he was pleased to see. Much of his life with these boys had to consist of acting as if they did not exist.

He didn't know if he ought to continue with Ramón. Not because of the trouble for himself—beggars aren't choosers—but if it was good for Ramón. They had come to the point where there was never a pleasant hour.

He said to Meg, "Are you hurt? I'll send him back to his father."

Harold did not begin to understand how profoundly important they were for Ramón, he and Meg and Terry and everything. They were all the horrible tension and security of home. And, what with the car, the softball, the poker, being smuggled into the racetrack, the typewriter, the incomprehensible conversation that flew over his head, they were school, possible future, world. Harold felt that his own life was so bare that he did not keep in mind, though he knew it well, how empty and desperate the street life was.

He turned with a wan smile to the guests.

"This is Joanna!" exclaimed Terry, in a tone to make it clear that he had never talked about anything else.

Joanna did not know what to make of the scene, but she was put off by the bleak poverty. Who was the crying boy? This was Meg, but who was Meg? She did not know what to make of Terry's account of Jason's poems. But she felt that the degree to which Terry seemed to cleave to all these was a loss of that much of Terry to herself. They were her rival The sex just now had been pretty good, but she felt that Terry was thinking about something else, if not someone else. She did not belong here. She wanted to leave. She wanted to get Terry to leave.

It was not that Vanderzee was offbeat or way out. Rather—she sniffed it at once—it was conventional and square in a way that peculiarly threatened her own middle-class.

6

"I was just going to get dinner," said Harold, with formality but obvious pleasure.

"No, I must pick up the baby," said Meg hastily, picking up her bag.

But Terry was enthusiastic. It was just what he had rehearsed, a repetition of the beautiful meal that he had manufactured with Connie. He was immediately busy with the concept of spaghetti and its intricate subdivisions. "Wait, Meg," he cried, "I'll walk down with you. For three people we need at least six pounds of *pasta*."

"But we only go together as far as the corner!" said Meg.

"Please?" he said with big eyes.

Joanna bit her lip and walked into the other room.

Henpecked, he followed her and whispered crossly, "Now what's the matter?"

"I thought we were going to eat in Greenwich Village and go to *Breathless*," she reminded him.

"What difference does it make if we have spaghetti here instead of on Macdougal Street?"

She did not choose to answer this reasoning. He would bring it up as a talking-point later, when they quarreled.

"Meg! Wait up!" he called out. Even though Joanna and he were not going to stay for dinner, he nevertheless had to walk Meg the five yards to the corner, saving with stubborn punctilio the remnant of his plan and his manliness. Meg thought that he was funny.

Bitterly he reproached himself as he came back slowly up the stairs. He was good at this since his childhood in the confessional. He himself had spoiled a lucky day! He had not, like a man, offered Joanna his community just as it was, whatever it was. He had tried to con his friend. Above all, he had not been cool; he should have known, from the first visit in New York, that the old man was not an easy mark, but a formidable opponent.

7

Then they were all gone, and Harold was alone.

Outside—no unusual thing—a squad car whined and wailed and turned up Hamilton into the dusk. It clutched at Harold's heart for the boy.

Next moment he was violently trembling. He tried to control himself, but his limbs spontaneously jerked. He went white and sat down. His feet kicked out in irregular automatic jerks.

—He was in the bedroom rifling the dresser drawers, by flashlight. But this time he had badly miscalculated. The room light switched on. The people had returned. He got through the open window badly scratched, and had sprained his toe by the first-floor jump. The police were everywhere.

Nevertheless, he had now got over the wall of a school building and he was hiding in the basement in a trash can. Outside, the squad cars whined as they went round and around the block, circling the school. He was nineteen. The headlights flashed through the little basement windows. It was in Seattle.

He heard the bulls tramping through the building. They were down in the basement. Their brutal voices were clear as they passed by. "Turn on the fuckin' lights." They were afraid because they assumed he had a gun. What he was feeling in his hiding place he did not remember. His memory was that he wasn't feeling anything. Now they had turned on the lights. They were again tramping through the basement. Their voices were clear as they passed close. The whining squad cars were circling the building.

But after a while it was again dark and after a while they had left the building and after a while the cars outside had gone away. He did not remember what he did. It was 1:20 by his radium-lit watch in the trash can. He had kept his hand in his pocket to hide the glow.

It was not till late the following afternoon that they picked him up in Portland and began the grilling. He did not remember much about that either, except that he had remained cool and kept his mouth shut, being the leader.—

He yawned, and drowsed. When he awoke he was able to get his book and study. Ramón had not returned. It was just as well, because the examination was on Saturday.

the mayor of vanderzee

1

The Powers in the metropolis, which was often called the greatest city in the Western world, set about throwing the artists out of their homes, though the artists were an important part of its being a metropolis at all. The bother with the artists was that they occupied big spaces at cheap rent. These they improved by their ingenuity and made into whitewashed studios for their splashes of color. But lofts like that could be much more profitably subdivided or demolished and replaced by $100-a-room efficiencies, or parking lots, or public housing for poor people, who could pay more than the artists.

Artists are prodigal of their spirit and personal lives, but in their economy and work habits they tend to be thrifty. As tenants they are a washout. They have noisy parties and pay low rent.

Naturally, people like that are tenacious, and how to dislodge them? Let me mention two effective strategies that were used. A quarter in which artists lived could be classified as a slum. Then all the tenants could be dispossessed and the area splendidly rebuilt. There was a lot of money to be made both in tearing down and in building up. Of course, the quarter might not be a slum; it might have a low crime rate, be kept up, and be even one of the most charming neighborhoods in the city, because of the labor and ingenuity of the artists. This could be tiresome. Some artists knew journalists and reformist sociologists who taught them to appeal in the courts and agitate, leading to a long delay of execution. Nevertheless the strategy worked, for during the interim of litigation the neighborhood would in fact become a slum. For some moved out because the house was coming down, nobody would move in because the house was coming down, and no bank would finance purchase or renovation of a house that was coming down. Finally, the court *had* to judge that the quarter was a slum.

Much more direct was for a building promoter to bribe

the Fire Department to find violations impossible to remedy, a method also excellent for getting rid of little theaters complained of by parish priests. Sprinklers to be installed at $20,000. In principle, artists' lofts were fire hazards because they contained paint and thinner, and since the artists could afford neither the sprinklers nor even counterbribes which tended to run to a couple of grand—their buildings were summarily condemned. To be sure, the lofts were not fire risks in the literal sense that no fires ever occurred in them; the artists were careful craftsmen, and jealously protected their stored-up treasures. But they were certainly, legally speaking, fire hazards.

As their hardships increased, quite a few artists banded together and issued a Statement: Under these conditions artists refused to exhibit their works in the galleries of the ungrateful metropolis! This was powerful economic pressure. New York art means big business. There was plenty of publicity; everybody talked about nothing else. But with the lack of community endemic among American artists, each of whom was competing for the galleries against every other, it all came to nothing.

2

Hearing about the ruckus across the river, Roger and Jason decided that the crisis was a great opportunity for Vanderzee! In Vanderzee were still dozens of big lofts unoccupied by our friends, and ideal for artists. And there were abandoned buildings that were never going to be demolished until they were burned down by the winos who camped in them for the night. An artist could take a shell like that and make a thing of beauty. Thing was to have the artists officially invited to come to Vanderzee! To open a couple of galleries for them. Twelve minutes from Greenwich Avenue!

Excited by their practical idea, the friends at once wrote a citizenly proposal to the Mayor, enclosing the relevant clippings from the *New York Post*, *The New Yorker*, and

Art News, and hinting rather broadly that Mayor Kavanagh too would get his name in the papers. Bemused, the Mayor asked them to drop around.

3

The Mayor wondered what the angle was. He did not ordinarily concern himself with the future of the fine arts in America. He was a cunning and stocky little man, but he did not have broad horizons. His most statesmanlike act was his proclamation, during one of the Cuba crises, that in case of nuclear bombing the rules for alternate-side-of-the street parking would be temporarily suspended.

Yet there was something teasing in the proposition of the young men. Just because it was entirely strange, the word Art had in it an intangible promise. He knew, for instance, about the Lincoln Center for the Performing Arts in New York; he had viewed the opening on television, graced by the wife of the President of the United States, sponsored by a national manufacturer of glass. Now that promotion, it had been explained to him, was a clever new way of getting a big government subsidy for slum clearance. Were Roger and Jason's artists like those artists? Tim Kavanagh didn't know. He was an ignorant man; he didn't know. Artists? He would have to watch his step.

4

Our friends when they came to the interview, were a striking and attractive pair, one dark and savage, the other quite blond. Taking advantage of the handshake, Tim examined their hands. (He had once been district attorney.) They were not punks or junkies, or coal heavers, or ladies' hairdressers. He had checked up and learned that Roger was odd but quiet as a mouse, and that Jason was a professor at the big University and had a pretty young wife. Jason was, indeed, impeccably dressed in a charcoal suit. Roger was rougher, tweedier, but he was probably the artist.

He sat them down across from his big desk. "And now, boys," he said beaming, "you do the talking."

Roger did, most of it, and made a lot of sense. His father was on the Chamber of Commerce in Wichita, and he knew how to discuss the tax base, retail grocers, and liquor stores. He had homely arguments like that artists were great eaters; and he had big arguments, that hundreds of people would flock to the new galleries to buy pictures, and people like that spent money on everything.

With tiny eyes, Tim Kavanagh kept looking for a clue. He understood that with professors like Jason—he looked young to be a professor—there had to be a considerable front. One could not get quickly to the point. He decided that Jason was an idiot, but *he* obviously had the real-estate connections. From time to time Jason interjected friendly references to the coming football season at Vander-zee High, and these were idiotic.

"Well!" said Mayor Kavanagh, "well! Who are these now artists? They Major Figures?" he asked, dropping the phrase he remembered.

Jason, businesslike, pulled an envelope from his breast pocket and showed him the names in the clippings. They were names unknown to Tim Kavanagh, but he revised his estimate of Jason and decided that he knew the Dealers. Unfortunately, *Art News* had embellished its story with examples of paintings, and these were not reassuring. They were even alarming. Jason wished that he had left that story home.

"What do you think this is?" said the Mayor, pointing with his pudgy finger.

"Yeah, that—that's a lulu, ain't it?" laughed Jason. He decided to handle it by laughing and being colloquial. He and the Mayor had a laugh together. Roger began to be annoyed. But the Mayor, though he did not know it himself, was also upset and annoyed. He was insulted. Who were they kidding? The shapes were crazy.

The poor man was in a bind. On the one hand, he knew, for some incomprehensible reason all the big-time publicity in the world was channeled through these eggheads, writer people and professors; and there was a lot of money connected with these artists. On the other hand, to get the publicity and get hands on the money, one had to *deal* with such people. But they deeply offended him. They made him nervous. He was out of his depth. How would he know not to make a fool of himself? Who were the all-rightniks in this line? What lurked? He was a cautious man. He had to be.

"I don't get it," he said. "Why does Wagner in New York want to get rid of important people like that? Explain me that. Now you explain me that."

5

At this, because the Mayor had been so friendly, our friends made an absurd mistake. They tried to explain their true motives, the real advantage of their scheme as they saw it. But their true motives were that they wanted to make poor Vanderzee stand for something for them to be proud of; they wanted to improve the look of the streets; they wanted to spite the brutal city across the river; they wanted to give the artists a crashing and humorous triumph; and they even wanted to do something for the community of art. In spite of themselves, they could not keep their voices from ringing with ingenuous enthusiasm, and one chimed in with the other. In brief, they oversold it.

And hearing them, Tim's heart filled with disgust. They were Holy Rollers! the kind that stands on the corner with a bugle and sings hymns. And the only cash in it is what you get by passing the hat. Grimly he lit his cigar and pulled back from the precipice. His beady eyes lost their cupidity.

Artists! They weren't junkies but what were they? Some people said that they were pansies. He wouldn't know. He decided he had had enough of this pair.

"Yeah! and what's about all this noisy parties I hear about?" he said. "Why doncha tell me the details like that?

Natcherly Mayor Wagner wouldn't want that kind of element."

The atmosphere was changed, and Jason started. He was sure that Kavanagh knew about the pot. "Noisy parties?" he said weakly.

"Loud radios all hours of the night!" barked the Mayor. "We get continual complaints. Con-tin-u-al complaints." He pointed down with his finger on the desk. "Look here. What's about these friends o' yours? I ain't saying it's you, but it's Artists!" And he handed them a report from the top drawer.

Soren—Terry—Harold—Stephan Simak—

"Complaints to Captain Ryan. Is this artists' wild parties?" asked the Mayor. "Let me tell you, young men, that this is a conservative community. How can we have continual complaints? Is this the element we need in Vanderzee?"

"Complaints?" said Roger, beginning to redden. "Complaints about what—what—what did you say?"

"I said *Noise!*" said Mayor Kavanagh.

"Noise?" exploded Roger, in a sudden blast of fury. It had been building up because of Jason's half-lies in what was a straightforward proposition. He was pissed off when they laughed at the pictures. He resented being called a young man by this punk. "Let me tell you some news, Tim Kavanagh," he growled, and wagged a finger under the Mayor's nose, "you've had it! You and that lousy sound truck barking through the streets. What a voice! Blah, blah, blah, blah." He began to roar. "You gotta register if you wanna vote! O.K., we registered. Now we're waiting for election day. For Chrissake, Kavanagh, can't you at least make a new recording? Ouch!—"

Savagely, Jason kicked him in the ankle. He had warned him to keep his big mouth shut and not lose his temper. He knew that he oughtn't to have brought him, but he himself had no head for the tax base. It was, of course, Barry Conklin who should have sold the idea to the Mayor, but how could he approach Barry Conklin?

Jason was wrong.

For at the first bark out of Roger, Tim Kavanagh turned pale. It was, God save us, the dread enemy that he had been warned against from his mother's milk, the threat of a Reform Movement in Kayser County. It was the authentic voice of the do-gooder used as a front by real-estate promoters and public-utilities contractors.

That wagging forefinger under his nose, Tim knew it well! It was the boss at the clubhouse. It meant, Give or get out.

"Now hold your water!" he said to Roger sharply, to show that he was not afraid of him, and he threw out his fat hand from his fat chest. "A thing like this has got a lotta bugs."

"Tell me, what goes on in this town anyway?" said Roger sarcastically. "Why did they just paint out the name of the contractor on the garbage trucks?"

"Snoutrage!" Tim vehemently agreed. "There's *plenty* in this town that needs a renovation. But the core of our democracy is sound. What Kayser County needs is a forward-looking reform administration, free of the control of the bosses."

"Roger," said Roger.

Tim did not imagine for a moment that Roger was serious about the noise of the sound truck, that his was the outcry of an indignant citizen. No such species had ever inhabited Vanderzee. He assumed that he was playing normal politics, picking on a detail and blowing it up to campaign proportions, in a world where neither party could very well mention the real issues. "I never give that sound truck a thought," he said thoughtfully. "I sure have got to get another record. Thanks!" he beamed.

It was at this moment that Jason said cheerily: "And by the way, Tim, ha! before I forget. There's something else I came to talk about. That speech of yours at the High School, on the Youth Workers. Ha ha. How can *I* get in on this racket? I used to play shortstop for Yale, and I can also do fancy diving."

Tim looked at him in stupefaction and terror. Too fast,

too fast. They were confusing him. How in hell had he found out about that? What did they know? What didn't they know? He was losing his mind. He oughtn't to have stared at that crazy picture. They were New Yorkers. They'd skin him and hang him up to dry. But he wouldn't sign! He wouldn't! Not until he really cased it.

On the other hand, *if he never took a chance, he'd never get to Trenton.*

Groggy, but still in there pitching, he wrote out a note for Jason to give to the Chief Magistrate.

To his astonishment, the two rose to go, as if that were indeed what they had come for. They were voluntarily giving him a breather.

Tim was grateful to them. They were gentlemen. They did not take advantage. No doubt the new alignment was so solid that it didn't need to be sold at all. What *would* the vote be on the new Assessors? At this moment he would have signed anything. And it *was* a pleasing idea: Hamilton Square, the Lincoln Square of Vanderzee! Timothy B. Kavanagh, Mayor.

Effusively he saw them to the door. "Thanks again, boys," he said, "I'll be getting in touch."

7

In the anteroom, waiting for his turn to deal with the Mayor, was sitting Barry Conklin and briefcase. Roger, for his part, was pleased to see a friendly face. He regarded Barry as a kind of specimen of the sociological zoo.

The Mayor was momentarily surprised that these people knew one another, but it figured.

They stood around joking. But Jason hardly knew what to say to the chap he had punched in the nose, and Barry was puzzled why Tim Kavanagh should be so buddy with a pair like Roger and Jason.

When the door closed behind Barry and the Mayor, Roger said, "Well, that's that."

"What, do you think he'll queer us just because I hit him?"

"No, he won't queer us. *He*'ll be the Reform Movement in Kayser County. . . . What are you going to do with that note?"

"That note?" Jason was still holding in his hand the note to the Chief Magistrate. "Use it!" he said with decision, and went out into the lobby to look at the Directory. One had the impression that he liked to deal with officials, even though he got cold feet. His heart swelled with emotion at the prospect of being a Youth Worker for the Townies.

Roger pointed to it. Room 302.

"Do you think"—Jason looked about if they were overheard—"they dig the pot?"

banning the cars from new york

1

A small yellow shadow appeared in the frosted glass door, and there was a tiny knock. "Come," said Terry. The little Indian looked to me about seven years old.

"Teree," he sang, "when you come down for de ball game?"

"Which one are you—Rodríguez?"

"*Sí.*"

"Rodríguez, you go tell them half an hour; I'll play ball in half an hour," said Terry very seriously. The child fled, leaving the door open into the empty hall.

I was touched—as I wearily got up and closed the door—at how good he was. He was good to me, programmatically trying to make me happy, and sometimes for a few moments he succeeded. I guessed I deserved it. Yet we were lucky—the grateful thought often struck me—to be able to use each other pleasantly, whereas so many people were impractical and got little simple satisfaction. I did not trust Terry, but the look of love and trust that was sometimes on his face in bed was genuine. He himself did not know what he looked like at such times. He could not abuse it.

We had to plunge again into the turmoil of the world. Even while we had our coffee, we were eager to begin quarreling, to stay in touch.

"What game do you play?" I was amused at the Indian's tiny size.

"You'll see. Chinese handball."

"They're not very tall."—I felt so sorry for him. His hang-up in school had started again. The sheets, the aborted beginnings, were scattered on the floor around the chair at the typewriter. But he had *told* me the little essay, in perfect outline, and I could, like a tape recorder, have dictated it to him from memory. I itched to do it and take him out of his misery. The idea was fairly original and would have done him credit.

Once he had talked it away, to an interested ear, it was

gone forever. He had no faculty to make an object, standing by itself, apart from himself. I no longer had the heart to nag him, even though I knew he would feel better if he finished anything at all and would be able to boast about something real.

"Some of them are tall. You'll see. They're assorted sizes and colors." He wanted me to see. The game was important to him. And indeed, this outpouring of service, to them and me, was his genuine vocation, but he was not proud of it and they did not give academic degrees for it. I was remorseful. I ought not to have agreed to his registering at the University when he was not ready. The bother was that I myself was hopelessly academic—school was for me, since my fatherless childhood, a comfortable home—and I always assumed that it suited everybody.

It roused my unbearable anxiety just to try to read one of his aborted pages. From the first sentence he began, acutely self-conscious, to comment on his comment and criticize his criticism, and strike poses, and founder in the shoals.

Lovingly he opened the can of apricots. For me. He favored a packaged dry cereal called Wheat-Chex, but for me he obsessionally had the can of apricots or pears that he knew I liked—I had once bought it—with heavy cream. I had an inkling how much security he got, which he badly needed, from this ritual of contenting me and sharing the hour. He was looking at me as I lapped it up. "I love you, Terry," I formed with my lips. He was as if thunderstruck. Perhaps it was amazement at the simplicity of his own feeling, whatever it was. I was not embarrassed but in pain, because I wanted to give him confidence in himself as well as in me, or instead of in me, and I didn't know how.

2

The floor was littered also with the literature he gobbled up, the *Esquires* and *Playboys* and *Evergreen Reviews*, for which, to my stingy dismay, he paid real half-dollars and dollars. These represented, as I have said, the normal social world of his generation, that they so interminably had to disgorge again, instead of leaving it alone to begin with. Terry had a remarkable finesse in understanding every nuance of what gave him nausea; he could do everything but vomit and become bored by it. I was in a bad spot. I was delighted by the motion of his mind and utterly uninterested in the contents of it. He had coined the term *avant-Kitsch* to describe what these magazines aspired to, the conversation pieces of Yale, the moral revolution of the convention of Door Hardware in Miami. He could point out infallibly where they succeeded and where they missed. In the right office he would have been worth $25,000 a year. But he was ashamed to apply.

Since I was not going to nag him about the school assignment, we had to start some other wrangle, probably ideological. (It always came to this anyway.) To keep at each other, continually probing, I being loftily hypercritical, both of us too attentive to each other and getting angry. We were the kind of people who interpret moment-by-moment behavior with big reasons; we used our close feelings as evidence, looking, as if sadistically, for proof. (Sometimes we came out surprisingly, with immense satisfaction in ourselves.) We could stop it at will, in the twinkling of an eye, by touching each other. Except that that would only end up in bed again, sweet but never enough.

I often put off lovemaking because we were not well matched. I liked to touch him, clothed or naked; we kissed greedily; he smelled delicious. I was never strongly excited by him, and after a while I would give in matter-of-factly to coming off, sometimes sweetly, sometimes because there was nothing else to do. But Terry had the same difficulty in coming to orgasm that he had in finishing a class paper or anything else. He was sometimes more excited than I ever was—or so it seemed to me, he sang strange sounds—but with rare exceptions he bogged down in distractions, lacked the resolution to satisfy himself, lost touch with his sensations. At first he used to torture himself about this, but it beauifully dawned on him that also this made no difference. He did not need to perform; we were together still. But it was never sure to me how much I ought to insist on his joy, and I no doubt often made wrong decisions.

I was disappointed, but it was the best I had in the world. There were moments of peace, sometimes of sweetness, and most important of all, there was never a moment, if Terry and I were alone together, whether lovemaking or quarreling or playing dominoes with absurd competitiveness, that either of us was ever resentful or bored. We both of us had a genius for coming across. When he was boring or hateful, I went *at* it. I was not going to abandon him and I refused to put up with him for a moment. And he refused to let me get too gloomy.

3

Even for the purposes of our quarrel, he tried to avoid mentioning his philosophers, since I became so jealous that it pained him. I was supposed to be Old Ironsides, always rational.

So I angrily took the side of his authors, of Mailer, Goodman, Krassner (who put out a brash sheet called *The Realist*). "At least they don't plagiarize the ideas of their betters," I said. "They have the courage of their own confusions."

I was sincere in praising them—even when I was petulant I was sincere. If Terry would be influenced by his authors for his own growth, I could easily overcome my jealousy, for I loved Terry like a son and wanted his advantage. I had no clue as to what he truly needed, what was truly in him to be. I kept listening for a clue. His potential nature was to me impenetrably dark—he was never enduringly enough in contact with the environment, or with enough environment, to express himself. There was no doubt that he was schizophrenic.

Was there time? Would he crack up before he found himself? Would the atom bombs fall? These were the circumstances in which we lived. Arabelle said that he needed three or four years to catch up with himself.

I *could* not talk to these kids with a clear conscience

about their authors. In my opinion, they were not good writers, not good enough. Beleaguered by a stupid world, they left out too much, just to cope at all and remain alive. I did not believe that the outcries of the marginal, or social justice for the deprived, would regenerate my country. This very leaving out was inauthentic, just as it was inauthentic to leave *them* out. Yet if I said this simple thing to kids who respected me, I found that it dampened their enthusiasm for their authors, like teaching them in *Contemporary Lit., English 553, for Seniors;* and this left the kids *without* authors. (Of course, I could not cope either, but I was not an author.) Instead, I became squeamish about my own frank opinion, and rather leaned over backward to approve. This was entirely phony.

Bitterly he said, *"You* can praise Mailer and Goodman, but who gets the big audience? Bennett and Goldberg steal what my writers make up in 1962 and give it out as the *avant-Kitsch* of 1963."

"What skin is that off your ass?"

"They have power."

It was the argument of Thrasymachus, as unanswerable now as in the time of Socrates. "Power to what?" I said ritually. "They can't get any more out of success than they have in their own small souls." As a matter of fact, these days, they did not even *have* their power. A mechanical system exerted a mechanical force, and the apparent governors were only engineers and oilers. Dutifully I pointed out to my young disciple, "You are giving, I ought to tell you, the argument of Thrasymachus in Plato's *Republic,* either Book I or II, I forget."

He was thrilled again to learn that there was something in the past that was real, in those great books that he could not read and for which he had a superstitious reverence. But his characteristic response was to adopt "Thrasymachus" as another hip role for himself, and to say glibly, when occasion arose, "I am saying the same thing as Thrasymachus." He was profoundly unteachable, at least by me. Whatever I said, he swallowed whole and used to his disadvantage.

But seeing I was distressed, he came across to me and

touched my face. We clasped each other. Greedily but not enough. I took my glasses off.

But we did not want to fall into sex, which would again have used up an hour of the time together that we both considered precious. "Let's see this game of Chinese handball," I said, disengaging myself.

I noticed that he no longer had to do up his hair *every* time he left the house.

4

Nine kids were bouncing a ball against the broad tan brick wall of the movie theater across the street. They were not exactly playing because they were incapable of organizing a game. For one thing, they were too disparate. A couple were seven or eight years old, a couple of others, Ramón and Chico, were fifteen and sixteen. They were Irish, Negro, Jewish, Spanish, and would never have come together except for Terry's game. And they were individuals, passionate, shy, brutal, or disdainful. All were taking advantage in order to be something by beating the others down, or at least to avoid being completely crushed themselves.

The ball bounded into the avenue among the cars and they cursed and yelled at one another, but no one would humiliate himself and get it.

Yet when Terry emerged and got it, there was a united shout of welcome.

5

"Foist!" "First!" "*Primo! primo!*" they shouted and crowded around him. Chico stood disdainfully aside, but I was astonished that he agreed to play at all.

"*I'*m first," said Terry decisively, since it was much easier to get harmony about being second, third, and so on. "Jocko is second," he appointed. Jocko was a shy tall Negro boy, age thirteen. There were two Puerto Rican girls, María and Constancia. Hymie was Jewish. I sat on a fender of a car at the curb.

And suddenly there was a game. It sprang into existence out of nothing. It was like busy clockwork along the wall. Ingeniously, pathetically urban. It was "Chinese" because the ball had to hit the ground before it hit the wall, and this allowed the game to be restricted to the sidewalk. Each player had a few squares of concrete as his field. When the leader missed, he moved to the end and all moved up.

The ball was bounding in rhythm. Slap-one-two, slap-one-two-three-slap. At once Terry awkwardly missed and went to the end of the line. On his first serve the shy boy missed and was overcome with grinning confusion; but the others, surprisingly, did not ridicule him as he wandered to the end of the line.

They were just learning our city game and were not good players. About Terry it was hard to tell, for he beautifully, as in everything else, took his coloration from the situation, sometimes as boastful as Ramón, sometimes as inept as the small fry.

—I did not have this adaptability. I always had to use what power I had, gently but decisively, just as in making love. I was too good for this league as yet, and that is why I sat out on a fender. As a boy, I was the champion of Washington Heights in Chinese handball, up to Morty Unterman more than a mile away, and I knew that the knack would come tingling back into my fingers. Maybe to sit out and observe was *my* way of being usefully adaptable.—

Oddly, Chico looked best. He had developed a little sleight-of-hand jab, with a lot of English, that required him hardly to strut about at all. They fell all over themselves trying to get it. He made monkeys of them, and smirked.

The chubby Jewish boy was a passionate orator. When he missed, instead of chasing the ball, he stood denouncing those who were at fault. They screamed, "Get the ball! Get the ball!" but he would expatiate on his alibi to the end, and then trot happily after the ball.

The two girls were silly about the game. They were as skillful as the others, but they did not seriously compete.

They never knew their scores. María, who was quick, made a deft shot, and then stood with her legs astride and her hand over her mouth, while Constancia giggled.

Pedantically, but with compassionate patience, Terry taught the shy boy how to serve on his next time around. It stopped the game, yet somehow—I could not understand how—there was no complaint.

The only pest was Ramón. He grumbled because Terry taught Jocko. When he was winning, he made the others feel as bad as he could by crowing, "I won you, didn't I? I won you yesterday too!" When he was losing, he accused them of cheating, and stalled the game by refusing to play. When one of the small boys made him lose a point, he waited till Terry's back was turned and, sharpening his knuckles, punched the little boy in the ear.

The child stood there unbelieving and slowly wept.

Ramón was dangerous to us. I saw, as if clairvoyantly, that he was going to do us great harm. But of course there is nothing to do with such clairvoyant visions not in the ordinary course of nature.

6

Yet it was not a school or social work, but a lively ragged game. Terry had organized it but he was playing it. They were playing hard and rapidly playing better. The ball leaped fast. It went out of bounds less frequently; when it did, it flew far down the street. As they became more purposive, they became more quiet, but when a play ended with a good shot, there was a unanimous exclamation.

The players were of assorted sizes and colors and they stretched in a thin line in front of the bleak bricken wall that had never before been put to any use. By the cosmos of their wills and passions they made the constellations in heaven turn otherwise, and they stayed, in so far, the breaking out of nuclear war.

My eyes were on Terry. It was hard to think that he was the same young man who was so tactless and rude. I'll ask

Harriet Young, I thought (I'll see her in Denver), if she has a job for this young fellow in the Settlement.

"Terry! I got 2! I got 2!" cried little Carmelito. They appealed to him as the final arbiter, whether the ball was out of bounds or just on the line. He was impeccably impartial. They were awestruck when he decided against himself. He did not seem happy but sober, as he shepherded the scores: "Now let's review. Who's got what? I've got 3. You've got 2, 5, 4, 4, 0, 1, 3, 5. What have you got, Ruby?" His problem, like any young man's, was to find a vocation, instead of monitoring the TV. Impulsively he came over to where I was sitting and touched my nose. I said to him in a soft voice, "You do it well." There was a derisive chorus of wolf whistles from the ten- and twelve-year-olds who never missed a trick. "Play ball. *Maricón!*"

Each kept his own score without cheating, except the girls who lost count because they did not care about the score. But the boys set them right.

There was a swift volley, and Chico won the first game. There was a unanimous shout.

7

In answer to it, the manager of the theater came out of the box office on the corner. "What the hell goes on here?" he said. "We gonna have this everyday?" He was a burly Italian in his shirtsleeves, and more than a little drunk. "Get in hell out of here. No ball playing allowed."

"Dere ain't no sign!"

"Where's de sign? Where's de sign dat says No Ball Playin'?"

"Fuck you," murmured Jocko shyly.

"*Maricón!*" said Carmelito, louder.

"What's that?" snapped the manager. Carmelito was about four and a half feet tall.

Terry confronted him and tried for a moment to be friendly. "Oh, let the kids play," he said. "What else's a wall like that good for?"

"I said scram, you cocksuckers. Don't ask questions."

They looked at their leader. For a moment Terry tried awkwardly to cling to his middle-class background. "You could keep a civil tongue," he said. "I'll ask all the questions I want." But he squared up to him. "What harm does it do if I play ball here?" he said.

Behind the man's back, Carmelito gave a Bronx cheer, and the manager shied. I had the impression that he had been slowly burning up in the box office and had actually fortified himself with the liquor. I wearily began to unwind myself from the fender.

"You can hear it inside the theater, stupid," said the manager.

White with fury, Terry pushed him in the shoulder, but not hard. "Don't call me stupid," he said.

"It's bullshit," said the shy boy surprisingly to me. "I sneak in yesterday an' you couldn' hear nuthin."

I believed him. The objection to the ballplaying was only that it existed, it was new, it was life instead of empty space. I stood up.

"Hey, mister," said the Irish boy, "how long you gonna stay on our court?"

I walked over and they groaned. "Jesus Christ," said the Jewish boy, "anudder one! Dey'll have a mass meeting wid speeches."

The girls giggled.

The manager turned on his heel. "O.K., you asked for it, I'll get the cop." He headed across the avenue. We watched him.

"All right, gang, play ball," said Terry, and they gave a shout.

But he looked at my face. The manager went up to the cop on the opposite corner. There was a terrible silence.

"He's getting the cop," said Terry. "Break it up."

"Terry," they said, "aw, Terry. Terry. Aw, Terry. *Maricón.*"

And blindly Terry walked away toward the Hudson River. I followed. They scattered from around me. I caught up.

"You said we had to be careful, for the Community!" he shouted at me.

"Don't shout at me," I said.

I was cold with self-loathing. I had betrayed natural society.

He was mortified because he had not protected them.

His heels rang angrily among the derelict houses as he walked. But I did not have an animal spirit to move me, so I stopped dead where I stood and watched him go.

He paused, and came back.

"Anyway, it won't do any good." I rubbed salt in the wound. "Tonight the kid will throw a brick and smash the box office."

"Which kid?" he asked, surprised.

"The shy one, the nigger. He went *in* the movie. It was a lot of bullshit."

"Jocko? Would Jocko throw a brick?"

"It costs $2,000 a year to process a kid in a reform school, Terry. Did you know that, Terry? See, Terry," I hectored him, "you don't know the facts. So why don't you keep your mouth shut?"

I was waste and sick to the stomach. But the incident had made him feel castrated. He hated me because we were powerless. We had come back very quickly to our quarrel about Thrasymachus.

I did not know how to reach him, so I decided on vaudeville. " *'We must provide these young folks an outlet for their energies,'* " I quoted from Mr. Rockefeller, the Governor of New York, " *'we must give them a sense of belonging.'* Thing is to get Jason to do Youth Work. He's going to start next week—Timothy B. Kavanagh, Mayor. Big shot Terry doesn't have an M.A., so *he* can't do it! He can't hand in his class assignments on time." I indulged my spite, the triumph of the powerless, and slashed about in every direction. What appalled me, as a city planner, was the thought of that bleak tan useless wall and the boring empty stretch of pavement, which Terry had made for an hour bound with ordered life.

"Why do you think he chased you away, Terry?"

My hope was by cruelty to make the tears come to his eyes, to thaw the knowing leer that I saw freezing on his face.

He rapidly narrowed the incident down to his personal confrontation, clenched fists, with the manager. "He was chicken," he said objectively. "So I should have been cool. Instead I copped out and pushed him. The bit was to feed him a few more drinks and ride him home in a taxicab. That would be sound administration."

"It's good," I said objectively. "You end up with a Little League ball team, HAMILTON THEATER across the chest. You get a percentage on the garments."

Thus we cut the incident down to size, our despair down to size, and our happines down to size. My country down to size.

"I'll see you," I said, and left him, and cut across, toward the terminal, the crazy little plaza with the verdigris statue of the father of the Hudson River Railway Company, striking the pose of Daniel Webster.

"Tomorrow?" he called after me in panic.

Yes, tomorrow, Terry, yes, I hoped. But I went.

9

In New York, I took a cab across town to WLSR, the Listener-Supported Radio—twenty-seven minutes, a mile and a sixteenth—and I asked to make my monthly tape for the daily Breakfast Commentary, Give People Something To Chew On All Day. There was no studio available. I said I would wait. And finally I was seated in a lonely booth with a metal microphone, talking to a spinning reel of tape in the control room.

And I poured out my heart in a plea for my fellow citizens to ban the private automobiles from the streets of Manhattan.

Vividly—I watched the tape unrolling—I explained how we could all have better transportation without those cars, by doubling the cabs and speeding up the busses. Pictur-

esquely—the technician signaled to me to bring the microphone closer—I described our city with half the streets
closed off, for planting and playing fields and new building
without relocating tenants. Responsibly—with an eye on
the clock to end on the minute—I provided peripheral
parking for the cars that came in from Mount Kisco,
Westchester.

It was a good performance. I did it because the manager
of a movie theater in Vanderzee became anxious at signs of
life on the street, and he shambled out of his booth to
still them.

It was a practical proposal. My colleagues and I have
continued to push it—the city will have to come to it anyway, and the sooner, the better. We want to put it to the
citizens for a referendum, to get a mayoral candidate to
adopt it as his program.

Because that ape took from Terry his place in our society
and made me sick to the stomach. But we could not fight
him off because we too were afraid.

But without the ordered cosmos of these lively games,
milk was poisoned.

I was doing the best I could. Unfortunately, I could do
nothing for Jocko or Chico, nothing for Carmelito, or
Terry or me. Though I spoke passionately into the microphone, looking at the clock so as to end on the minute.

10

I had no technique to live on except by denying that facts
were necessary, although the existing facts are always, inso-
far, necessary. I looked past them to their causes, to undo
them. But I did not take the causes very seriously either.

Instead—and this I did with all my will and apparently
indefatigably (but I will one day drop with weariness)—I
invented a different practical world than this world that
made no sense and took the heart out of me. Instead of
resigning, I reacted, in moments of despair, by thinking up
something else, and behaving as if this more pleasing landscape might indeed come to be the case.

I, like anyone else, would like to accept my only world as it is. But it is not viable for me. I do not find enough in it to celebrate. When I have found something, I have celebrated it! Yes, ask anyone who knows me if it isn't so! I am even easy to please.

But my praise has to be authentic. I do not like to make allowances. How can one be in love, making allowances?

Of course, I had a spiteful satisfaction, in my dismay, in offering utopian proposals that were so practical that people felt stupid and ashamed not to put them into effect. I did not offer them for spite, but out of dismay. I hated the money and power that made my country base. I loved my countrymen. It was a time of unrest, under a calm surface.

I often wished I were an artist, a writer or musician, so that I could actually create for people a piece, though small, of lovely and sensible world, without being balked by intractable powers and, worst of all, by the almost universal psychology of this beaten people that Nothing Could Be Done.

As it was, I went about the country angry and quarreling, urging people to do what they wanted but feared to; what they wanted but couldn't; what they didn't want at all but that I thought was good for them. It was an ungrateful kind of hectoring and badgering. I was often boorish and often boring. Yet I was not a fanatic. People could shake my confidence. But they had to convince me with reasons.

11

I got home from the radio station late for dinner. My wife and boy were clearing the table.

Polly was waspish, and I was not eager to explain. I rarely missed the evening meal with her and Hugh (my daughter was at college again). No matter how good a time I was having elsewhere, I cut it short to get home, as I cut short my pleasure with the students in order to go to the Administration's reception. I earned the freedom I insisted on by plenty of responsibility. But I had had to make the tape in order to revive enough animal spirit just to move my feet. How to explain that?

She was jealous of Terry. Since I concealed nothing, she had soon figured out that I was spending a lot of time with him and was no doubt in love with him, in my familiar manner. My loves were nothing new. The trouble was that she didn't like Terry. He seemed to her empty as well as rude and shifty. This was too bad, but I didn't expect my life to be easy and convenient. I was sure that when she came to know him better she would tolerate him, if only because he was needful and she was just and kindly. Her jealousy, like my own rages of jealousy, was only an incident in our long experience as partners.

Yet, after Hughie had gone in to do his homework, my wife burst into tears, and they were certainly not tears because of a callow youth. I rose from my chair and came across and touched her face. "Don't talk to me, go away!" she blubbered. "You never talk to me!"

It was true. I didn't find her conversation interesting. But of course she was interesting when she was real, like now. I explained why I was late, and she understood perfectly well, except that she could never understand why I hoped for anything different, since her own fortitude was deeply stoical.

She told me that she was tired and aging.

It was her job.

I thought she liked her job. Her work was important to them—it was a news agency, and scheduled the tickets and maintained communications to the farthest corners of the earth. She met world-famous people whom she liked to talk about, and there were numerous parties which to me, when I occasionally went, were quite boring, but I didn't belong to the club. She definitely did, and I suffered twinges of jealousy at the tone in which she spoke of this reporter and that photographer. But I hadn't noticed that she was coming to see—what to me had been evident immediately—that the enterprise was not *bona fide*. The Agency was pretty venal, and some of them were thick in the Cold War and overlooked stories that were inconvenient.

To my pleased surprise, Polly had suddenly joined the Women's Strike for Peace. But I ought to have taken it as a terrible sign of how desperate our situation was, for Polly was not one to cry out except in a matter of life or death.

"Why don't you quit?" I suggested. "Serve them right. They can't do without you."

"I did quit," she said, and again wept. "Now what am I going to do with myself?"

It became clear what she was after. (In this kind of scene, she was always after something.) She was forty-four and wanted to have another baby before it was too late. She let slip that she had had lunch with Connie.

Why not? It seemed to me to be a reasonable motive to have a baby, to have something to do, having quit a lousy job.

12

Inevitably she was boring, conversation with her was uninteresting to him, because deep down she balked against what he stood for, what he spent his life for—or perhaps just that he spent his life. When he got himself into trouble, as happened from time to time, she was almost disloyal: she did not side against him, she did not approve him. Instead she sat there sullen.

So he could not explode in his indignation about the issue, as he saw it. Yet he did not explode in his indignation against her disloyalty, because he knew that this made her nearly lose her mind.

He tried in quiet tones—ill-muffling the impatience in his voice—to explain what it was about, and she began to yawn.

a youth worker

1

"I'll nail you, you black cocksucker!"

From behind, the tall Negro had slashed the ball out of Schiller's hands.

The whistle blew.

"Two shots!" said Jason, holding up two fingers.

They lined up. Schiller's knuckles hurt and he was a sorehead. He missed both shots, and his teammates jeered him. The game was being played with a real lousy spirit. The ball flew down the other end.

Jason whistled.

"Charging."

"*Maricón!*"

The electric light was dreary, but outside it was dark and drizzling. Jason hated the whistle that stopped the game, but he had thought it through and he was going to blow it. If they were going to get anything out of playing, it would be by playing the rules.

"Pass it! pass it, you white mother!" said little Roy in a pleading whine. Jason kept the teams mixed, and one of the results was that they never passed the ball.

He whistled.

It was the Irish and Germans who said "cocksucker," but the Negroes said "mother-fucker." Jason was curious about the difference in psychology and had discussed it with Connie and Harold. He was aware of too much for this company, but nobody is ever aware of enough.

Schiller wore on his fourth finger an imitation ruby class ring from St. Aloysius'. Cleverly he lashed out and drew blood that, on the black cheek, shone the same color as the ruby. Nobody saw him do it.

Schiller was the black jacket Jason had crossed with at the Amstel on the night that he knocked down Barry Conklin. When they recognized each other, Jason was

156

pleased at the chance to work with him, and Schiller thought whatever he thought.

As if stung by a wasp, the tall Negro boy wiped his cheek and looked at the streak of blood on his yellow palm.

2

Jason had earnestly thought it through and read the authors. The usual Youth Worker theory was to accept their standards and prejudices, and try to calm them down and con them into adjusting. But the better writers pointed out that in the long run this unethical approach wouldn't work anyway, because it didn't take them seriously as people.

It was obvious that these fellows had no objective world, to lose themselves in, and grow, and find their identities. They lived by kicks and empty interpersonal relations. They needed something different from one-upping one another and spiting everybody else. From their panicky proving of prowess. From their interminable hanging around with nothing to do, and hanging together in groups that punished any gesture of initiative or individuality by instant ridicule and blackmail.

Jason wanted to get them interested in *anything,* individually or collectively. He thought of photography. Sex was good if it was affectionate. Even driving was good if one was going somewhere and could make himself useful. Making music and dancing were very good. Political action —to Jason this meant the peace movement—would be superb, and would win them the gratitude of mankind.

He set himself the goal of getting one of them to read a book.

Working with them, he was dismayed. They would not concentrate for five minutes on anything but tormenting one another or waiting for a fix. They seemed to have no sexual drive; they could not persist after a girl for half an hour before feeling rejected and withdrawing or becoming insulted and slapping her in the face.

3

Athletic games, he thought, were ideal for his purpose. The athlete gave his body and himself as a sacrifice. The individual lost himself in the team. The team lost itself in the competition. Afterward everybody was exalted, purged, chummy.

He was mad for form and style. He was himself a fine all-around amateur, sometimes, for a flashy moment, as good as a professional, and always eager to play hard. He liked these young fellows, some of whom had strength and speed and reflexes that delighted him. He was sure he could transmit to them some of his own athletic joy. He was a good coach, and technically they improved fast. This lulled him.

He did not cajole them with personal praise or con them with flattery. When he cried "Good shot!" he meant it. Sometimes, when he was carried away, he said, "Beauty!" Often he said, "Too bad!"

He was a fine fancy-diver, with the stylish self-possession of his blond body that he lacked in his pathetic self-reproachful poems that could not yet cope with the town. Diving into the deep, or when he went up after the ball with his mind set on it, and therefore, toes dangling, he leaped four feet from the ground, he felt great and looked it, and also knew he looked it. Within a week, he was in condition again.

In short, he set it up exquisitely to get a kick in the balls.

4

It was a close game. Jason had picked the teams well.

To his delight, a few of them—Luis, Roy, MacGregor—were suddenly really playing, to win, but fair. They were angry and impatient when he blew the whistle, but not at him, at the foul. They knew that he didn't like to blow it either.

They began to pass accurately and with brains.

It had got rapidly darker outside. The electric light was less feeble and unpleasant.

He whistled. They groaned.

"He carried it," he explained apologetically—his first sign of relenting. (He had been tempted to let it pass.)

Those who were interrupted in the game to which they were sacrificing groaned at the interruption. But those who were trapped in their own conceited souls, through clenched teeth sucked in a sadistic breath at the interruption.

They were sixteen to twenty years old, much too old to risk playing ball games. When they had no useful jobs, when their families were like hell, when they were stupid, when they had a monkey on their backs, when they were unmanned. Jason understood that God loved the adventurous sacrifice of playing basketball as hard as one could, and He would renew with interest the energy we squandered. But most of these juvenile delinquents did not understand it at all. They laid side bets on the game to make it worth playing.

Deftly little Luis passed the ball to the tall Negro who had stolen away from Schiller in the corner. And the tall boy flipped the ball, in a languorous arc, neatly through the hoop.

There was a great shout. The score was tied.

Excitedly Jason tossed it up in the center, and it was again tipped to Luis.

With a fierce blast of the whistle, "Foul!" shouted Jason angrily. Schiller had outrageously swiped the forward. Jason grabbed the ball.

"Toin off that fuckin' whistle!" cried Schiller.

"Two shots!" said Jason, holding up two fingers, while with the other hand he tossed the ball to the forward.

Schiller kicked him savagely in the balls, and Jason fell screaming to the floor, doubled up and writhing.

They looked at him lying there, and then all of them, except little Roy, fled, crowding at the door, to the locker room, to dress and get away. Roy bent over the writhing man, as if to try to help him, but he remembered that if the man died he would himself be questioned by the police. So he too ran away.

It was late at night that Connie returned from the hospital. Pedro was waiting in the street outside the door, in the rain. He was drenched and cold. It was the last week of October. What did he want? she wondered. Why hadn't he waited in the bar across the street, until a light went on? He wasn't thinking. It was unlike Pedro.

She fed him tea with a shot of rye. Indignantly she poured out the story about Schiller in the gymnasium, as she had got it from Jason. Her eyes sparkled with indignation. It was extraordinary to see Connie in this mood. For a change she made no effort to understand everything and pardon everything. All she knew was that her man was hurt, doing his duty.

Naturally, Jason had told the police nothing. His version for them was that there was a mix-up on the floor and somebody had kicked him in passing.

"Somebody kicked him in passing—" she repeated her husband's sentence. "He did not know who it was." And as she said the sentence, she realized that it was not a lie but the truth. The glow of anger slowly faded from her eyes, and the tears came. Luckily they were wearing sneakers.

Pedro could not, of course, comfort her by holding her, but looked at her with a courtly and stiff concern.

She was now about eight months pregnant and looked like a pretty little tent. Pedro looked at her, as always, with soft eyes. She suspected that he was in love with her; she did not understand that he adored her. He was confused; he did not know how to look at her, and averted his eyes. But when he took a sip of tea, he flashed her a look from behind the cup. He stood up tall from his chair.

To her surprise he was kneeling before her. She had the vivid sentiment that it was a ritual act, something medieval.

"May I listen to your baby, Señora Connie?" he asked in his impeccable English.

"Yes, Pedro. Whatever you want."

Avidly he pressed his ear to her belly, holding her fastidiously about the waist, and he could indeed hear the foetus in motion.

160

He got to his feet, put on his wet jacket, and left.

She was baffled by this behavior. He was altogther un-like himself. Why had he come in the first place? He had said almost nothing. Usually, when he came with Harold, to figure out the evening's trotters with Jason, Pedro was talkative, full of anecdotes, often quite amusing. He was one of the best human beings she had ever met, and Connie met many fine people, inevitably, since when they were with her, people showed their good side. She had an alto-gether biased, yet true, opinion of the human race.

6

It was not until hours later, at five in the morning, when it was beginning to be dawn, that she awoke terrified from sleep in her lonely bed and knew that Pedro had come simply to get the name of Schiller, and had perhaps killed him.

a physicist

1

"We have tended, as Terry there pointed out last week—"

It was as if by accident that Terry had wandered into the Physics lecture. He had decided to flunk out of the University and he had decisively cut the lab section. But after that he had nothing scheduled—he still did not know how to waste the morning, too early for lunch with Joanna. He was again in his accustomed seat in the fourth row on the side, from where his arm used to shoot up when he had a bright idea. He lost what color he had. *Again* Professor Davidson was singling him out for special mention.

He knew that the honor was never quite serious. But the other students envied it and therefore he boasted about it, having so little real to give him confidence.

"We have tended," said Davidson, looking away from him, "to find new particles when we have new apparatus. J. J. Thomson, you remember, took a Crookes tube and redirected the beam, and so he analyzed out the charge and mass."

Terry *had* said it; it was the kind of "germane" idea that struck him. He was bitterly proud that he was again going to disappoint Professor Davidson and disappoint himself. He was distressed that he had come, but if he hadn't come he wouldn't have known this mention, bitterly to mention later.

"The last twenty years," continued the lecturer, "with random bombardment by the atom smashers, we have of course been getting a random proliferation of particles and antiparticles, antiprotons, hypermesons—"

Davidson was a good man as well as a great name. He was really at the University as headman of the reserch contracted by the University with the Air Force. At $25,000 and no classes to teach. But he felt that there was something indecent in these bogus faculties that did not teach. He had been taught. So he took over the Introductory and was telling them all about the particles. His elementary approach was not so much popular as historical rather than mathematical.

He belonged to the princely line. Thomson taught Rutherford taught Chadwick taught Davidson. He assumed it matter-of-factly, although it was a British line and he was an American Jew. He refused to change the spelling to "Davison." "Analyzed out" was strictly American. His own best was a young, already world-famous, Chinese.

When he singled out Terry, it was only partly as a lecturer's gimmick. He did not much go in for gimmicks; he preferred to hold up the subject in the space before them, and let it shine. But Terry puzzled and disturbed him. Being in a mathematical science, he was used to white faces and borderline-schizophrenic eyes, but he could not understand how this young man could grasp so much so quickly—and even intuitively, mathematically—and yet learn nothing at all. The report from the section leader was "hopeless."

"Good!" he went on. "There is an inventive virtue in the apparatus. We can envisage these men doing. Doing with hands and eyes—men—increasing the energy in the magnet, making a bigger whirlibang. But now let's look at the other side of the process. And that's the subject of my lecture today. Most of these particles, as some of you may know, were *theoretically* predicted long before they showed up—or were produced—whichever way you want to put it. We could not find them without the apparatus, but we did find them because we were looking for them. Take my teacher's neutron. Who remembers from last week what a neutron is? . . . No, not quite. Yes! That's exactly correct. I'm delighted you put in about the cloud chamber."

But Terry, as he sat there—his was not one of the hands that had shot up—no longer knew exactly about neutrons, though he had known. Reminded, he remembered about the cloud chamber, the absence of trace and charge, but he had forgotten it. He knew he had forgotten it. He no longer fooled himself as he had at Columbus. It was not "their" fault; it was somehow his own. His face was white. He loved Professor Davidson—he found it very easy to love. If it didn't require knowing the subject, he could gladly have devoted himself to a career in physics.

He was puzzled and disturbed by Professor Davidson. What was he doing up there? Nobody in this Introductory was going to be a physicist—so Terry had made up his mind for them—and yet Davidson, with obvious affection, and remarkable skill, was earnestly going through a song-and-dance. Why was he?

In spite of himself, Terry was fascinated by the orator of the Western world, the beautiful spirit. "So there it is, a neutron!" said Davidson, at the blackboard, underscoring an equation, his blue suit dusty with chalk. "Picture it! it was partly just on grounds of elegance and symmetry that we demanded, Produce it! It *must* be there! And within two years after the equation, the French *did* produce it!" His voice rang with pleasure at his teacher's triumph. "What are you thinking of now, big eyes?" he suddenly demanded, fourth row on the left. He was curious what that mind thought of *that!*

"Who? me? Do you want to know what I'm thinking?" said Terry, snottily. "Sure. They're at each other like a gang of bops. The war counselors versus the hippies. Each is one-upping the next to prove he has a hard-on."

"I beg your pardon?" said Davidson, and the crowd cracked up.

"But you can't prove it!" cried Terry hysterically.

The bell rang.

At the bell Davidson had a blinding insight into what it was that disturbed and puzzled him with this generation of youth.

2

He caught up to Terry at the door.

"You don't mind my picking on you, do you, young man?" They emerged from Thayer Hall, past the marble statue of *La Semeuse,* scattering her grain.

"No. The professors always do . . . the good ones," he said, not boasting, but confused.

"Do they? Why do they?"

"I don't know. I used to think it was because I was bright. . . . I'm flunking out again."

"You are bright, it goes without saying. I know you're flunking out. Do *you* know why?"

They walked across the big quadrangle, and past the verdigris statue of *Le Penseur,* with his back, as the joke went, to Philosophy Hall. The campus was crowding up. It was five to twelve.

"*I* know," said Professor Davidson.

Terry looked sidewise at him, with the whites in his eyes showing. He knew that he did know. All these fatherly grown-ups understood him. He said, "Is there something missing?" He almost meant, "Do you think I'm crazy?"

"No, it's not only you!" said Davidson hurriedly, apprehensive. Many of his colleagues *were* pretty crazy. "Tell me, Terry, tell me something. Why do you think the Old Man— or Rutherford or my teacher—*bothered?*" So asked Professor Davidson in the fourth generation. And in the past behind them all loomed, like the fabulous Emperor Chow, Clerk Maxwell. "Do you really think that those men were—what did you say?—hippies? one-upping? And—impotent?" He smiled at the idea and Terry's way of putting it.

Terry said nothing. He was beyond being combative.

"They were in love with her," said Professor Davidson. They walked along in silence. "They wanted to see her better, know her," he said.

It was, in the crowd, as if there were a silence on the campus. He was that sure.

"She favored them," he said.

At this, Terry would have burst into tears. He gave Professor Davidson one look and bolted in another direction. He was not yet ready to burst into tears. That would be later, for the asylum.

Davidson stood, and watched him go. He knew what was wrong, but he did not know how to cope with it. These young people simply did not understand what the enterprise was about. It was not their enterprise—he could not imagine why. They were never going to take it upon themselves. They might go through the University, but they were not going to commence. Some of them—technically the best, morally the worst—imagined that they could *master* the subject. Master it! With others—Terry, vanishing in the crowd—if they were visited by an idea, it was not because of the nature of things, but because of—interpersonal relations. Or to please Professor Davidson.

He felt dirty. Then he became angry at being imposed on.

3

In his haste to have it over with, Terry ran back to catch Professor O'Connor emerging from Philosophy, to tell him that, though he had tried, he could not write the assignment, and he was going to drop the course. He took a pride in himself for this manly statement. He no longer silently ran away, as he used. He watched his behavior like a fever chart and saw good and bad indications.

This professor too walked him across the campus, more and more crowded as the students poured out for lunch. The big bells began to boom noon.

O'Connor was saying: "Get out of this place, it's death. They'll put you in a mold like Jell-o. Like—heh heh—like cold shape, as my English colleagues say."

Terry looked at him sidewise, with narrow eyes, as they passed the black statue of *Le Marteleur,* leaning on his sledgehammer.

"This University is run like a bank!" exclaimed O'Connor with spiteful enthusiasm, demonstrating an unpalatable truth. "Figure it out. I wanted to give a little seminar on Hobbes, to six students. No, it wouldn't pay. The cash take on my afternoon lecture, at $40 a point, 88 students, is $10,560." He had spent the morning calculating. "Now deduct my salary, one-third of a twelve-hour load. . . . Who *gets* all that money? Young man, if you want my advice"— Terry had not asked for it—"escape! Escape while there's time! Go some place where there's sun! Go to Mexico! Travel! See for yourself! I take it that you want to be creative"—this assumption too was uncalled for; Terry would certainly not have put it that way—"then *be* creative! Why do you need lessons? *Make* those poems and stories and pictures, just as they rise up in *you!* Directly!" He jabbed the air with his exclamations. "You kids all say the same thing, you'll start working when you have the equipment. Take a tip from me, you won't get it here. *We'*ll see to that. We'll *kill* your confidence, as dead as we can. And we're stronger than you!" he concluded in triumph, stretching out his arms to embrace—everything.

"Why would you want to kill us, Professor O'Connor?" asked Terry.

"Are you kidding?" said the professor, looking at him in surprise. "Didn't you ever hear of resentment? What do you think that Nietzsche and Scheler are about? Take Scheler—heh heh—Scheler couldn't get a job because he happened to like to screw. The great Husserl—Scheler applied at Marburg—Herr Professor Husserl said, *Nein! niemals Scheler!* So poor Scheler didn't have a job. Did you know that?"

Abruptly Terry left him, and wandered off.

He wandered off, around the gilded seated statue of *Alma Mater,* spreading her offering hands. He had been biting his lips to keep from expressing his contempt. He was glad he had not spoken. What bullshit! If a young man could write down directly those poems, etc., that were apparently teeming in his mind, did Associate Professor O'Connor really think that he wouldn't be able to write a little class assignment on the relation of Husserl and Descartes when he had actually read the two books? A mind strong enough to educate itself would be able to put up even with the University. He'd quit, he wouldn't flunk out. So far as Terry knew, O'Connor had never asked any student a personal question. (Yet there *were* eighty-eight in the class!)

What Terry most resented was that the whole gripe came out of *The New Yorker* magazine. He resented being exploited as a coward's vicarious rebel, age ten, beaten at fourteen, like the adolescent in *The Catcher in the Rye.*

He found himself alone, in a small red-paved quadrangle with a grassy border. From here the lunch-bound crowd had vanished. There was no symbolic statue. Terry himself was standing there—he was self-conscious—like a symbolic statue.

And to his wonder, he was engulfed by an academic nostalgia, a yearning for his fellows, for his fellow students at the University. It expressed itself as another daydream in the biography of Terry. Terry was going, as the champion and ambassador of the students, to the offices of professors, of deans, to plead for the Community of Scholars (which he had also picked up from Goodman). Maybe, after all, people did not understand one another and all really had a common aim. Nobody spoke up. Why not he? He came to the Dean with a proposal to abolish grading. The Dean looked up at him and asked, "What are *your* grades, Mr. Terry? By what warrant are *you* in the University? Are you part of our Community?" asked the Dean.

In his daydream he flinched, and the depression of the young men of the United States, of England, of the Soviet Union, crept into his breast—

With a start Terry awoke, and looked about at the big unimpressive Georgian buildings surrounding him in the square, of the great University of the greatest city in the Western world, that stood for not much.

And he went back again—this time running—across the quadrangles. Toward the Laboratory, for Professor Davidson had been heading in that direction.

4

He caught him in his lab with the goods, actually putting on his leaden gloves, about to close the door.

Davidson was not annoyed to be interrupted by the breathless young man who called his name. He had plenty of confidence that She would always be there waiting for him to resume their dialogue. He did not think that Teaching interfered with Research.

Terry was pink with indignation, the first time that Davidson had seen any color in his face. "Twenty million of the annual budget," Terry gasped, "comes from government contracts, and most of that—*you* know—is from the National Defense!"

Davidson looked at him blankly.

"That's 40 percent of the running expenses of the University," said Terry.

"Is it really?" asked the professor ingenuously. Forty percent was surprisingly high. "Where'd you get those figures?"

"President's Annual Report, 1961," said Terry, accurate and documented.

"Hm. I shouldn't have thought—that's a big slice of the pie, isn't it, for an academic institution?" Suddenly the implication of Terry's "*you* know" struck him, and he reddened with anger. He was annoyed at the boy's effrontery. He was also a little sad, and disappointed, that Terry had such thoughts of him. "I'm busy," he said roughly. "What do you want?"

Quick as a flash, Terry chose a gambit. "What are the gloves for?" he asked.

Davidson tightened his lips, but he was big enough not simply to dismiss him. Indeed, he did not think that Terry believed that he was there for money or that his research was oriented by a business contract. Nobody was that stupid. But what disappointed him was that Terry, particularly Terry, should need to make such a spiteful attack, and at such a level, just because he could not learn physics. He was always saddened by vindictiveness, yet he understood it—he understood kids—they had to win victories, to retain a little dignity. Yet it was tiresome. He had thought that the boy and he had made a personal contact.

"The gloves?" he said. "Oh, I always put them on because they're stylish on TV. Do you have any other problems?"

"Is the radiation dangerous?" asked Terry.

—Was the boy a moron? "Look," he said, "don't bother me. You're a moron. I have office hours on Thursdays at four, but don't come unless you have a question." This was too harsh. "It doesn't need to be about subatomic particles," he added kindly. What *was* it in Terry's eyes? Was the boy *concerned* for him?

Suddenly the situation had become, inexplicably, extraordinary. Terry was standing there in front of him and suddenly, inexplicably, he thought of the last time that he had seen Niels Bohr. But Terry didn't look anything like Niels Bohr.

"Do you mean I should go away?" said Terry with suppressed fury, but his eyes were blazing with appeal.

What did the boy want to say? Terry was looking at him with doglike respect. He certainly was not accusing him of venality or timeserving. Yet he was accusing him of something. Why the twenty millions? Forty percent *was* a surprising figure; he should have known it. And why the gambit—Davidson understood that it was only a boring gambit—of the gloves?

The physicist felt sick. He was swept by a wave of nausea. For a moment he panicked. Had he been careful in bombarding the lithium? He gripped onto the bench.

Why was human communication so unbelievably confusing, almost as bad as the proliferation of the mesons? In dismay he had seen, year by year, almost month by month, the theory degenerating into a chaos of *ad hoc* explanations that could not possibly be Nature.

Astoundingly young Terry said in a pathetic voice, "Don't you know that you are like a father to them?"

"What is it, young man? What do you want from me?" wailed Professor Davidson, the present heir of J. J. Thomson. He needed to spell everything out, to have it spelled out, simple and clear. "You *don't* think, do you, that I am working on this problem because Washington, D.C., pays me to?" He was ashamed of his question, and he said, "I'm ashamed to ask you such a question. I know you don't."

"I! You!" cried Terry, too amazed to be offended. "Don't you feel well, Professor?" he said with concern, for the man did not look well. His admiration for the great man began to mount so strongly that he was afraid that he would become speechless and not be able to make the direct appeal that he had come for. (He wished, wistfully, that he himself could learn physics.) He was ashamed of his bit and returned to his own skin. And when Terry was alive in the world, and was not cowering or playing roles, he had no passions in his soul so strong as indignation and admiration; and now both these welled up, conflicting and yet reinforcing each other, and he became a very beautiful youth. He had the persuasive force of the future of mankind. It is what moves serious people.

Davidson was a seasoned veteran and quickly recovered from his panic. "Like a father? I see," he said quietly, and even cheerfully, for it was interesting. "Here I have been disappointed in *you* young people, and all the while, it seems, you have had cause to be disappointed in *me*. What can that be? Explain. Sit down. Come into my office." He took off the gloves.

"Not especially in *you*, Professor Davidson—"

"Ah. You mean, in my generation. The mess we have made of the world, and all this?"

"No, sir. I think it's more specific than that."

Davidson sat on his desk and looked at him candidly.

"We are disappointed in science," said Terry.

"Aha! In science," said Davidson.

"If you would stop the war—refuse—all of you from Pugwash, Russians and Americans—it would have a tremendous influence. The students—my fellow students—" He faltered and paused because he was flunking out.

"Go on, Terry, say it."

"They'd be—" He was abashed at the thing that he was going to say. "If the whole Physics Department—"

"The whole Physics Department!" roared Davidson merrily. "Where do you think that is?"

"If the whole Physics Department would take a stand," said Terry, "the students would be very proud of the University!" He paused—and blushed. "Can I be frank?"

Davidson averted his eyes. He was afraid of what the young man was now going to say.

"Last week when you stood there in front of us, joking about the lies of the Civil Defense, smirking and making wise cracks like a junior clerk or a griping sailor—Professor Davidson!—"

For the man started and, to Terry's dismay, blushed a deep scarlet for shame. And he remembered it, the blazing gloomy look of Uncle Niels when they gave him the Peace prize. For a moment he was badly shaken.

His agitation left Terry without support. Automatically the youth tried to retreat into his own callow defenses, except that, precisely when confronted with a boyish shame that responded to his own boyish shame, he could not retreat. So the two were, for a brief spell, in scalding pain, wishing that the earth would open and swallow them up, each by himself, but they were chained together, as they were going to be on another day. Terry cursed the inspiration that had occurred to him in the small quadrangle, to serve as an ambassador for his fellow students. What he had not counted on, in his daydream, was that his intervention would meet a response. He had not believed that the professors were men. He had simply wanted to spite them, by holding up the mirror to their ugliness, because they were powerful. Now he had to take the consequence of human contact. How could it be pleasant in our times?

Again the veteran recovered first. "You've got a point," he said. "I'd have to think about that." He looked at the youth frankly and somewhat humorously. "Thank you, Terry." He held out his hand. "Don't drop the course. You get more out of it than you think. You enjoy the play of mind—better than a movie."

Terry was afraid to take his hand—took it out of politeness—because their touch might be unbearably sensitive. But it was not so bad. Their palms were hot and dry.

"Forget that idea about the whole Physics Department," said Davidson. "There is no Faculty in this factory. Put it this way. Suppose that among the students you appealed to all the—what do you call them?—*majors* in Physics, the ones who are waiting for Bell and Westinghouse to tap them, the ones who are primed for General Dynamics—"

And because they were his fellows, Terry hung his head.

"Do you happen to know what in fact I am working on these days?"

"Of course," said Terry surprisingly. "You think that something is wrong with the method. You don't like the smashers, but it's deeper than the smashers. Something *must* be wrong, because there are too many particles. It doesn't add up. That's right, isn't it? Naturally you can't *say* this till you've got hold of something, but you're a lousy actor."

"You listen close," said the Professor. "There must be *something* you could learn, son."

5

By the time he was sitting at the lunch counter with Joanna, he was nearly delirious.

Under the intense bombardment, the particles were flying off in all directions.

The students ate at the counter like pigs at a trough. They jostled his elbow and his coffee was spilling in the saucer.

He envied Joanna. *She* had the philosophy assignment to hand in. What she did was thoughtful and honest, not phony. He did not want to belittle it. He had no right to belittle it.

She had an inner check that enabled her to walk out on the party when she had work to do.

But he was bitterly resentful that she had gone home to her parents over the weekend, and left him to his fate. She did not see that he was taking too much pot. Why didn't she see?

His doughnut was on the floor. He looked at it. She looked at him.

She was in a dilemma. She needed him to be wild and exciting, but if he flunked out again he was going to fall to pieces. He said that he was going to go away to Poland among the communists or to Ghana among the Negroes.

He could not, he would not, tell her about the conversation he had just had with Davidson. Because it was real. He resentfully withheld it, just as he lost his hard-on. Inevitably he was beginning to forget that conversation, like something he had dreamed.

His coffee kept spilling in the saucer because of his own shaking hand. He could not even turn surlily and say, "Watch where you're shoving."

Some One had robbed him of his alibi.

With humility he realized that he was an outlaw not because it was admirable, or good for him, but because he couldn't manage otherwise, just in order to survive. He bent his head.

She took his hand on the counter. She moved against him closer. She was terrified of her lust. Clinging to Terry would be her ruin. But she did not see about her any other young man who was worthwhile.

king ubu

1

"Of course I have sex with him," said Terry, "I love him."

Hearing it, Joanna became momentarily depersonalized. It was too strange to her. She did not feel a pang of jealousy. Terry was trembling with his own statement.

She knew that she must not interfere with him in this, nor try to prevent it. She would fail and arouse bad feelings that would never subside; or worse, if she succeeded, he would be defeated in a way that she did not want Terry to be defeated. She realized that she had known that Terry loved him; she had seen it on his face when he came from him.

She took a breath and decided that she was going to live with it.

At once she began to be frightened and confused. As soon as she accepted him, the man seemed like an over-powering force, not an evil force but just too strong for Terry, something like her own father. If Terry had a stronger character, if he had found himself, she would be less uneasy. As it was, he was swallowed up.

Suddenly she understood that the old man felt this too; he was her ally. Terry had long ago been swallowed up; the task was to persuade him to emerge. This man was wise and experienced; he certainly knew better than she. Even if she could, she did not dare to deprive Terry of his help. But she could not help hating him, something like her father.

"He needs me. Don't you see he needs me?" pleaded Terry, trying to bring them all together, so that he could have them all together.

2

"He means O.K., Terry," said Douglas, whom Terry was putting up during these months, "he's a good man. But he's shieldin' you from the hardships o' life an' it ain't a natural situation." When his own envy and frustration were strong, however, Doug sternly declared, "You're becoming effeminate, man."

Being a Negro, it was hard for Doug to get a job. He made it worse by a suspiciousness and touchiness that were pretty nearly paranoiac. At the personnel desk he would hand back the blank without filling it out; or he would balk outside the door of the employment agency without going in, while his hostility rose till he banged his fist against the wall; and he came home in a sullen depression. Next day he could not get out of bed at all. But as he lay there cursing himself, in the other room the two were making love, trying to be quiet but not quiet enough. Or they were carrying on their interminable quarrel in the kitchen, looking—he knew—in each other's faces.

Terry cheerfully, out of his few dollars, fed Douglas and gave him money for carfare and cigarettes, and paid for the pot that they smoked, never making any demand. Thus day by day he deepened Doug's guilt at being dependent.

Sometimes, visiting, the old man paid attention to Douglas—for half an hour—and he could, with a few piercing questions, bring his distress to the surface. He thought that Doug was much too bright and talented to be a messenger or stock boy, the jobs that Doug could not get, and he encouraged him to go back to school, which Doug could not do. Naturally, the Negro responded to this kind of concern both by falling in love with him and being fiercely resentful of the invasion of his secrecy and independence.

But of course the man had come to see Terry and not Douglas, and he often callously—for Doug's silent reproach could be a drag—avoided him, as if ruling him out of existence, so as not to get tied up in long conversation, there being so little time. This was pretty brutal.

"He's using you! you're being had!" said Doug. He was twenty-six, and spoke with the authority of an older brother. "He'll coddle you and discard you and you'll pay your dues anyway. He cain't protect you." He felt that the atmosphere was decadent—the kind of language he used—and resolved to move out as soon as he could get a job. He

176

passionately himself wanted to protect Terry, and also to see him learn his lesson.

Terry said: "Doug, have a heart! He knows you want to have another serious talk with him, but he's tired."

"You talkin' about me behind my back!" said Doug, fiercely controlling himself. "I ain't angry but I don' want nobody knowin' my business, understand?"

"He comes here for a little rest," said Terry, "and we're at him like cannibals."

"I told him about my stomachaches, and next thing he tells them to you behind my back! I gotta have my privacy, understand?" It was hard for him to live in somebody else's home.

3

But the college boys who descended on Fridays, to shack up with their weekend chicks, took Terry's weird affair more at face value. To them the old man was a sloppy creep, with unpressed pants and false teeth. He used to set fire to himself with his stinking pipe, and his dirty sweater was full of holes made by the flying sparks. If he sat down with a cup of coffee to talk to them—when he wasn't letching—he sounded off so you couldn't get a word in edgewise and he gave lectures like History 406. Professor Corcoran at Wesleyan said that his scholarship was twenty years out of date. Who in hell *was* he, who did he think he was, to put them down the way he did? And then taking Terry by the hand and leading him into the back room. If it wasn't so disgusting, it would be like a cartoon in *Playboy*. But the chicks were offended.

"He came out to our school," said one sophomore, "and shacked up with the president of the Peace Union. And damned if the old creep didn't make a pass at him and try to crawl into bed. Saunders—he was president of the Union —didn't really know how to handle it. He had to be polite to the guest. What can he say? So he lays there frozen stiff. Till morning. A man oughta have some consideration, don't you think?"

When he heard that kind of thing, Terry was speechless. He kept swallowing. He couldn't throw them indignantly out of his house. He couldn't protest, because their realm of discourse was too disparate from anything in his own experience.

4

What Terry saw was how his teacher at a banquet or in a TV studio—for he often took Terry along to show him the way of the world—got to his feet to speak, with a neat tie on and his hair almost combed for the occasion, and minute by minute, by some strange process, he would rumple, his tie pulled awry, his hair standing up wild, and his fingernails slowly becoming dirty—as he made a rambling sense, in an earnest voice. Then Terry loved him.

He hesitated to tell him what the others said. He knew that he was a very willful man. Joanna, once she had had time to observe him, said that he was like Jarry's King Ubu, a fearsome drooling baby.

But since all these people told him that the situation would not do, Terry gradually began to believe that his weary friend was already dead. He had no strong convictions of his own.

part three

part three

election day

1

Then it was Election Day, and we were out picketing one hundred feet from the polls with our signs, DON'T VOTE! STRIKE FOR PEACE! We handed out our leaflets, trying to get at the citizens before they went in, but the police kept removing us to the corner across the street. A thrown-away copy was flying high in the winds of November; and here it is, just as it flopped around:

> The governments of the world have put us in the danger of nuclear total catastrophe and are wasting wealth and destroying health and spirit in waging the Cold War. Especially, of course, the United States and Soviet governments; but it is likely that the Common Market government will soon be an equally fearful third.
>
> The Soviet government proceeds with no democratic check by its people. But in waging war and making war-preparations, the United States proceeds almost equally unchecked. For almost 100 percent of the candidates of the overwhelmingly major parties, however much they differ in other respects, are unanimous in this crucial respect. The electorate has no choice to vote for peace. Like the Soviet government, our government drifts toward catastrophe as one bloc.
>
> Therefore, to vote for any candidates in this present election—except for a tiny few who have proved their will to peace by their records and their brave campaigns —is to legitimize with the popular will the insane policies of the nuclear nations. Since the government as such means war, *do not vote at all*, especially for national candidates. (There are no acceptable candidates in northern New Jersey.)
>
> To vote is the most essential act of political societies. It is the act by which, in small or large communities, the citizens create the kind of world they

181

want to live in, so far as this can be done by political means. Then it is a sacrilegious farce when the vote has come to mean rubber-stamping one of two rival candidates who both share a policy that no citizen can sanely will.

Yet we cannot merely abstain from voting. Voting is too important, too existential an act. We therefore urge the citizens to engage in *active non-voting*. Picket the polls with your protests. Join us. Urge others not to vote, and explain why.

A vote invests the Cold War and the nuclear war with legitimacy. Refuse it.

Support the General Strike for Peace. Boycott civilian goods produced by big war manufacturers. Don't vote except for Peace candidates.

This was really high level. People who took the leaflet and gave it a glance, rather than stuffing it into their pockets or handbags while they proceeded in to vote, would often stop dead in their tracks and, with puzzled frowns, read it right through to the end, before going in to vote. The trick of the leaflet was that the beginning was cleverly confusing, so that one asked oneself, "What in hell is this about?"

We had printed it off in modest type, without bold face. For we found that bold black letters made 75 percent of people refuse to accept a leaflet altogether; it was agitational and frightening. A quiet reasoned statement was best—and not good enough. It was really pointless to ask for acts for peace in Vanderzee, but it was as sensible to engage in our futile work there as anywhere else. Anyway, we lived there; it was our community.

But what was galling was for little diddledybops like Carmelito or Jocko to pass by us and shout, "Communists! Go back to Russia!" Once we were picketing, they no longer recognized us. They of course had no idea what we were doing, but we were doing something, and this was too disturbing for their insecurity.

Quite a number of them passed in the course of an hour. And each one independently shouted, "Communists!

Go back to Russia!" They were rugged little individualists. Carmelito, Ramón, Chico, Franky. They vanished, with secrecy and anonymity, into a condemned house down the block. It was obviously their meeting place, likely where they had hidden the whiskey on the day that Harold chased them out. In this, as in everything else they did, their behavior was as cool and quiet as could be, and one look at them and you knew they were up to no good.

Arm in arm with Connie, Terry was singing out, "Buddy, Get Wise to Yourself! Don't Vote. Ain't got time for loose talk, folks, but Take a Tip! Don't Vote!"—It was sad; he had just turned twenty-one and it would have been his first vote as a citizen of the United States. But he threw himself into whatever he was doing, and he was soon madly acting out his *Mad* magazine fantasy.

Connie stopped at the corner to give a leaflet to the poll worker for the Republican candidate for United States Senator. Soon the two were deep in conversation. One young lady was handing out her brochure to vote for Henry C. Devereux, and the other was handing out her leaflet not to vote at all; but in fact they were both professionals in a lay world and were more interested in the gossip of the trade than in the merits of the case. The cop had made them both cross the street, for the town was Democratic.

Terry was interrupted in his noisy strutting up and down by an elderly woman who engaged him in a long discussion about religion. She could not see why a nice Catholic boy like him was attacking the Holy Church. What did he have against the Cardinal, that saintly man? Surely, she and Terry agreed, it didn't make any difference what church you belonged to; everybody should love one another.

"Twist for Peace! Ball for Peace!" bawled Terry.

2

Upstairs, the Puerto Rican gang did not mention, or otherwise seem to notice, the absence of Pedro their chief. Since he was in bad trouble—it was not yet clear how bad (Schiller was alive)—the thought of him was more than they could cope with. They were incurious about his fate and blotted out his memory. If he ever reappeared, one would see. *Que sera sera.*

Nevertheless, their lives were electrified by Pedro's absence. They were fiercly free and breathing defiance. They were thirsty to wreak the havoc that he had always prudently inhibited. Also, they had to spite him. Since he undertook to care for them, he must not get arrested and leave them flat.

"Now we will get Harold!" Their thoughts of insurrection focused on Harold. Harold who played favorites! Who were the favorites? Pedro and Ramón!

"He slap me *por nada*, for noughtin," said Chico, "driving down a play street." At thirty-five miles an hour.

They had treasured up every detail of humiliation and resentment. Carmelito remembered that Harold was cheapskate because once he had sent him down for ice cream for everybody and had not given him a tip. The unforgivable —they could not even mention it—was that he had laughed at them for their ineptitude.

Ramón was in a desperate plight. He had had sexual relations with Harold. If now he was not hot to rob him, humiliate him, take revenge, it was proof that he himself was a faggot. This was what they were thinking. They did not need to say it.

With scorn and bravado, to put them off, he talked about how Harold lost his hard-on. He mimed his ridiculous efforts to revive himself by masturbating. "First he tickles him. Then he rubs spit. Then wham! wham! like a crazy man. This does nothing, so he goes back to petting like a pussy. But it stays just as flabby as before."

The silence hung heavy. They did not laugh. In fact, the gambit was a fatal blunder. It indicated that Ramón was *interested* in Harold's penis and not entirely indifferent. The code was to allow the faggot to touch or suck your penis, but not for you to acknowledge the existence of his penis in any way. If he tried to embrace you in such a way that his penis touched your body, it was necessary at once to express revulsion and punch him in the jaw or, if that was impractical, to return as soon as possible and burglarize his house.

"*Como el deja á Harold chingar,*" sneered Franky, "*pues vamos nosotros!*" Since he lets Harold, let's get to work ourselves.

"*Vamos! Vamos!*"

"Liar! Liar!" Ramón screamed his denial.

They lunged for him. Breaking a beer bottle off at the neck, he backed into a corner, facing them with the jagged edge. They hemmed him in.

They wanted him to steal Harold's car. They wanted, above all, to break up the relation between him and Harold, because it had advantages.

Chico tripped him and he went down. They got the bottle from him. While he thrashed and bit, they held him down and ripped his buttons and took his pants half down. A key fell out of the pocket. Chico grabbed it.

But nobody was interested in raping little Ramón. Nobody had a hard-on, and that fact also would have been embarrassing to reveal. Instead, they began to call one another faggots.

"*Maricón!*"

"You! *You're* in such a hurry, go ahead! Go ahead!"

"Say that again, I kill you."

They fell silent and didn't know what to do.

"*Don't be a litterbug. Ban the bomb! Did your government make the atmosphere dirty again today?*" It was the voice of Terry, loud across the street. "Ladies! when you see that fallout piled up in the sink, do you ever feel a headache coming on? Sure you're tense, jittery, irritable. Control yourself. Don't take it out on everybody else. Doctors say, Don't Vote!" His confidential voice trailed around the corner.

"Communist! you spick communist!" Pulling Ramón to his feet, they began to punch him, guilty by association, while he could not defend himself because he had to hold up his buttonless trousers. All that they had experienced of the eerie strangeness of middle-class life, the existence of books in the house, the incomprehensibility of intellectual conversation, they dissolved by punching and bully-

185

ing Ramón. The powerlessness and anxiety of every day of their lives was made whole and manly by conforming to America and its mighty system of weapons. In their politics, they were deadly earnest.

But he could not get off by being a political scapegoat. For there persisted the underlying fact: he either would steal Harold's car for them or he wouldn't. Faggot or communist, they were not going to let up. He looked in fright from face to face.

Like a suicide, he rushed to the window and shouted down, "Go back to Russia! *Maricón!*"

The man below looked up inquiringly. He was a worker for Tim Kavanagh's organization, and so had not been sent across the street.

The others crowded to the window, and, over Ramón's shoulder, shouted, "Communist! *Maricón!*" They were still not berserk enough to throw down bottles.

"*Qué es este llave?*" said Chico, holding up the key. It was not Harold's, because that door, they knew, was always open.

3

Walking by our pickets, Roger accepted a leaflet, stood, and read it through. "It's a good leaflet," he commented, and proceeded on into the polling place.

Unlike most of us, Roger had actually registered to vote, and he was certainly going to vote if he could. Our disposition was to act breezily on probabilities, but Roger was more honest and always gave them every opportunity to state their case before he said, always, "Naa."

Once he was in the booth, however, with the curtain drawn and faced with the names on the machine, he was stunned beyond expectation at the insult to his intelligence. He collated the information about the candidates that he had gathered from campaign material, speakers on the sound trucks, and sometimes private information; and he was frustrated. His disposition was to reject outright those who used the sound trucks, but what when this involved choosing the *rival* candidate? He was in principle willing to entertain the idea that choice in our times was not *for* anyone but rather *against* the opposite number, a process called "Choosing the lesser of two evils," but how could one vote for the opposite number when it was Harvey F. X. O'Reilly? or Lulu D. Polenta? He was at a loss. But what was insulting to his intelligence was that in no case in this election was there a single issue, a fundamental difference of policy, offered to the voter. Either to ban the sound trucks from Vanderzee or to take away the franchises from the TV giants, or to stop poisoning the atmosphere with nuclear explosions. There were dozens and dozens of candidates, but there was not a single one who was concerned about furthering a peaceful and sensible world. Of course, this was exactly what the General Strike leaflet had said, "There are no acceptable candidates in Kayser County,"—an accurate assessment after all, breezily as it had been arrived at! And Roger could draw no other than the same conclusion, "Don't Vote!"

Inevitably, all this research and reflection took a considerable length of time. A line formed outside the polling booth.

The manager became impatient and rattled on the curtain.

"Hold your horses!" growled Roger. "I'm thinking."

"It's against the rules," said the manager. "Time allowed is five minutes, crippled and handicapped fifteen minutes. That's the rule. You been in there twenty-five minutes."

"Fuck the rule!" said Roger. "I came here to not-vote, and I *will* not-vote. Let a man take his time."

The manager went and got the cop, and the cop ripped open the curtain, while the party watchers feverishly wrote in their notebooks.

"You got no place here for a write-in vote!" cried Roger. "How can I make a write-in not-vote? And you didn't leave any pencil. You got this fuckin' machine, you don't even provide a pencil any more."

"Here's the place, stupid," said the manager, beside

187

himself. The party watchers gasped at this browbeating of a citizen, and they wrote and wrote.

"Hell it is!" said Roger. "Try it! I tried it. It's stuck." It was stuck.

By now they were frightened at the irregularity, and they brought a knife and unstuck the little lid on the machine. They servilely brought Roger a pencil to write in his write-in.

"Thanks," he said, giving the man back his pencil. "There's nobody I want to vote for."

4

The key was Meg's.

"It belongs to the whore," said Ramón, with a shiver of joy.

It was on Meg, he decided, that he must take revenge. This would clear him of everything.

They were so generally hurt and sore that they could pick and choose on whom to take revenge.

He had finally badgered her into it, into letting him "get away with everything," and since then she seemed to him loathsome and revolting. He was visited by nightmares of incestuous guilt. He snatched the key from Chico's hand. *"Haz te caso de mi! Listen to me! Escuchad!"*

In the dresser drawer, she kept a hundred dollars. Sometimes a hundred and fifty dollars. He used to steal fives and tens, when she wouldn't notice they were missing—to be sure, she would have given him the money if he asked for it; she did notice that the bills were missing; and she knew that Ramón was the thief. But in this also, she was passive, curious, astonished. She unwittingly increased the amount of guilt in the world by letting herself be abused.

On Wednesday nights, explained Ramón—and they crowded around him, and he was the Chief—she drove with Harold to the trotting races in Yonkers, leaving the baby with Connie. That was the time! He held up the key.

He was in ecstasy; he was the chief, revenging himself against Pedro. Now he was *macho,* a man. As vividly and

188

as callously as possible he described his liberties with the woman, assigning to himself the role of perfect Chief. The manly ideal was immense satisfaction and utter lordly detachment. To the gang his revelations were bombshells. Their eyes shone with respect; they laughed with raucous joy. It was like a revolution in which there is dancing in the streets.

They did not identify with Ramón's prowess but with Meg's degradation. "I don't believe you," said Chico enviously, "that she touched it with her right hand."

"Touched it with her hand!" crowed Ramón, "she ate it with great appetite."

"Tell again how you sucked her milk and she moaned."

"And you rubbed your hand in the crack of her ass."

He was both their Achilles and their Homer. It was too much for one hero. They were all stroking their bulging crotches, as they drank in the images that they called upon him to sing. And he neither shocked nor disappointed them, for in this line they had an exquisite conformity to a standard.

Their voices were vibrant and rather fresh and happy.

"*Ahora!* You have put your *macho* hands on her hips—"

"You are about to pull down her underpants and take them off!"

"Her shoes! her shoes!" said Chico.

"Her shoes had very long pointed high heels," invented Ramón freely. No mention of dirty bare feet.

It was little Carmelito first who took out his penis and began to masturbate to the story. Most of the others started to masturbate, dreamily or vigorously, according to their characters. Sitting on the floor, or on broken chairs tilted back, that they had salvaged from the alleys. In masturbating, too, they meticulously observed all rules: they held their breath; they did not move the pelvis; they sought for immense satisfaction and masterly disdain. They raped themselves.

Ramón, however, was not permitted to satisfy himself, for they held him inflexibly to his role. "Tell it again, all from the beginning!" they demanded. "The part about she puts it in her mouth." "No, no, more onward," said another hoarsely, "when you shove it hard in." They were too demanding. The little poet felt compelled. He began to be unwilling; he began again to be frightened. He knew he would not be able to control them. He dreaded the moment after they came off, when they would no longer be in the grip of the lust he had aroused.

Chico also did not masturbate with the others, but disdainfully sat on the windowsill and watched them, his face set with disapproval. He felt that it was cheapskate to masturbate. Privately, to be sure, he masturbated as often as any; but by some special logic the imputation that applied to the others did not apply to him. When they were in this mood, as when they were careless about their clothes, he regarded them as lower class.

5

Roger took a sign and picketed with the rest of us.

"You see, folks," sang out Terry, "national brands are lousy brands. They have no taste a-tall." He was very sweet when he was enjoying himself, like an awkward innocent child. People smiled on him benignly.

But our number had now grown to a dozen, straggling up and down the block, and we were making a lot of noise. A squad car pulled up at the curb and rolled down it's window. Terry walked over and gave the pair a leaflet. "Strike for Peace, officers," he said. "Smokey the Bear is *against* firestorms."

These rapidly gathering, rapidly dwindling, demonstrations had become a frequent feature of our cityscape. They meant nothing and they meant everything. They exerted no influence; they meant that people were powerless and at a loss what else to do. But they meant that people had had it and would no longer put up with it, even if all they could do was to carry a sign.

One of the cops signaled to Roger, and our hearts sank. The cop assumed that Roger, by his grave demeanor, must be the leader. There was no leader. But we were apprehensive because with Roger there was never any tell-

190

ing. If he became outraged, he might say or do something dreadful and get his head bashed and his ribs kicked in.

Unlike the rest of us, Roger did not have a spontaneous dislike of policemen. Rational and compassionate, he understood that they were earning a living and doing a job, just like anybody else. But their work put them in dangerous situations and they were therefore apt to respond with anxiety and stereotypes, as when a pair of them clubbed, and kicked in the head, the Negro mechanic on Burr Street, when he was locking up at 1:00 A.M. and made the mistake of opening his mouth to explain what he was doing. Yet that had occurred after another cop, their buddy, had narrowly missed being hit by a sack of water dropped on him from a roof on Fourth Street. "If one of us," Roger pointed out to us, "were a huge motherly or fatherly figure, and could take a cop in his arms and stroke his hair and calm his fears, and draw out the sorrow and frustration of his little soul, he, like anybody else, would soon burst into tears and be grateful and affectionate."

The bother was that in dealing with the police in the hurlyburly of existence, one had to maintain one's rights and honor as each occasion arose. And here Roger was not cool at all; he could not maintain the right symbolic distance. He could not stoically take their insolence whence it came, from empowered anxious stupidity, to be stolidly obeyed so as not to make them more anxious. And he was not political enough to do what we advised him, to take down the man's badge number and say, "You'll hear more about this through the proper channels, from your superiors." At any moment, Roger was likely to reply to an insult by being offended.

Harold was on tenterhooks. (This was rich, because Harold was of course the only one of us who might become thin-lipped and really kill one of them.) "Shut up," he said to Terry, "don't antagonize them."

Terry was abashed. Again he realized he had tactlessly lost touch with the environment! He buttoned his lips and put on a spiritual face and slowed his gait. He held his sign in front of him like the True Cross. "Shhh! this is a peace demonstration," he hissed at the two junior high students who were chatting away.

"A-OK," said the young astronauts, "what you want us to do?"

"Meditate." And he himself began to meditate about the tragedy of Hiroshima.

"That's a lot of crap! *Strike for Peace!*" bawled tiny Timothy, in his turned-round collar of a bishop of the Old Catholic Church.

But Roger was quietly talking to the two policemen in the car. There *was* no altercation, for they really wanted to inform themselves. The police were piqued and teased by these odd people who acted so wrongheadedly, flouting the authorities and disregarding the wisdom of the experts, exposing themselves to ridicule and physical suffering, and without, apparently, being paid. Mostly they were not even communists. In Headquarters the current theory was, pacifists were drifters. It was proved by their careless dress. To be sure, many demonstrators dressed conventionally, like businessmen or ward politicians or communists; and others were strictly disciplined by their marshals to shave off their beards and wear shoes, especially if there were going to be news photographs. But the captions under the photographs always pointed out that they *had* beards and wore sandals; so there you were.

Seated comfortably in their car, the police good-naturedly asked Roger about red or dead, and why didn't they picket the Kremlin, and people like the Russians don't understand nothing but a big stick. Resolutely, Roger declined to wrangle. "You two are simply brainwashed," he said. "If other people were in power, you would say different things. Facts and thinking haven't any importance in your lives; why don't you stop bullshitting?" This left little room for discussion.

"Did you go to college?" the younger cop suddenly asked him. He was a good-looking Italian boy.

"To college?" said Roger. "Yes, I did. Why do you ask?"

"What about them? Did any o' them go to college?"

Roger surveyed the ragged line. "Why, yes, I guess about half of them went to college," he said.

"You see?" said the young cop to the senior officer. "They know more about it than us." And he turned on the motor.

"Who is the little man with the clerical collar?" asked the officer.

"That's the Reverend Timothy Slotkin," explained Roger gravely. "He believes in a community of love."

"He sure makes a lot of noise," said the officer, and they drove off.

Harold's presence on our line was disturbing.

6

Harold had now passed his examination with a good score and was waiting to be assigned to a plant that manufactured guided missiles. What was he doing in the General Strike for Peace? But day passed into day and no one had the heart to call him to task.

They did not notice, meeting one another on the circling line, how Harold, who carried no sign, looked at them with a kind of disdain. "They behave this way," he thought, "because they are not important people." He took it for granted that they were burning with competitive envy like himself. But he himself was walking on the pacifist line with them because, dumbly, he could not refute their reasoning. He stubbornly would not accept it either. He walked—but without a sign.

Connie was smiling at him with irrefutable affection as she came on, and he was confused. Connie was not an unimportant person. His friendly nature rose and he called out to her, "Tell Jason if you see him in the hospital—" She passed by. On the next turn he completed the sentence, "—the Goose finished in the money again yesterday!"

"Oh, good, I'll tell him!" said Connie. She too was a partisan of Spangler Goose who always placed or showed.

He was envious—it bordered on dislike—of the tired man who in his clumsy but self-confident manner kept stepping out of line to offer a leaflet to a passerby, with a cheerful smirk. The leaflets were spilling out of the pocket of his torn overcoat—he could afford a better, just as he could have chosen other friends. As if despite himself, Harold found himself saying, passing, "I'll pick you up on Thursday morning and take you to Idlewild."

Up the street came two of the *boricuas* whom he had begun to hate and fear. (Yet he shared their views more than he did these others'.) They passed him by without a word. "They're on heroin," he thought. He did not know the immense excitement they had been through.

Harold *knew* that he was stupider than his own capabilities, but it was something that he did to himself. One cannot *simply* be stupider than one is.

shit

1

Meg came home at midnight, the baby asleep and heavy on her arm. As soon as she opened the door, she knew that the place had been burglarized; it was a wreck. A powerful stench struck her in the face. She tripped on something and hurt her shin.

She switched on the light.

They had tipped over the chairs and tipped the books off the shelves.

There were stinking piles of shit on the floor. She saw three in the living room. In the kitchen—she switched on a light—there was a pile of shit on the round table. In despair she tugged open the kitchen window—it was hard to do, holding the heavy baby. She went into the bedroom to put the baby in her crib. She switched on the light.

One of them had climbed also into the crib—there were dirty shoe prints—and shat.

Gripping onto herself, she laid the sleeping baby on the floor and proceeded to replace the sheets and blankets, making a dirty pile. And as she did so, she could vividly— she could not help but—reconstruct the scene. He, whoever it was—she did not think of Ramón—in his moment of burglary, was tempted to commit the early crime of them all: to shit in the baby's crib.

But the rest—of it—was aimed at her.

She turned and went to look in the dresser drawer. The money was gone. She now knew that one of them was Ramón. He had also stolen the key last summer. They had wantonly cracked the dresser mirror. She saw her face— split.

She finished making up the crib and tucked the baby in, and switched off the light. She saw her face in the mirror, in the dim light from the other room.

Once one of them had committed the enormity, she could reconstruct their frantically mounting excitement.

Their need to get into the act like monkeys. It was really funny—she found many things funny—but it was hard to laugh.

2

She started to clean the house, but she suddenly gagged. Unlike herself. She was not a sqeamish woman. She had kept dogs and bred puppies, and there had been moments as bad as this. It was the shit on the kitchen table.

They had left the door of the refrigerator open. They had drunk up the soda pop she kept for Ramón. She was angered because they had spitefully smashed a bottle on the floor, dangerous, for the baby. Her anger and anxiety gave her support, to go on—with the disposal and scrubbing and sweeping, that simply had to be done.

The November air took away the odor. But it was cold.

But she could not finish, not beyond the absolutely necessary. She could not right the chairs, put back the books. They had stolen the record player, ripped it from its wiring to the speaker. But the picture album on its antique table was undisturbed, and it sat there like something silent.

She felt so sorry—she sat down exhausted—for Harold, who had to cope with this every day. For a change he had won a little at the races and they had driven home from Yonkers in a merrier mood than usual. She asked herself whether she ought not to tell him at once, to warn him. On the one hand, in the passive serenity with which she accepted everything in the world, as interesting or funny or that's the way it was, she did not like to inform on Ramón. It was tattle-telling, as she said it to herself in her language of age eight. On the other hand, Ramón could do Harold harm.

3

Instead, as she sat there beaten, after she had done what absolutely had to be done in order to live on at all, her brain began to seethe with hatred for pretty Terry and the man she loved. Because they *had* things. Terry had Joanna and he had his wife. And they also had each other. It wasn't just.

She beat stiffly on the table with her fist. There was no chink where she could enter.

She was impractical. She did not wish well to the people she loved. In her worst moments, she wished that harm would befall them. This is impractical.

What she could not bear—it suffocated her, it blinded her—was how they were able to talk to each other, the words dropping from their mouths, and each one was eagerly interested in what the other said.

Terry's door was always open, and she had gone in, and stood in the corner in plain sight, and saw it all. Standing there in muffled silence. But they were so concerned with each other that they did not even notice her.

It was not what they did, but that, when they were together alone, or believed that they were alone, they murmured to each other and looked understandingly at each other.

She used to barge in on pretexts, when she suspected that they were together, in order to prevent their being alone together. There was point to this, because she knew that it was hard for them to snatch a few hours alone together, since both of them had so many things to do and places to go and people to talk to and make love.

Once she had come, there she was. In the way.

Sometimes they were impatient with her. She could tell.

But it was impossible for them to be rude to her because they were good.

The worst, however, was when she broke down in bitter sobs, and then he impatiently complained that she spoiled the little happiness he had; because she could not bear to see him unhappy, since he was so generous and citizenly and overworked.

Such were the thoughts that Meg had as she sat, seething with hatred of her loved ones, exhausted from cleaning up the shit of the Puerto Rican boys who had burglarized her house.

a conference on democracy

1

Where was Harold?—I was more anxious than usual, because he was usually punctual. It was less than an hour to plane time. At last the phone rang.

Ramón had stolen the car.

"Did he?" I said. "Are you sure that it was he?"

"It was he. They robbed Meg." Harold's voice was tired. Meg had come too late, of course.

"I'll be back the day after tomorrow," I said, and grabbed my bag and ran for a taxi. But it was today, maybe, that they needed me.

As the cab took me across the Triboro, my heart did not stop pounding. As we sped along the Parkway, I had a bitter taste in my mouth. If Harold reported the theft, Ramón would certainly take revenge and cry cocksucker. If he didn't report it and lost the car, it could lead only to further blackmail. I overlooked the third alternative, that Harold would do nothing and Ramón would be arrested anyway. Yet that was inevitable. I assumed that I myself would be somehow implicated—I didn't much care since I had no secrets—but I was dismayed for Terry. Where was Terry?

It was too late to go back and get Terry.

Those Puerto Rican kids were so stupid. We were so stupid.

I made the jet for Denver.

Five minutes later we were high over my stupid city, and climbing. My forehead and my eyes were glued to the window, looking at the wormheap where I should have been, instead of flying to Denver on "The Possibility of Democracy in Contemporary Urban and Technical Conditions." The panorama spread to the horizon. And there it was! The suburban sprawl, dominated by the central towers, the impossibility of democracy in contemporary urban conditions. What a poor use of land!—we were ten

miles farther—farms and forests ruined—and standardiza-
tion, as far as I could see ahead.

The height was beautiful. My forehead and eyes remained glued to the window. From a mile up, the cars in
their parking lots were vivid wampum. At three miles, one
could no longer see them even as tiny ants crawling on the
ribbon roads. The oil tanks were pretty polka dots.

The earthly details vanished, and there began to be
bright clouds in the gorgeous blue.

"Do you wish a magazine, sir?"—I turned sharply. My
neighbors were reading *Newsweek* and *Sports Illustrated*.
I too, on the almost weekly flights I took, often tired of
the miraculous dream of space and sank back from the
window, but not into magazines but literally asleep, into
my own troubled dreams. "No, thanks," I said to the
hostess's mechanical smile.

The skyscape was piled with mile-high towers of pink
and gray, and we were flying deep through their grand
canyons. And like an emblem, the shadow-cross of our
plane in its glowing circle of sun moved slowly along the
cloud with us as we came.

I looked and looked because my soul was thirsty for
simplicity and grandeur. The blue was gorgeous, and the
horizon of rose and pearl was gorgeous. I lost sense of the
time.

Before I expected him, there flashed below the fat-
bellied meander of the Mississippi, spreading away into
the hazy south and vanishing in brightness. Our American
plain. A sparkle, tiny as it must have been on its wave,
easily leaped to us and gave a bright signal. It said something friendly. I read it correctly because I was otherwise
so unhappy. I sorely needed that friendly little signal that
said, "The ingenious animal man devised the machinery to
give us this long view."

I was alone, with no one to whom to tell my excitement.
Luckily my eyes were heavy, and I sank back asleep.

God, were we stupid! Overworked and stupid. The way we set it up, we were bound to be overworked. With the best will in the world, the managers and professionals, and even if we had excellent brains, were too few minds to attend to the multifarious problems of the Americans. Yawning and overstimulated, we worked eighty or ninety hours a week. And because we were too few to make so many decisions, we tried to cope by using standard procedures.

Dozing, I began to have a kind of low-grade nightmare. I was trying to put things into standard boxes. Many of them did not fit in the shoeboxes where we were trying to cram them. All the white rats were becoming stupid.

Ignorant consumers were making stupid choices of goods. An ignorant electorate chose stupid rogues to govern. These made even stupider decisions, and everybody else became stupider.

And then, because they had a dangerous machine that was slowly bearing down on us to crush us, we began to unravel the stupid reels of red tape to clog up the wheels of the stupid machine.

I awoke without a start as our wheels jolted the ground in Denver. And at once, like a dying well-trained horse, I recalled, even to the alliteration, the title of my afternoon sermon: "Centralization, Style, and Superstition." I intended to speak for decentralization, to say that it was an empirical question, which areas of urbanism, industry, education, and communications could be practically decentralized, and how far, and how. But modern people were so mesmerized by the stupefying logic of central planning that they did not make the relevant empirical investigations, nor pragmatically try out the alternatives. That was what I intended to say, and in fact that was what I did say.

I wished I had brought Terry, for company.

3

At the hotel—I was not astounded—were the same faces that I had been meeting for a couple of years at every other conference. I banished from my mind the distress of Harold and my apprehensiveness for Terry. I shook hands with Irving, of the National Council on Child Labor, and I warmly kissed Judge Amy Watkins of California. Harriet Young was there, of course—I remembered that I must ask her for a job for Terry—"Well, well, fancy meeting *you!*" we both said.

I was mildly surprised to see Dr. Blumberg at this conference. What would this bureaucrat have to contribute to the problems of democratic initiative? When I arrived, he was holding forth in the center of a little ring in the lobby. He dressed too carefully. "Excuse me for interrupting," I said. The rest of us were anarchists at heart, roving the world without portfolio.

Blumberg was in the middle of a story. "I'm explaining what did happen with Broad Outlook," he politely briefed me. "So like I told you," he went on excitedly, "we worked at it child by child. Tailor-made. That was the point. Tailor-made. And on a shoestring. It was $9,300 for J.30, and we boosted the I.Q.'s of forty children! There was not one penny spent for administration!" He pointed down with the forefinger of his right hand on the palm of his left. "My staff and I worked sixteen hours a day. Naaa!" The thought of it put him in a rage. Red in the face. "To them, if it was good for J.30, Brooklyn—where I had my own staff, mind you—why shouldn't it be good for seventy-five other schools in five boroughs? Write us out a schedule, Ben! Why shouldn't everybody go to the Yale-Harvard football game, in busses with soda pop and waving banners? *Everybody* goes to see *West Side Story*—was that a lemon! Standardize it, Ben! You get bargain rates and administrative convenience. And with a staff of shlemiels under me— believe me. Needless to say, they diluted it to nothing. What's the use of talking? I was made an Associate Superintendent of Schools." By now he was purple. "I *fought* for my Broad Outlook—I didn't take it lying down—" He looked at us appealingly from face to face, as if we were his accusers. "A lot of them are smart kids, even if they are niggers or can't speak a word of English. . . . O.K., O.K., I'll stop hocking you a *tchainik*. Now I'm the special adviser on school dropouts to the President of the United States of America. They have tied my hands behind my back."

We let out a shout of laughter. The facts of life always turned out to be a Jewish joke.

Ben looked at us surprised. What was so funny about it?

"Don't laugh so hard," he said. "I'm calling a conference in Washington for February, 1963. And *you* shall be invited. You Conference Bums. Yes, every one of you because you think it's so damned funny!"

4

We were Conference Bums and roamed from Conference to Conference, putting up at the hotel or the college. (My misfortune was to be on two different circuits, education and community planning.) But unlike the tennis bums, staying at rich homes, we had very uninteresting food, formal dinners of roast beef or roast chicken, choice of filet of sole on Fridays.

In the end we played for one another. Sometimes beautifully and profitably for ourselves. For instance, if we said, "Columbus was a good Conference," or, "The American Institute of Architects was an authentic pseudoevent"—as we might say that the National Open was bang-up or the Gulf States Invitation was badly seeded—we meant simply that we contestants had learned something new, the spirit was lovely, we had made a new friend; or, on the contrary, that the format prevented any discussion or a stuffed shirt from official circles had bored us for hours. We did *not* mean that the Conference had any point, that we had made a beginning, or failed to make a beginning, in remedying juvenile delinquency, the ugliness of towns, the threat of atomic war, the devolution of democracy. I might say appreciatively, "Irving, that was great! I never thought it was that grim!" meaning that he had spoken even better than usual and that his statistics would be used by me in my own future speeches.

By now we were used to one another's styles, and this improved the game. I could say, modestly, that my own brash interruptions pepped up the tone of all the Conferences in the circuits that I played. Soon the other panelists learned to interrupt too. We sometimes had a real roughhouse. People in our league were in strong demand when a civic group or a student body was *engagé* and wanted earnest thought with existential vitality. But let me be fair. We were athletes, not entertainers. We often performed best when there was no audience at all and we had been called together by some august sponsorship just in order that, on some pressing matter, there might by a Conference.

At Denver there was no audience, just ourselves, the Conference. A great Foundation had summoned us, in deep concern for the future of the Republic. And we had gathered because of our deep concern for the future of the Republic. We were Conference Bums.

I had toyed with the idea of bringing Terry, as I sometimes did. I hadn't proposed it to him because it was only for a day and there were no students for him to mix with. Yet he would have enjoyed the flight. He could have gone on a ride into the Rocky Mountains, up to Lookout, while we were conferring. He could have seen the grave of Buffalo Bill.

5

There was a pall over the Conference at Denver.

Unofficially—but we knew that it was true—our informant in the White House had told us that they were going to begin exploding bombs again. There was not going to be any disarmament. (Of course, there was a disarmament Conference—I did not belong to that circuit.) By the end of the week, the President would address the nation.

This made us somewhat futile. Not that we were not

futile anyway, for we were only Conference Bums; yet we were now, how shall I say? even more futile.

Not—make no mistake—not that there was no use in improving our garden if in a few years we were all going to be blasted anyway. That was not the reasoning that threw us. We were all going to die anyway, whether late or soon, and nevertheless we did our work, did it because it was worthwhile and because it was the work that we chose. But we were futile because—these human beings—our countrymen—suddenly seemed too base. One gave them up. They were impractical. They were not worth thinking for. We did not like to look at one another. We were ashamed of being alive. As if each one of us were asking, Where now can I drag my days out and erase this awful memory of my country? What can I work at?

6

In the evening Amy gave a remarkable performance; it cheered us up for more than two hours.

Drawing on her judicial experience, she made a pitch for fair play for the criminals in evading the police. With the new electronic machines, Judge Watkins pointed out, a little crook picked up on suspicion in Spokane found himself, at a twist of a dial, confronted with his fingerprints and record from twelve years ago in Tallahassee. That prejudiced his case, especially if he had reasonably denied that he *had* any record. And add the wiretaps, and so forth.

She painted for us the horrifying picture of our vast world in which there was no asylum. Mighty sovereign States—there had been recent instances—hounded down refugees, and handed them piously one to another. (In fact, we had rejoiced because one fellow escaped by suicide.) She quoted the awful sentence of Gibbon: how in the majestic unity of the Roman Empire, with its wealth and civilization and symmetry of institutions, there was no place for an honest man to hide.

Unfortunately, she had no counterproposal except Bob Kastenmeier's bill for a Public Defender, who would try to give the captive a fairer day in court, since the police were able, by their huge capital investment, to amass so much evidence against him. This was probably better than nothing; but the real problem, it seemed to some of us, was how to keep out of the court altogether.

I went to bed morose.

7

A mighty pounding at my door awakened me.

"Are you out of your mind? What do you want at this hour of the night?" It was Irving. It was hardly dawn.

"We're going on a ride to Red Rocks. Put your sweater on and let's have breakfast."

I was pleased. I was disappointed that Terry was not there to come along, though I knew that just in such a case he would have been a nuisance, dawdling, taking half an hour to comb his hair.

Irving had been upset because I looked so gloomy. He knew that seeing the mountains would enliven me.

We met Amy in the coffee shop. Soon we were out in the fresh morning. There was a hired car. Irving had hired the car just to cheer me up—the thought of it was hard for me to take. Why did they cater to me? I must *somehow* have deserved it, in spite of my bitter remorse. But all of us came across for one another.

The sun rose from the plain behind us as we climbed up the mesa. We descended on the other side, and it set. We drove a dozen miles in the dim light among blue spruce and ponderosa, up into the snows. There began to be rocky mountains all around. The rocky mountains were the Rocky Mountains. The sun rose again from the hills behind us, tinging the snow red. Some of the rocks began to be bloody red.

And we got out at the Amphitheater hewn from the red rocks and built of the hewn red rocks. On each side that theater is bounded by an enormous, man-dwarfing, red rock fallen there at some ancient time. One of the rocks is called Creation and the other is called The Ship. Amy cried out with delight as we got out of the car, for she had never seen this thing, though her hair was white.

It was here that fifty years ago a couple of friends had come exploring, and one plucked a fiddle between the rocks, and the other, high up the hill, heard it clearly. Then another man thought that we could make a theater here. Another carful arrived. One proved to be an Australian tourist starting out early in the morning because there was so much America to see. He had just come from Hollywood, he said to me, and I was deeply ashamed.

"They built this in the thirties," I explained to him. "During the Depression. It was a WPA project, to make useful work."

"I've heard of that," he said brightly, "alphabet soup."

"The actual work was done by the CCC boys," I explained patiently. "Those were work camps for unemployed teen-agers."

I was proud of my Red Rocks Amphitheater. I was sure that the boys, when they came back to visit as men, were proud of it.

"Don't judge this country too quickly," I said to the Australian. "Just now my country is dragging its behind. What you'll see is lousy television. If that's what you're looking for!" I said angrily. "Have you tried the stage? Listen to this."

I bounded down the red steps to the flat stage, and I stood in the middle. The giant rock sounding boards flanked me on either side. And because I was angry because he had just come from Los Angeles, I bawled up at him at the top of my lungs, although I knew better, "Hi! hi! Can you hear me?" The shouts and echoes are rattling down around me like hail. I am ready to run for cover.

"Certainly I can hear you," he calls down to me in an ordinary cultured tone, like a Stradivarius.

I have been surprised by my own vehemence. I am astounded by the sweet clarity of human conversation. Now that the sun is up, it is warm. The snow is melting and running in runnels down the steps, as in the springtime. My country is beautiful and various, where I go about, checking up like a proprietor.

I write her jealous notes like to my wife.

8

The afternon was a catastrophe.

The lunch had been heavy—the roast-beef-and-dumplings variation—and now the Foundation had saddled us with a keynote speaker who rose in his glory at the microphone, while the waiters whisked away the remnants of the ice-cream cake, and longingly we whispered for another pot of coffee.

He—I don't remember who he was, but he was not a college president or even a politician; he was not anybody who had ever engaged in any activity at all; he was a kind of dollar-a-year man of serious thought, but I don't remember from where—Washington? the United Nations? I don't remember.

His subject—I don't remember that either. In fact, even the first time when he spoke it, I don't think that I heard a single sentence, though he had a loud clear voice and, so far as I can remember, the public-address system was in order. Were there sentences? Perhaps he read from a typescript prepared by a staff writer. Or maybe, as some do, he familiarly crooned words into the microphone, strangling the neck in his hands. I don't remember.

This was pretty cruel punishment after a heavy meal. Because we were so small a number, it was impossible to decamp, since why should any particular one be privileged, and we could not all steal away. Aha! something comes back to me. I thought that he had the talent of talking to a small group as if he were addressing the camera on TV. So surely he said something abut Educational TV, about the use of TV in the revival of democracy. He *must* have said something about the televised debates between Kennedy and Nixon as a revival of the Town Meeting.

And now I remember the syntax! Yes I do. It was Harvard 1940—perhaps he had been the associate editor of

207

the *Lit.*, a rich boy, destined to be a public spokesman for —A Public Spokesman, period. The basic texture of his style was old-fashioned frayed Santayana, sweet-and-pungent periods with a dash of irony; but rewoven by the Jewish jurists who preened themselves on their elegant writing, Cardozo, Frankfurter. Maybe he had gone to the Law School! He gave out these periods with a little smirk at the closing of each one.

I fell asleep, my head slumped on my shoulder, but only lightly snoring. Irving let me be.

9

Starved for reality, I had a vivid dream of things I had failed to notice when awake.

In the shadow in the corner stood unnoticed Meg, beside our untidy bed. Her eyes were a pair of flashing red traffic blinkers, the fire leaping from one eye to the other.

"Take me with you," Terry was whispering in my ear, but, intent on coming off, I did not hear him. He had been continually saying this for two weeks. He was afraid to remain in New York, where his Times Square cronies were feeding him too many narcotics for his precarious sanity. I ought to have insisted more on his reaching orgasm.

Suddenly he had vanished. And there was nothing left but a green traffic light suspended as if above a lonely road. Go!

"Go! Go!" it bade me, but there was no place that I wanted to go, without love in the world.

I was being awakened, shaken by the shoulder.

"Telephone, sir, from Vanderzee, Kayser County," said the bellhop.

I awoke. The public spokesman was still at it.

"Telephone, sir."

In the general stupor, I doubted that anybody had noticed that I had fallen asleep or that now I was being delivered from America, even though by this green-suited messenger of death, as, groggy, I followed him out into the lobby and accepted the call. "Go ahead," said the operator.

"I'm sorry to bother you," said Terry on the phone.

"Yes, Terry. What is it?"

"People just came for Meg, Harold, and Soren. Understand?" He had picked up Understand from Douglas.

"I see. But why Meg? Why Meg?"

"They found Ramón."

"I understand. But why Meg?"

"Same thing. Primary education." He had carefully figured out a code. Lord knows where he was phoning from.

"Meg?" I said in unbelief. "And how in hell did Soren get involved?"

"The whole community has fallen to pieces," he said in a flat voice. "I thought you ought to know."

"Don't say that, Terry. Explain about Soren."

"Soren says Ramón is a liar."

"Is he? Did Soren?"

"Oh, how would he know!" he said, exasperated. How *would* Soren know whether or not he was having sex with anybody? "They went to Connie's too, to look for the tomato soup. Hello? I can't hear you," he said.

I suddenly recognized that he was high. "I'll take an earlier plane," I said. "Did they find any?" I asked, with a sick feeling. I knew that because Jason was still in the hospital, Terry had taken the pot home with him. "Where's the can now?"

"Everything's O.K.," he said. He was lying to me. He was lying to me.

I didn't know what to do. "Tell me, do our friends have money for tickets?"

"Yes. Meg was able to put through a call to a Mr. Duyckman. She said you know."

"Oh, *isn't* that lovely!" I said. "*Such* a lovely family!"

"Hello?"—He had kept asking me, in a hoarse whisper, to take him away from himself. But I didn't know what to do. I never could think on the phone. I kept seeing the green light of my dream. I thought of the right thing the moment after he hung up—I should have told him to go out to the airport and wait for me. At once! And left this pointless Conference. And taken the first plane. Something for him to do, to cool his heels. He not only had the pot; he was pushing it. I *knew*.

"Where is Joanna?" I asked in despair.

"She's in Mount Kisco," he said bitterly. "She has a term paper in medieval history."

"Did Ramón mention—my name?"

"Oh, I guess he explained everything he could. Now he's a big shot."

"Once they got him started," I said. I could see the three or four of them hovering like giants over the poor little animal, now offering him a bribe, now giving him a slap in the face. "Terry!" I called to him. But I didn't know which airport. "Hold on a minute; let me think." I didn't know which airport. I kept seeing the green light. "I'll see you tonight!" I said. But I didn't know which airport.

And he at the other end said in a choked voice, "I love you."

He had hung up.

He wouldn't be there tonight when I arrived. Of course I should have said any airport at all—what difference did it make?—Newark. Connie had no phone. Meg was in jail. There was no longer any way to get in touch with him.

I was surprised that Meg had had sexual relations with Ramón.

So poor Harold was not going to be cleared after all for the job that he had so patiently studied for.

My colleagues began to stray into the lobby, talking in still-depressed tones after their ordeal.

I began to feel again in my midriff the vacancy that I had felt before I took the plane for Denver. As usual, I began to rally, against my woe, my indignation at the meddling police who would be bought off for $3,500; but by then the damage was done.

Wistfully, dutifully, I drew Harriet Young aside and asked her if I could send a young fellow up to the Settlements to apply for a job. Who was he? His name was Terry. He had a genius for community—for rallying people together—for coming across. I never knew such a person, I said, for coming across. No, he didn't have a university degree.

"It's no use," she said. "We have to maintain standards to stay on the city budget. Tell him to go on and get a degree. It's the same everywhere."

It was no use. I did not argue about it.

I bit my lip and did not argue. Terry was not a strong case to argue for. I did not trust him to shine in an interview. Rather, he was likely to make a pain in the ass of himself. He was a borderline schizophrenic with obsessional defenses. It was not accidental that he did not have a university degree. He just happened to have a genius for shepherding together.

11

I had no fight left in me. My indignation could not ward off my woe. I certainly did not have a practical proposal. Simply, our way didn't work. We didn't have the power. We were stupid anyway. I didn't have the wherewithal to be indignant.

Almost immediately after the takeoff, leaving the wall of the Rockies behind us, our plane ran into a storm. The plane bucked and sagged. The pilot climbed, but never quite got above the clouds. People became sick, but I was too grievous to be nauseous.

I was not squeamish. It did not bother me if people threw up into their little sacks. There was plenty of air.

Maybe I misunderstood the nature of our society entirely. My doubt in myself assailed me more and more strongly as I grew older, because I was sexually unhappy as well as tired. That too was all of a piece—unrealistic. But being dissatisfied made me all the *more* vehement, and all the *more* likely to be in the wrong. Sometimes I felt that I had been outrageous. (I was not in Denver.)

Why didn't they refute me if I was wrong? Instead, people crowded and applauded me, and said that I spoke their thoughts. Naturally. We were the dissatisfied. (It was not a matter for applause.) There were a lot of us. I spoke for *some* people when I said that our society was worthless. But certainly my anger was not making myself happy.

I was now fifty-three years old, and I could count up very few happy hours that I had had. Simply, my formula did not work. I could not make good the degree of freedom that I wanted. And today, when things went badly with my friends, I was remorseful, if perhaps I was responsible for influencing them, who could not cope even as much as I could.

The dusk was darkening fast, and as we flew East into it, even faster than it ordinarily would. We could not altogether get out of the clouds, but there were a few stars.

Naturally, the powers of the nation and the corporations proceeded on their way as if I and my friends did not exist, except when, for reasons of their own, they chose to scatter us like chaff, or drag this one or that one away. What was I doing? The wise course, taking everything into account, was to compromise with them for a breath of life, and otherwise avoid them.

But I couldn't agree to it, for they insulted me. They preempted my space. Worst of all, they bored me. In this, at least, I was justified to complain. Everybody has a right to his own sensibility.

Tough shit for me! if I couldn't find my city and nation interesting unless a hundred million TV watchers had other standards more like mine! They certainly would not change for my sake.

But they never did anything that I admired or was proud of. What a world to live in! where there was almost never a subtle decision, an inventive solution, an ideal motive, a forthright act. One could die of inanition, of the deprivation of meaning. Yawning and hungry, people fell asleep.

Outside the porthole, the storm was extraordinary. It was terrifying. I was not terrified. Orange and white in the clouds, the thick lightnings flashed and flared. A miles-long fork of lightning wandered from cloud to cloud. I felt myself baring my teeth with joy. Breathing freely with delight. The plane took a great drop. Despite my seat belt, my head thwacked against the cushioned ceiling. We must have been over Illinois or Indiana. The black cloud below was not unbroken, and I could see the blue-and-white constellation of a town in which I had no friends. Three or four chambers in the clouds were simultaneously lurid with yellow lightning. I was breathing full and freely. This kind of thing did not take my breath away. I wondered what happened when lightning struck the plane. Probably nothing.

Other passengers seemed to be frightened and were holding their breaths. If they were as wretched as I, they wouldn't hold their breaths!

Tired and disappointed as I had been, I was going to suffer even more without the youth who had the ability to enliven me and make me feel not so old. I knew that I was not again going to meet anybody like him who, unaccountably, wanted to please me and knew how. He regarded me, I think, as a piece of valuable horseflesh who was going, if he was preserved for another dozen years, to win the Nobel Peace Sweepstakes or something. He worked hard to keep me young and sexy. He was disturbed if I took an airplane in a storm.

By now they had hold of Harold's fingerprints from Oregon. (Perhaps I could use Amy Watkins to do something for him, though she was from California.) Poor Harold! We were unavoidably responsible for him since he was so useful and decent to us. But what were we supposed to advise him? To live more prudently? A man had to have some life in his life, even if it could not possibly bring him any peace or satisfaction. I could see his stony face, that did not even feel the fear and guilt he felt.

Neither Harold nor any of us would bear any grudge against Ramón, because we were understanding.

12

I got to Vanderzee about midnight, but Terry was not there. Harold and Meg were in jail. Jason was still in the hospital, and there was no point in waking up Connie. I wondered what provision had been made by the State, in its wisdom, to care for Meg's baby. Vanderzee was not at her best.

policemen

1

The police cuffed the Spanish kids around a bit, but not worse than the gang did to one another. At one time Domingo fell to the ground, whimpering as though he were going to die, but it was only that a cop had adroitly knocked the wind out of him, and he soon got up. The kids were afraid of the brutal-looking blackjacks, but nobody used any blackjacks.

From the viewpoint of the police, the affair was routine, unnewsworthy. They pinned on them a dozen of the reported burglaries, some of which they had indeed committed. They located the pot, identified the junkies, and heard the names of the same pushers as they already knew. After that the ritual was useless. There was no space in the reformatories anyway. The police did not like to cooperate with social agencies and probation officers any more than was necessary.

But suddenly the address that Ramón gave rang a bell. The cops went into the office to look at the record. When they came back, three of them took the boy into another room. They decided not to tell Harold, for a few hours, that his car had been picked up with an under-age driver.

2

Singled out, Ramón was in terror. He was in a storm of confusion, of hatred for his friends who had got him into trouble after all, of nostalgic guilt toward his grown-ups whom he had wronged. Now they were going to pin the blame on him for everything. He had not even been driving the car—he had screamed from the back seat, "No! No! maricón!" because he saw that you could not squeeze between the standing garbage truck and the parked cars. Then they could not even open the doors and abandon the car; they were caught cooped up, screaming at one another.

214

He could have wept at the injustice of it all. He was in the right, in everything. He could prove it. Nevertheless he was singled out for punishment. Somebody had sung that he had stolen the car, but they had forced him to steal it, hadn't they? Was this what it meant to be the Chief? His morale was undermined by the sneaking thought that he was a usurper, a chief-killer who did not have the power to make it good; and this accusation was confusedly echoed within him far into the past, returning reinforced like thunder.

Yet even more deeply than he hated his friends and himself, he loved the police: they were so strong and terrible. They certainly were not cheapskate. He had never been arrested in Vanderzee, but he had been told that they were even more brutal than the police of New York.

Gripping onto the edge of the chair where they put him, he faced them white-faced.

3

But it was not to be like that at all. Instead, the brawny man in the gray shirt and with the black gun in the holster, was smiling at him. The thin man with the eyeglasses went out into the corridor and worked the machine and brought him back a frothing bottle of Coca-Cola. He drank it greedily; he needed the comfort of sweetness. He could not think of anything, except this painless timeless moment with the bottle of Coca-Cola, gurgling down his throat. Afterward, if he ever spoke to anybody in the world again, he would say that they had given him a bottle of Coco-Cola.

He sat back a little in the chair. They did not ask him about the car; they did not grill him about the burglaries. "Don't be so nervous, man. Just tell us about yourself. You seem to be the one who can talk English." The two of them did not even loom over him, but stayed a little away. There was a third cop over on the right, but Ramón did not yet dare to look away to look at him. But they just wanted to ask him where he lived, and who those other people were.

They knew all about the other people anyway! To his surprise, they did all the talking. They kept telling *him*. The big cop was named Joyce; the thin one was Harriman. Pretty soon the atmosphere was more relaxed, and Baby Ruth candy bars appeared. Ramón didn't like that kind of shit, but Joyce and Harriman munched away. Joyce obligingly offered him a cigarette. Harriman lit it for him with his lighter. Ramón drew deep. For a moment he looked away.

He stole a glance at the third cop, sitting silent on a table and leaning against the wall. Ramón didn't like him; he was a Dago. (He was the youngster in the squad car that had stopped to interview Roger.) He had a pad, and from time to time he wrote something down. Ramón didn't like that. "What's he writing?" he asked.

"He's taking notes," explained Joyce. "Hi, Giuseppe! Meet Ramón! He wants to know what you're doing. Stromberries! Everything has got to be put down in notes." Yet Joyce himself was doing all the talking—just, sometimes, Ramón contradicted him and set him straight. It was kookie.

After a while it was even funny and even Ramón had to laugh. The most hilarious subject was Soren.

"After that we go to the third floor!" crowed Joyce, chuckling in anticipation of his own anecdote, and slowly working up the vindictive fury in his insulted soul. "On the third floor, ladies and gentlemen, we meet the Savage Beatnik in his Den. Hey, Beppo? Do you remember them paintings on the wall? Oh, boy. You tell 'em; I'm still blushing. Go ahead, Beppo! You tell 'em. Oh, boy. Oh, boy. Stromberries!"

The young Italian said nothing. He thought that his colleague was contemptible and disgusting.

Joyce looked at his dossier. "Here it is. Complaint about a noisy radio. September 15, 2:05 A.M."

—They had knocked at the hour when the soul is not too well attached to the body. Finally, Soren threw open the door to them and stood there naked. He was wondering why anybody would bother to knock and not just walk in; and it was hard for him to think of more than one thing at a time.

Joyce was confused by his nakedness and could not take his eyes off his crotch. Soren was not flattered, as he might otherwise have been, but querulous. They had interrupted him in writing his *Ode to the Victim Hood*—located in Buchenwald, Nagasaki, Sing Sing, Riker's Island. When he finally comprehended what they wanted—Beppo impatiently walked in and turned the radio off—he asked plaintively, "Why ditn't you to it in the first place if it annoyt you?" He hit his *d*'s very high because his front teeth were missing. Then he remembered his lower-middle class Danish manners, and said apologetically, "I ditn't remember it was on. I can't keep two things in my mind at once. Won't you step in?"

"For Chrissake put some pants on," said Joyce. Soren obediently, wonderingly, put on a pair of pants—he noticed that his feet were filthy—apprehensive about what would happen now. His thoughts were in Dachau. He realized suddenly that they were cops.

"Ain't you cold, boy?" said Beppo. Soren noticed that Beppo was Italian and good-looking.

It had got chilly in the small hours. Soren realized that he had been shivering. He realized that he was faintly hungry—he had forgotten to eat for a couple of days—so he offered them some of his Tiger's Milk, an orange concoction of vitamins that he believed in, and a soda cracker with a dab of crunchy peanut butter. Joyce turned away with a snort, as if he were being poisoned. Beppo looked into the bare and unused refrigerator, and took a cracker politely and nibbled at it.

Soren kept nervously buttering the crackers and stuffing them into his mouth, the flakes falling from the corners of his lips. He had two little locks of black hair that curled, comically, on either side of his noble white brow and made him seem, with his wide gray eyes between, like a peculiar being.

"Shall I read you some of my new poem?" he said.

Beppo again agreed politely, and Soren, shifting from

foot to foot like a small boy on the stage at Assembly—but he was six foot two and not too skinny, despite his diet— read a page in his stammering Detroit accent. The other cop, however, took the occasion to look at the lewd pictures on the wall. They were fragile Pre-Raphaelite pastels drawn for Soren by the young woman he loved in Detroit. They were lewd in that they showed the genital parts of the figures somewhat as they exist in nature.—

These were the pictures that Joyce described with brio and gusto. In this one a horse had a couple of balls, and in that one there was the unmistakable crack of a girl's twot. Joyce remembered every detail. "Oh, boy!" he kept saying to Ramón. "Hey, kid? Oh, boy!" As if carried away and letting himself go completely, he confided how he couldn't keep from getting a hard-on. The entrapment was hopelessly amateurish, but Ramón was tickled pink to be included in the intimate society of such powerful and prestigious persons. "D'you ever see them pictures?" he asked Ramón, and Ramón started to crow also and add an item or two to the saga of Soren.

At a signal, Harriman dealt him a blow in the jaw that knocked out a tooth. Blood spurting from his mouth, Ramón lay on the floor in the overturned chair, dazed. Then he sat up, spat out the tooth, and started to bawl.

4

As the police saw it, the case of Ramón and his older friends required delicate handling to extract the maximum advantage. It had angles. Primarily, there was the paying off. The more people who could be involved in paying off, probably the better. The questions were, Who? How much could these people afford? Who had friends to cover for him?

There was also a more craftsmanlike angle, to win renown by cleaning out a whole nest and being very busy and effective policemen. There might even be interesting names that would make headlines in the newspapers. It happened that at this time the police of Vanderzee sorely needed to demonstrate that they were guardians of the King's peace and of public morals. But superficially, at least, this kind of reward conflicted with the paying off. The problem was to manage so as to get a clamorous indictment, a handsome bribe, and a muffled suspension of sentence.

There was a community background to the case. The police were citizens of Vanderzee, and these people were still the New Yorker intruders. With correct management one might make it uncomfortable for plenty of them and maybe dislodge them. But even this was not unambiguous. Kavanagh himself seemed to be of two minds, whether he wanted to get rid of the New Yorkers or wanted to invite more of them. Who belonged to what faction? A little Puerto Rican thief with a record of Times Square arrests was not much of an object for citizenly concern. How to separate him from the rest of the gang and present him in a more attractive light?

And always underlying was the fact that the policemen, like everybody else, were day and night struggling with their own insoluble problems as human beings, abreacting their nightmares, revenging their frustrations, righteously condemning the hidden wishes of their own hearts, and building up their conceit to be as perfect, powerful, and manly as all get out. Yet this pleasant vindictiveness and meddling also had tiresome difficulties. To be carried away by their moral feelings might jeopardize more practical objectives like money. And one had to be sure to be safe from counterattack. Harriman was right to slug the punk, but he ought never to have knocked out a tooth. He was sometimes so fucking careless. Suppose they got him to a doctor? Now it was necessary to keep the kid from having recourse to the middle-class faggots, because they had lawyers.

If the police of Vanderzee had been aware that a woman was to be involved whose family connections went up to Councilor Duyckman and beyond—if they had known what those connections meant—they would have turned tail. But, being ignorant, they were able to follow their instincts.

5

They let Ramón bawl a long time. They were used to bawling kids, whom they made bawl. He was bawling with the relief that came to him because he was going to betray everybody he knew (with a curious exception), whether his Puerto Rican buddies or his grown-up benefactors. This was a lot to lose, including the contradictory motives that were the fabric of his emotions, so he had a lot to bawl for, and the cops were experienced enough not to interrupt him. He was bawling with the blessed comfort of throwing himself on the mercy of the authorities. Lucky for the peace of this confessional, he did not begin to understand how dishonest and malevolent the police were. He was bawling with the pent-up distress to which he had been subjected by his gang for the past couple of days, and his speechless jealousy of Harold and Meg that had lasted for months. Also, his face was throbbing painfully. With his tongue he felt where he had lost a tooth. But he was no longer afraid, only bawling. Freed of the years of anxiety of his life on the streets—the years of anxiety that more fortunate children accumulate in their middle-class homes—continually in danger, always in the wrong. But now someone was going to take care of him. Bawling, he was able to achieve for a few minutes at least the sublime fatalism that Pedro had in his heart eternally, the complacent acceptance of damnation, and hell as exemplified in interrogation rooms in police stations. It was a religious experience.

Washed, he was able for a few minutes, until his sins recommenced, to recapture the original innocence, which was, in his case, to show off and be an admired tiny rooster. He had a genius for performing for his grown-ups, and when he was childish he was very likable. Even though his face hurt, he was radiant at being the center of attention.

"Don' hit me no more," he wailed. "*Maricón.*"

"Cut out the bullshit and give it straight. Nobody hit you, do you hear? Nobody hit you and nobody's gonna hit you. Not if I can help it," said Joyce.

Harriman stood over him ready to kick him.

"Get off the floor and stop sniveling. Give it straight.

Pick up that chair you knocked down and sit on it like a little man. Now, what goes on with this faggot you live with?"

Ramón could see that they were really interested in the song he sang. They were not questioning him just to torture him. He was a born little actor and he became enthusiastic. He watched their eyes light up. When he mentioned having sex with Meg, they slapped their thighs. Sometimes, if he embellished, they cut him short. It was hardly necessary to draw him out.

He was high. He was the Talking Chief, the Actor Chief.

Beppo closed his pad and stood up. "Aw, cut it out," he said to Joyce and Harriman, and left the room.

Ramón was taken aback by his departure, but not crushed. He hadn't liked him from the start. Instead, he redoubled his efforts with his authentic audience and threw in a hint about Jason with the potheads. It led to a sharp question. It opened a whole new chapter.

6

But about Terry he said nothing.

This was strange. His soul was crowded with scenes and information of Terry's crimes and accomplices. He had snooped, but he found that it wasn't even necessary, for Terry willingly told him what he wanted to know. Maybe it was because he knew everything that he didn't have to blab anything. He and Terry went to Times Square. When the college youth came for the weekend, from ten campuses, to shack up and ball and smoke, Ramón often came down for Sunday breakfast, and it was amazing for him to see what they were like. How, the question is, how, when he was singing so freely, could he censor so much that was interesting? In fact, it was blotted from his mind.

It was entirely blotted from his mind because it was another order of reality. It was the world of the mystical community. It was the Vanderzee that Puerto Rican hustlers, or the police of Vanderzee, or the folk of Vanderzee, including our friends, did not much see with their accustomed eyes, knowing minds, and hardened hearts.

In that world, if an angelic policeman had asked Ramón, "Now, what about Terry and that old man, aren't *they* faggots?" a wiser Ramón would have answered, "Oh, no! they are in love." "Then what about that whore who spends the night with him, afraid that her mother will phone her at the college? She and Terry peck at each other as if they wanted to peck each other's eyes out." "Oh, no, neither one wants to hurt the other. They are desperately trying to find a basis on which they can marry and have children." "The spongers?" "Oh, no," said Ramón to the cops, "those young people do not come to sponge on Terry and one-up one another, but to find themselves and one another as the community of youth. And I too am, wistfully, a part of it!" He did not star. He did not need to star.

Nobody needed to star. And yet they formed a constellation. If you looked, through the eyepiece down into your reflector turned to heaven, new stars appeared, out of the Milky Way, in their millions and billions, shining their brilliance to us from outer space, the clouds of light resoluble into stars. And I am writing here about a young friend of mine, while I make up fictions about Terry, whom they have locked up in jail far away, and we cannot think how to free him to return to us, although we continually try one way and another. With him absent, the joy and interest have dropped out of our lives. But the crowds of stars you see in your reflector stun you with awe.

The cops tried a number of leads. Why did Terry always come home after 2:00 A.M.? Who was that chick he shouted at and slugged on the stoop? And what about the old creep who came so often during the day and he and Terry went to the Jamaica Diner? Those beatniks who showed up on the weekends—and one of them a Catholic boy from Fordham! . . . Was Terry? Did Terry? What did Ramón think?

But Ramón was blank. He knew only that Terry lived downstairs on the second floor.

It was as if he had to preserve a secret inviolate from them in order not to collapse into utter shame and die.

"O.K., now shut up, you conceited punk; you've had it."
And Joyce gave him a good backhand slap as punctuation.
For the time had come to be cold and reasonable, and get
him to sign a paper. If he didn't sign a paper, they couldn't
get a warrant, and all this beautiful and useful information was for the birds. They began to impress on him the
enormity of his offenses and to lie to him about the penal-
ties that were in store.

But if he kept cool and signed the paper that they'd
bring him, and followed through in front of the grand
jury, then he could count on them to be his friends. They
would separate him from the others for special treatment,
and provide him with a lawyer of his own, because in the
case against the New Yorkers he would be on the side of
the State.

By agreeing to be used this way, Ramón was dooming
himself. The others were out on probation the next morning, but Ramón was remanded to the reform school to be
on tap as a witness.

terence and clarence

1

Terry by this time was quite crazed, and began to split up six ways like a psychiatric classic. He had been tactless of the environment at best—it was not much of an environment at best—but after a couple of weeks of overuse of the chemicals he began to be unsure of his own name. Sometimes Terence was Clarence. (There was also a Vince.) Sometimes his personalities quarreled.

Clarence wore dark glasses and slouched like a crane, and he was a Negro who passed. He passed because of his fair skin and green eyes and because he had been born of white parents in Akron. He was the Connection, the one who carried the heroin from the pushers to the junkies, while they waited for him in anguish—there was a play by Jack Gelber.

But Clarence was restive, he didn't *like* being put in a costume. "Shove off, white boy," he said, "an' let me smoke my pot in peace." He liked the Negro bit, though he had a poor accent, but he kept mislaying the dark glasses.

"You've *got* to wear the glasses," Terence lectured him, "because when you're high the light hurts your eyes."

"Light don' hurt my eyes, white boy," said Clarence. "You jes stop dressin' me up an tellin' me how to stand. Friggin calisthenics."

But he liked being the connection. It was a real community service, and he worked at it gratis. In his moment of glory, when he was actually coming across, he was Bacchus, and the spotted animals of various colors fawned and leaped about his chariot. He petted them on the head and generously doled out. And every face lit up, where'er he walked. Why would you want to watch a scene like that through dark glasses?

To be sure, there *was* no community. The little tribe of pimps and junkies who kept plying Terry and dusting heroin into his pot and calling it the newest from Panama were entirely cynical about the white youth, and laughed in his face as they abused him. But they were not secretive, just treacherous, and Terry understood them perfectly. They *had* to use him as a brute object, a thing to discard and even to try to destroy for revenge, because they were ex-slaves and outcasts; they could not enjoy the luxury of humanity. Since he meant to be their friend, he had to take them where they were. And there they were. He had the situation under perfect control. Every act he performed, making it up as he went along, added to his own Enlightenment.

For five-minute spells he was utterly miserable.

He had nowhere to rest his head and sleep it off. He was afraid to return to Vanderzee because of the police. One of these days he planned to phone Joanna, but this required figuring out the conversation beforehand. From time to time in the phantasmagoria, he came back to it and jotted down the repartee in his notebook. His teacher, he remembered, was dead.

2

During the small hours they sat at the big window in the screamingly lit cafeteria and watched, in the way of business, the hurrying shadows pass on Forty-second Street, sometimes sharply outlined as a whore, a plainclothes man, another pimp. Later, to smoke or sniff, they sneaked up to the roof of the Columbia Hotel; and taking off his glasses, Terry saw the grand view of New York blue before the dawn. "All that mighty heart was lying still."

One didn't go north of Forty-second Street or south of Fortieth. One could go west as far as the Bus Terminal on Ninth Avenue, or east maybe as far as Sixth Avenue. Why would anybody want to go to Fifth Avenue, where there were white stone lions?

One night they took him to shack up—he remembered climbing five flights of stairs—and he was inside a Jewish girl. He did not come off. She was vaguely familiar. (She was Angela, the one who had fallen stoned to the floor at the Amstel. He had met her at Connie's.) He was trying hard

225

to reach her, to know her, to save her; but she wasn't enjoying it, she was hard. He could not come off. Then he was fighting her off, and refusing to inject the needle in his vein; he was afraid to fall asleep because she was a witch. He was on the brink of getting her to kick the habit, *it was that close!* Comatose, he started awake in anguish; and he could not come off.

It was that close! Starting as Bacchus doling out, he was also the Rescuer of all poor creatures, of batty young women and of pimps who did not have the benefit of a middle-class education. His story contained a long chapter of his saintly deeds. Except that, interrupted, he never quite came off.

Mostly they spent the early mornings furtively haunting the upper corridors of the massive midtown hotel. There was little surveillance; one could enter an empty room and sprawl on the bed. They were like mice, padding the carpeted corridors.

3

Naturally, he had impulses to flee in panic, especially Clarence who had more sense. But Terry had the situation too perfectly under control just to run away.

"I sick an' sleepy, man," moaned Clarence. "I jes wanna go an' hide."

"No," said Terence, who was an ass, "you misinterpret your impulse. What you want is to Fare Forward and cut loose from all ties."

"Yeah, man. How you know which way's forward?"

"Cast the responsibility for action upon Brahma!" said Terence. "Everything in this world of maya is only a prop."

"Bullshiit," said Clarence. "You never read dat Hindu poem. Don' bullshiit me. I ain't walking further'n Forty-fourth Street. You said you was gonna phone up Johnny" —this was his pot name for Joanna.

For a horrible five minutes he was sick and lonely.

He stole out to the all night cigar store on the corner of Seventh Avenue and dialed the number at Mrs. Gray's, where Johnny lived. He let the buzzer ring a long time, into

the empty silence, until finally Mrs. Gray crossly answered
—it was 4:00 A.M.—and he hung up. *It was that close.*

The man who used to be his teacher was dead, killed
in an airplane accident somewhere between Denver and
Allentown. He never did get back into the New York
region. It was tragic, but not surprising, for Terry had already watched him dying for a couple of weeks, in the
deepening furrow behind the bridge of his eyeglasses and
the despondency of his drooping shoulders. Desperately
Clarence tried to reach him and enliven him with a little of
the Panama; but the man stubbornly shook his head from
side to side as he boarded the airplane at the International
Airport: *No Smoking Beyond This Point.*

"Are you sure, man," asked Clarence shrewdly, "dat
they ain't dustin' dis pot wid a little shiit?"

"How often must I explain," said Terence, "that the
personality revealed under hasheesh is the same as has always been there waiting, underneath?"

"Yeah, yeah. But what if down there, man, you're a
schiz?"

4

Terry decided, with a stiff face, that now was the time,
when he could do anything—except come off—to begin to
educate himself as Professor O'Connor had advised. The
bit was first to go to Painter and Oak's, and steal the books.
This required going as far south as Thirty-seventh Street,
but it was broad daylight.

At Painter and Oak's there was rarely anybody on the
second floor where the heavy reading was, so Terry was able
to smoke his pot in comfort as he made a careful choice of
Chinese classics and the *Mahabharata.*

But it was a drag that in the handsome four-volume set
of Haiku for the Seasons, the book of Summer was missing,
and indignantly Terry slowly descended to the main floor
and complained in no uncertain terms. Luckily, the sales-
girl was able to find another copy in the basement, and he

courteously thanked her and took it upstairs. He liked it when there were no hang-ups.

When he had about ten books under each arm, he saw that there was a red light on the wall and he opened the window there and went down the fire escape, to take his treasures home. He had no home, however, and it would be a drag to carry two armloads of books up and down the corridors of the Columbia Hotel. But it was no sweat, because he took the books to the Bus Terminal on Ninth Avenue and put them in one of the lockers and pocketed the yellow key.

On the way back to cafeteria, he realized that this yellow key could be very damaging evidence of theft, so he dropped it in the trash basket on the corner of Eighth Avenue: *Don't Be A Litter-Bug.*

5

Clarence sat clutching his belly, whimpering.

The pimp regarded him with massive indifference. "Man, on this street you gotta pay your dues," he said. He was a self-righteous pimp and took a keen satisfaction in the moral. From his boyhood in Harlem, Jeff knew that pleasure was inseparable from torment, and in his business on Forty-second Street he had had plenty of opportunity to add confirmatory evidence to this grand law of Compensation. The sin of Vanderzee, in his opinion, was that they followed up fucking with affection, and did not charge a fee. Now it was good for the white boy to suffer. It did no harm to add to it a bit.

But Tony, the little pusher, was queer for Terence whom he held in awe as a brain. Being psychic, he could see that the white youth was endowed with a mysterious future that he could foresee but he wasn't saying. "I see it! I see it!" he cried, with eyes closed and stretching out his hands like swimming the breaststroke, to open wide the veil, "but I ain't sayin'." All he would say was that Terry must quit his friends in Vanderzee, who had grossly offended him on their one exploratory visit. "Boy," he said prophetically, raising a finger, *"their* way is not *your* way! But Terry, you my boy. Understan'? Uptown, downtown, crosstown. Understan'?" He gingerly brushed his fingers across Terence's crotch, ready at any moment to withdraw into his offended dignity if rebuffed. He was a tiny little man.

—With narrow eyes, Terry watched them one and all. He saw the sadistic self-righteousness of the pimp and the lascivious sentimentality of the little pusher. He knew from long experience that Terence was a fool who parroted ideas that he didn't understand. He was sad for Clarence who had started out on this binge only for a high and was now so sick with the gripes. At this moment, Terry thought, he could get up and leave, if he wanted. *It was that close.*

But he had not noticed that another character had come in and sat down in the chair with him. This was Vince, packing a toy six-shooter.

Now, Vince was really only a spiteful child of five or six, burning up for the many reasons that little fair-haired boys have. But when Terry slowly turned his eyes and beheld him, he wonderfully costumed him as an Existentialist, an authentic Savage out of a TV Western. "They comes a mo-ment," drawled Vince in rich Texan, "when an hombre has got to fell his father afore his old man fells him." And he skillfully rolled his reefer with one hand, and with the other hand he put on the dark glasses.

6

In half a year, Terry had quieted down in Vanderzee, with his friends, his psychotherapy, and a reasonable amount of sex. He had entirely sloughed off some illusions that he had arrived with. He had sloughed off the illusion that the phony images of Madison Avenue and the Front Page were necessarily the real world at all; and he had sloughed off the illusion that hipster role-playing in that world gave any real power at all—he no longer believed the argument of Thrasymachus. He saw that there was finally little difference between a hipster and a cop.

We sanguinely hoped, we who loved Terry because he loved us, that now he would start to grow up, from the bewildered child who had been left back in bad schools. And he would gradually unfold to us, and to himself, who he was to be, for we had no inkling of it, except that we would be proud of him. Arabelle's opinion, as I have said, was that, on a sober estimate, it would take three or four peaceful years for Terry to develop enough identity to be trusted.

But we could not cope with chemicals any more than we could cope with the Cold War or the police. The argument of Thrasymachus was irrefutable. They had power.

7

During the long hours of silence, and passing the joint, and brief phrases, there slowly developed, by accretion, a groovy scheme for Clarence to drive up to Montreal and bring back a consignment that had arrived there on a ship.

The idea was obvious, for nobody else would be able to get across the border.

But passionately, as he saw the lazy pot-hazy evolution of this idea, Clarence resisted it. He was willing to admit that he, like everybody else, had to pay his dues, but this wasn't paying dues; it was death.

Terry was infatuated with the task. It fitted exactly Terence's conception of Clarence as He Who Passes. It was dialectical! It was a Project. And Vince dryly concurred that it was a "criminal arpeggio."

Terry, Terence, and Vince were definitely for it. Clarence would have to give!

—It was a means, thought Terry, by which he could give way to his animal panic and bolt. If he stole a car, he thought, he would drive it very fast.

"Clarence!" he commanded, "get up on your feet."

He was merciless to the troops under his command, to the dozens of personalities under his command.

"Naa, naa," whined Clarence. "Yo' after me again for that fuckin' calisthenics."

"It could be apocalyptic," Terence said, with shiny eyes.

"You can say that again!" snorted Clarence. "Use yo' head, man. What in hell you mean, a consignment? Me? Whadda I look like? I'm supposed to give the man a bill of ladin' or sompn? Na."

"Clarence?" said Terry warningly to his vegetative soul.

With a quiet smile, Vince worked on his hair-do.

Suddenly they began to scuffle within the soul, leading to the fatal subjugation of nature and good sense, leading to the depressed and strutting posture, the frantic thoughts and irrelevant behavior of many a young fellow in 1962. It takes a lot of bad education, a venal economy, and a really insane foreign policy to achieve that hoodlum strut, that junkie slouch, that hipster cool, that college aptitude. And Terry's mind was leaping, leaping to and had conquered, move after move of the breathless adventure on which he was already rolling. (His animal lay crushed under the wheels.)

He had stolen the car and now he would drive to Canada with Johnny. Her company was not only inevitably appropriate according to the movie, but he realized that, having the situation perfectly under control, he was certainly going to crack up along the way if he did not have somebody to hold his hand. That too was dialectical.

He had to compel her to come along at gunpoint. She liked that.

It was a gas to pick her up in Mount Kisco, out of her father's split-level ranch house. But alas! that wasn't authentic. It was imprudent, especially because of her father. To take needless risks just for kicks was Not In Good Faith.

But the bit was to drive fast, to drive fast and come off.

And once arrived in Montreal, he was now taking a ship for Poland that was on the other side of the Iron Curtain, and had been highly praised in the *Evergreen Review*.

times square

1

With a stiff face and a weak jaw and wearing a small smile, Terry slouched through the lobby of the Columbia Hotel and out onto Forty-second Street. He was fortified with four packets of pot and was making deliberate speed on his breakneck adventure that was taking him to Nigeria, highly praised by Clayton Bernstein of Rover House Press.

The fresh air was shocking, and the sunlight pained him in spite of his dark glasses. The street was being shaken by a terrible noise, louder than the cars or busses. When he reached the corner, he stood fast in amazement.

In fact—he saw it through his glass wall, not making much sense of it—a throng of humanity was packed on the island in the middle of Times Square, pullulating around the black statue of the priest. And scrawled signs, like an ocean of whitecaps, tossed their message NO TESTS EAST OR WEST. Long blue-black cordons of the police hemmed in the crowd, in a determined effort to keep the roads open for traffic, but the cars hesitated to venture down into the throng.

On the sidewalks of Broadway and Seventh Avenue were deep ranks of spectators, without signs. But some of these were also demonstrators and started to chant, "Ban the Bomb!" Assailed from all sides, the police were frightened. And by moments, the chant spread over the entire multitude, making a formidable shout. It smote Terry.

Now it penetrated to Terry's hazy mind that there was to have been a demonstration of something or other. All the community was going to appear in the demonstration.

He did not know what day of the week he was at. He was looking for Johnny, and he knew that she was somewhere on the Square, because she always did what she promised.

As vehemently as the shout, other demonstrators said "Shhh!" either because the chanting was unseemly or because it was provoking the police.

But it was this strange hiss, more than the loud shout, that made the horses rear up. Police sat on about twenty fine chestnut horses in a line, facing the island. The horses were restive because their riders were uneasy. They pawed the ground and clumsily backed up. They shied their heads, but the police kept reining them to face the crowd.

None of it was comprehensible to Terry. He did not know what he himself was doing. But he was amazed. As if he were looking for Joanna in that crowd, as if he were joining the demonstration, he drifted onto the roadway toward the pacifists.

Half a dozen of the police whistled shrilly. They were edgy. The horses shied because of the whistles. Their iron shoes struck sparks.

Terry was engulfed in the crowd.

2

The President of the United States had now addressed the nation and announced that the Americans were again going to shoot off more of the big bombs, as the Russians had done and would do. As previously agreed, all pacifist groups, from the tamest to the wildest, converged on the center of America's biggest city, for a monster futile demonstration of protest. It was a great spectacle.

Surely, we deeply trusted, out of the concerted futile protest of so many thousands bravely saying "No!"—saying "Don't!"—saying "We won't!"—there must emerge a positive practical idea that was not futile, a way to exist in the world simply at peace. That seemed to be a reasonable confidence, didn't it?

During those years the powers of the world hardened their wills and narrowed their ideas, as if no contrary desire of the people of the world existed at all. And the people of the world, in more and more frequent and larger demonstrations, expressed their futile protest with less and less willingness to be disregarded.

A fierce quarrel had broken out among the pacifist leaders, on the corner of Broadway and Forty-fifth Street. In fact there were no leaders—the futile demonstrations were largely spontaneous—but the spokesmen expressed a real conflict in the situation.

A tall thin young orator was saying with a ringing voice, "You *must* stick to the agreement. If there are any acts of civil disobedience, we will have to separate our groups from the others and demonstrate elsewhere. The agreement for this united demonstration was that there was *not* to be civil disobedience. You are putting the lives of hundreds of people in jeopardy against their will."

He was a classical radical politico, even to touching off his points on his long fingers. He was a fine young man but he seemed a little old-fashioned in the middle of the twentieth century. He was obviously a little of a bureaucrat, a top-down decision-maker, who, one felt, disciplined his own instinctual life too strictly for his own good, just as he wanted to discipline the spontaneous pacifist movement. But he had common sense and he was concerned. In order to extend our influence, he pointed out, it was necessary to cooperate with the police, since they in fact (as yet) had overwhelming power. To foment a riot by civil disobedience would be unjust and dishonorable to the conservative pacifist groups, the academics, the left-wing liberals, some of the church people. They had not come to support illegal actions and be arrested as bystanders and get their heads broken.

But those on the other extreme who wanted to engage in concerted civil disobedience also had a reasonable position. But their leader was not interested in arguing it, simply in commanding it to be done. He was more like a charismatic leader and spoke in a sharp and suppressed-hysterical tone that alienated one's feelings from him, and that was both terrible and boring. "Maintain rigid discipline. Sit down. Stop the traffic. Maintain perfect quiet. Do not resist arrest. Go limp. Fill the jails. Those who cannot maintain the inner discipline of nonviolence, separate from us at once."

There was evidently something phony in calling this calculated hostility of his "nonviolence" and "winning over the enemy with Soul-force." Nevertheless, these fanatical objectors were sincere, for they could not conscientiously tolerate what the State was doing, even if it did have overwhelming force. And there was a profound practicality in their desperate idea. If the continuing Cold War was a matter of life or death—and we believed that it was—it was practical for each man desperately to risk his individual life in order to stop the universal juggernaut.

Yet these extreme views quarreling on Forty-fifth Street on that Saturday did not, in my opinion, truly represent the spontaneous movement that had sprung up against war. Most of us at that time were not political or moral pacifists at all, and we did not engage in demonstrations as *either* tactics or strategy. Our thoughts and feelings were simpler. We rejected the possibility of nuclear war as not human. It was unthinkable, if one thought with one's living brain instead of a computer. Saddened and sickened by the long history of violence, some of us became impressed by the philosophy of nonviolence. Others of us could see nothing wrong with angry fighting or guerrilla fighting, yet we totally rejected the organized senselessness of modern war. Some of us were convinced that the Cold War was intrinsic in the power structure of the Sovereign States and we became interested in anarchist ideas. All of us were "pacifists" —we wanted the nations to cut it out. Surely, we felt, given so many beautiful resources, mankind could make a better world than we had.

Inevitably, as time went on, the very simplicity of our elementary compassion and simpleminded reasonableness seasoned us and made us balkier and balkier. We could not be discouraged from believing what was obvious. We became less and less sentimental. But we were certainly confused.

Perhaps if we had known the shape of a peaceful future, of any peaceful future, we would have rallied immensely to effectuate it, and we would have known what to do on Times Square more than jumping up and down. But years of stupefaction of the citizens, in soul-paralyzing emergencies, had atrophied practical imagination. People could conceive of no alternative to what they did, even though they were no longer going to put up with what they had.

Our remarks on Forty-fifth Street were pretty shaggy. "How in hell would I know whether or not I'm going to sit down in that road and block traffic? Depends on the provocation. This country is for the birds, but what social order are *you* thinking of?" We were meticulously anti-Soviet.

"Balls! I'm damned if, when I come here and make a public fool of myself and risk getting my head broken, I'm going to accept somebody's discipline. I'll chant 'Ban the Bomb' whenever I damned well feel like it. Do they expect people to picket for peace and not be themselves?"

"All the same, it's awe-inspiring, the unity of so many people on such simple and irrefutable propositions! 'No Tests East or West.' Period. By God, it's what we used to call solidarity."

"Yeah, but five million would be a hell of a lot better than five thousand. I came just because you've *got* to do *something*."

4

The crowd accepted the command of silence, and it fell.

Honking a horn, a car ventured to drive up Broadway.

In the silent crowd, forcing his way—but people courteously opened space for him, since he was looking for someone—came Terry. He was looking for Joanna, if that's what he was doing. Whichever way he looked, he was hemmed in by hundreds.

Suddenly he was face to face with Soren and Meg, who were out on bail. They exclaimed with delight to see him, bad as he looked. But he did not know them, and the next moment he had gone away from them in the crowd that closed around him. They were eclipsed.

They did not fit into his scheme of Faring Forward. The car, he thought busily, was running out of gas. Thing was to get hold of a credit card. He could also use this to buy some tropical suits. It was best to come on like an Important Person and wear a hat.

"Johnny!" he called in the silence. There was something familiar in people he had just seen, and it might have been she. His voice rang in the silence.

5

With a little click in the neck, he returned to sanity, because he knew that he was among thousands of his friends. He took off his dark glasses and, in confusion, he saw the people plain. What day was it? What was he doing? He put the dark glasses in his pocket.

"Joanna!" he cried out frantically, and he knew that he was looking for Joanna. The people were crowding him and suffocating him. He thrust his way with his elbow. "Don't shove," said a woman angrily.

And he saw the scrawls that people were waving high above their heads, NO TESTS EAST OR WEST, JOIN THE WORLD-WIDE GENERAL STRIKE FOR PEACE.

"Joanna! Joanna!" he called out, because she must be here with these, our friends.

"Shhh!" hissed loud voices.

"I won't Shhh, you mothers!" snarled Terry. "I'm looking for my wife." This was how he chose to regard her when his world was falling out of order.

"*Ban the Bomb! Strike for Peace!*" bawled out a voice nearby to support him. He turned, and recognized the Reverend Timothy Slotkin. "Hi, Terry!" said the little man, and waved to him cheerily.

They were not an easy crowd to discipline.

6

There was now a sea of signs—he was getting toward the edge of the crowd, the road—and they were tossing about like whitecaps before a storm. ONE WORLD OR NONE, STOP POISONING MY BABY'S MILK, NO TESTS EAST OR WEST, THIS HOUSE HAS NO FALLOUT SHELTER. Some of the signs were formally printed in nonviolent type; others were dripping gore like action-paintings.

N.Y.P.S.S.C.D.P.C.: the New York Public School Students Civil Defense Protest Committee was an association that had as many members as initials. And its sign was held up by Hughie, the son of the old man whom Terry loved.

"Hello out there! O Terry!" said Hugh, who was just beginning Latin.

For Terry was looking at him in utter disbelief, as though he were seeing a preternatural being.

"My father says there is going to be a riot," said Hugh. "I'm not allowed to go to the barricade."

With horror at himself, Terry realized that he did not know the day of the week.

He had missed the appointment! He remembered phoning to Denver. (But the plane had crashed. The plane had crashed!)

"Connie can't come because she went and had the baby," said Hugh. "She's at North Baxter General Hospital."

Terry wanted to speak. Perhaps he wanted only to know whether the baby was a boy or a girl. He could not. He swallowed but he couldn't find his voice. He tried to look up but the light lanced his eyes. It was like when he lost his voice and he could not call out Help. But this time there was no one to rescue him. He began to fall to pieces.

"Harold drove her to the hospital," explained Hugh. "My mother is going to have a baby too—she had a rabbit test."

There was a world—Terry was hemmed in by it—and all of the folk our friends held up their signs. But Terry knew that it was not a world for him. This is what it means to lack Grace, to know that the only world there is is not a world for oneself. How can one then take a step, or learn anything?

"My father says," said Hugh, "the police will cop out and ride their horses right into the crowd." He became sober. "This is for real. My father usually is right." He began to be scared by his own words. "Ban the Bomb!" he shouted, in order to give himself a little courage by his own words. "I've got another dog," he said.

Terry saw that Hughie was scared and needed to be touched, and yet he could not stretch out his hand to him and touch him. There was an appeal, and he could not come across. But he had no other way to be in the world.

Then the tears of pity for himself welled into Terry's hurting eyes—which he had a right to, for they were for a young man.

"Ain't you looking for Joanna?" said Hugh. "She's out there by the barricade with Jason."

7

She was with Jason and Professor Davidson, a small group from the big University.

Elbowing his way to a position at the sawhorses of the police, for a while Terry did not see them, for he was face to face with the cordon of police in the road. He was appalled by their faces. They were determined, ugly-brutal, and continually shifting their eyes to the left for a signal. They were the Riot Squad. They were tactitians and would certainly create more trouble than was necessary. They did not know how to cope with the confusing silence, with the peculiar peaceful recklessness of these people, from which, indeed, anything whatever might emerge, if they became desperate.

He saw Joanna. It was Professor Davidson!—They were the University. But he did not belong to the University either.

How pathetic it was! It was because of Terry's intervention that the great physicist was there, justifying the University by his presence. It was Terry who, by his noisy love that could not be brushed aside, had made the Professor understand what it was that the students expected of him. Terry had well deserved of the University, in his way. And now his heart should have swelled with honor, he who had so much need for something real to boast about, and *here* was something real. Everybody could see it! and Terry knew the facts. Instead, he looked and saw with mild surprise that it was Professor Davidson with Jason and Joanna.

Davidson was not a well known face, but a few people recognized him and said, "That's Davidson!" The word spread around. A man pointed over Terry's shoulder and said, "That's Davidson, the one in the tweed coat." What Davidson gave them was not the prestige of his presence— the situation was far beyond that—but the astonishing security that perhaps they were in the right, because here was Professor Davidson, who *knew* about the radiation. *He* ought to know! He *ought* to know.

"Terry!" screamed Joanna. She saw him and was frantically calling out to him. She was fighting through the crowd to get to him. He looked about, which way to run away.

8

A car was slowly coming down Broadway, and three of the Committee for Non-Violent Action went over the barricade and sat down in the roadway in the front of the car, that jolted to a stop. The crowd stirred.

The Riot Squad was caught by surprise. With frantic whistling and obscene shouts, a half dozen cops converged on the sitters and grabbed them. The sitters went limp and made themselves difficult to drag away. Startled, one of the horses reared and was momentarily out of control. And the pent-up fear and ugliness of the police got the upper hand. Two who were trying to handle one of the sitters began to beat her on the head and shoulders with their sticks. She did not cry out.

At once a large number of others climbed over the barricade to come to the girl's support, by sitting down beside her in the road. There must have been twenty of them at once.

To the Riot Squad everything now seemed to be out of control, and now they really laid about them with their sticks.

"Shame! shame!" called Professor Davidson, laying his hand on the barricade to support himself in his grief. Young Terry saw this awful moment. He saw Joanna caught in the press and looking back at him in despair.

"Take your fuckin' hand off that barrier!" barked the cop at Professor Davidson. Davidson removed his hand and, quietly ignoring the cop, said in a loud voice, "Shame! Shame! Shame!" At the scene that was taking place in the middle of Broadway, in the middle of Broadway.

"Shame! shame!" called out Terry and others, to support him.

Terry was surprised to find his voice. It was inhibited and he could hardly call out at first. But by the grace of God he had found a relation with the nature of things, and he found his voice and meant what he said. He was too ashamed of himself to think of himself as yet, but he was able to see the shame of the cops as very real, very real.

In the road, a cop pushed his stick against a woman's breast, and, "I just hope you provoke me," he snarled, "because I'd love to smash your face in."

"Why—Why, you don't even know me," stammered the bewildered woman.

The reinforcements of police came, assembling in a hurry at the barricade, getting set, coordinated, but not yet making their move, but blocking off ways to join the sit-down spreading. They closed in to contain the crowd in their cordon, while they brought up their trucks in the roadway.

Brutal men were mishandling a gentle elderly fellow who held a sign simply asking the government not to poison his grandchildren's milk.

"Shame! Shame! Shame! Shame!"—The provocation was intolerable to the police; they had not heard it since they stood, as small children who had pissed in their pants, with bowed heads, in the pool.

241

9

Then a cop was swinging his fist and his club at somebody behind the barricade, and then the cops on his flank were swinging and those on their flanks, and the cops began to charge, knocking over the sawhorses, and more and more people were screaming, "No! no!"

The cops wore gloves and had long clubs weighted with lead, swinging on leather thongs. They were cursing, coming in fast, as a phalanx of gloved fists and clubs, and blue cloth, nickel badges and brass buttons. And the chestnut flanks of horses were pushing people down. The people were screaming "No." For no reason at all the police were charging their horses into the crowd that was not threatening anything.

10

They singled out Professor Davidson because, in his intellectual and objective and Cambridge-trained voice, he called out, "Shame!"

Awkwardly, but expertly, Terry thrust his way through the crowd to come to the side of his professor, from whom he had learned, and could learn, nothing. And it happened that on his way he passed by Joanna, who was the young woman whom he was going to marry if he was going to marry anybody, but it did not seem so; and as he passed, he grabbed her hand roughly and excruciatingly squeezed it, in such a way as meant that it was she whom he was going to marry if he was going to marry anybody. She remembered this.

Davidson was coming toward him with blood pouring from his nose down both sides of his lips, down the channels of disapproval. Jason, wincing with pain from his recent injury—he had just been discharged from the hospital and ought not to have come—was throwing a long punch at a policeman. But the cops were throwing short chopping punches, blocking and feinting and hacking with their billies. Then Davidson was overwhelmed and swamped in cops. As he went down, Terry could see a gash on the top of his delicate pate and his sparse hair wispy and loose in the wind. He could not see, after the Professor went down, the cop kick him and break two ribs and puncture a lung. So much subtile love of nature.

The tide of the police forced Terry back. He no longer knew where Joanna was.

And Terry was red, from head to foot, with shame. It is the feeling that remains when exhibition, self-expression, and maybe eagerness to come across—the things that could make one great, effective, and loved in the world—have proved unacceptable, out of place, in the world. Maybe one was conceited. Maybe the world is not up to our offer. Then the capillaries on the surface of the body contract violently, for one has been too outgoing, and there is a hot blush.

Terry knew that he was sometimes crazy.

When Professor Davidson called "Shame!" it was not in shame for himself; he was confident of himself. He was blushing for the world that he saw: it was not up to a man's normal impulse to belong to it. It had no honor.

But Terry was ashamed of the world *and* of himself. The world had no honor and he had no manliness. This left him nothing. It left him nothing now and no future either. The feeling of shame, like being in love, does not permit one to make Projects. There is nothing to do but flame, and sink into the ground.

Suddenly Terry fainted and fell down, having nothing by which to support himself upright.

11

The melee surged into the crowd almost as far as where the boy Hugh stood. He saw a lot of it and he was crying. He was not afraid anymore, but looking with big eyes, the tears rolling down, and sometimes saying, "Oh, you mustn't. You oughtn't to do that."

His careful father had predicted that there might be trouble, and Polly had wanted to forbid the boy to go to the demonstration at all. But Hugh wanted to go, and it

243

was better for him to do as he wanted even if there was a (small) risk.

But his father would have preferred that he didn't see some of these things, though he was eleven years old.

Naturally Hugh followed with intense excitement Terry's progress into the fight—the one he knew—and he was gripped by anguish when he saw him fall and then couldn't see him any more. He liked Terry, with whom he played chess.

Then he began to cry as he watched and said, "Oh, you shouldn't."

12

The tall young politico was stalking up and down, shouting, "Order! Be orderly! Go away as orderly as possible! Let's try to have as few hurt as possible."

Naturally, when the showdown came, he did not at all try, as he had threatened, to withdraw from the ones who had broken the agreement. All were in it together. But he was now seething with rage as, responsibly, he stalked about, risking a conk on his high head from a nightstick, shouting, "Order! Go away as orderly as possible!"

Understandably, his rage was even greater against his friends than against the police.

harold

1

Harold had steeled himself for the interrogation. He denied everything—and waited. He was plausibly sure that if he once got to the grand jury he could face down the testimony of a little hustler.

But the cops made no effort to break him down. They hardly went so far as to bring up his previous convictions. He was perplexed.

In fact, Meg had already affirmed everything that Ramón had said, so far as she knew, correcting only an occasional exaggerated detail.

It simply did not occur to her that this was not what one did. Being innocent in her own mind, she did not feel accused of anything. The facts, so far as they went, were largely true. She did not try to explain to policemen the meaning of the facts, because that was not the *kind* of thing they asked.

She somewhat understood that it was a lawsuit. When she had bailed herself and Harold and Soren out, she went to see Councilor Duyckman, and he thought about it whatever he thought. His plan was to separate her case because of extenuating circumstances and prevent (for a sum) any indictment. But Meg was stubbornly unwilling to be separated from the others.

The police were enthusiastic about this bail money, this early appearance of affluence, which often did not show up until they had turned the screws several times. They raised their fiscal sights another couple of thousand dollars, and their approach became much more high-toned. They celebrated by at once having Harold fired from his job, for failing to notify his employer that he had been in prison eighteen years before.

2

When he learned that Meg had simply affirmed Ramón's story, Harold was so puzzled that he was not angry. For the first time in many years he began to be deeply confused. He was in love with Meg; he respected her. What she had done seemed to be the behavior of an irresponsible moron.

"I don't understand," he kept saying. "You said—you said to *them?* that you had sex with Ramón? You *signed* that?"

"It was all true, the way policemen look at such things."

"The way policemen look at such things—" echoed Harold, unbelieving. "But Meg! Where does this leave *us?*"

"Oh! does a person have to think about that?" she asked, surprised.

"Anyway, how do *you* know what was true between Ramón and me?" he said with a touch of anger.

She became frightened. "I didn't tell them anything that you didn't tell me yourself," she said.

"You didn't tell them anything that I didn't tell you myself!" he echoed. To his astonishment, this remark sent him into a kind of rapture. He had, in fact, been unusually frank with her, the only one in the world. It had made him fall in love with her.

"Besides," she said, and darkly blushed, "one night I—watched."

"You watched? Ah, you watched."

It had been hard for her to say, and she became speechless with guilt, first for the eavesdropping and then for everything else. Maybe her invincible ignorance—what would she know about being arrested and what to do?—had now made trouble for the people she loved?

But Harold could not get beyond the eavesdropping. "Meg! You watched? And did you tell—*them*—that you watched? and what you watched?"

Speechless, she looked at him with eyes burning with her customary reproach that she could not understand what the grown-ups were doing.

"When did you watch?" he asked with melancholy pleasure. There were different scenes of his disgrace and humiliation.

"I'll go back and tell them that everything was a lie!" she cried. "I probably don't remember it right anyway," she said, with her customary abnegation of a petulant child who gives up even what she does know.

For the first time he noticed that lurking behind her reproachful eyes was a look of infinite mischief, almost of malice. This wickedness excited him. He saw that her childlike frankness was partly innocence but partly defiance. It came to the same thing! He was overwhelmed by confused excitement at the idea that lordly, well born people, well brought up, regarded the police as so many dogs, though watchdogs. They accepted the system because it was their own system. They were more than *macho!* They disdainfully did not even agree that they were emasculated.

"These police of Vanderzee," said Meg with acumen—she had brooded over it for some time—"imagine that they can be important by meddling in our business." She did not quite come to say "in the business of their betters." But she added, "Especially because we are New Yorkers."

To Harold a thought like this was profoundly new. He was always so trapped in his defenses, and made narrow-eyed by his need to counter the grilling, that he had never enjoyed the luxury of looking at anything in an objective and sociological light. He had never entertained a political thought in his life. It was a new world. He was able to guess at its existence now because he identified with Meg and she spoke and acted with the gracefulness of power. He was thunderstruck with admiration for her. He felt oddly, in spite of all, secure.

Suddenly he felt a little courage trickle back into his genitals. It smote him like a blow in the nape of the neck that fells an ox. He made a wry face. He was engulfed in a woe of uncontrol. He sat down. His legs did not twitch.

After a moment, assuming the authority that he naturally had, he insisted that Meg take the Councilor's advice and get out of it promptly (for a sum). There was no sense in *her* being in jeopardy. How did that advantage the others? On the contrary, Harold believed, if one friend had good luck, it made it better for everybody else, something like a philosopher's stone. His own loyalty was so absolute, except to himself, that he could not understand the existence of disloyalty.

So Meg went back obediently to Councilor Duyckman, and diligently the Councilor got her off because of extenuating circumstances (for a sum). A part of the settlement was that she had to get out of Vanderzee.

3

When Soren heard that Meg was out of it, he flew into a rage. Meg and Harold, he cried, the rich and the cunning, were ganging up on his poverty-stricken naïveté, of which he was very vain.

He felt betrayed. Since he was indeed out of touch with the world, its incursion into his asylum threw him into delusions, and he lashed out with the petty-bourgeois frenzy that was at the bottom of a good deal of his Beat ritual. Unluckily, he had at this time a spiteful girl friend named Evelina, who hated Meg because she was a woman, and hated Harold, Jason, Terry, and so on, because they were men. Soren she loved and protected because he was her genius. And now, in this crisis, she kept devising plans and consulting experts for them to "protect their interests" and "leave these squares out on a limb." Soren was mesmerized by her vindictive energy, so different from his poetic lethargy. Fortunately, they didn't have any money, or Lord knows what havoc they might have invented.

Soren complained to the community. "I ditn't do anything," he said, "and now you put it all on me." We were gathered lugubriously at Jason's.

Wearily the tired man tried to explain to him again that it was Harold who was in danger. He had already lost one job, he was not going to get the new job for which he had studied so hard, and he was the one who had kept Ramón. No matter who admitted what, the circumstantial evidence was entirely against Harold.

"Nobody ever came to see *me* on the third floor," said Soren astoundingly, "except to come and eat my peanut butter."

He said that we visited him to eat his peanut butter.

We were at Jason's to see the new baby. To Harold's utter confusion, they had called it after him, Harold.

"What do you mean you didn't do anything?" said Jason brutally. "You yourself told me that you used to jack each other off to dirty pictures."

"But I explaint that to the policeman," said Soren. "My girl Chrissie in Detroit sent me a book of Chinese prints for my birthday. They are *supposet* to be an aphrodisiac. And it's better if anyboty else helps along, so each one can relax with his revery."

"Did you *say* that to the policeman, honey?" asked Evelina, wincing.

She hated the name of Chrissie. She was righteously indignant at people relaxing with their reveries. Her view was that sex must be strenuous to be worthwhile. At this moment she hated poets too.

"I offeret to read them the preface," said Soren, "but they mate fun of me."

"I don't know why you're so upset, Soren," said Connie. "Jason says that you'd get only thirty days. I think that you would find it interesting in jail, seeing what the people are like."

"Do you think so, Connie?" said Soren wonderingly.

With a scream Evelina flew at Connie and began to scratch her face and milk-full breasts. Connie cried out, wounded.

This was the darkest moment of our community in Vanderzee, when the friends fell apart and Connie moaned.

4

Harold was in an extraordinary life situation. For a few days he had no secrets. He was not hiding anything from anyone except himself. Thanks to Meg, so to speak, the ordeal of the grilling was past. His jaw and shoulders, which were chronically tensed to ward off torture and diabolic questions, began to relax themselves. They ached. His lips were less tight.

And he vaguely remembered an early scene—early for him, though he must have been nine or ten. (Mostly he existed for himself after fifteen, when he was leading the gang.) He was a small boy in a garage, and there were grown-ups. It must have been in Boulder, before they went to the Coast. Now he realized that it made no difference what it was all about, because it was always the same thing: they were grilling him! One of the men was his stepfather.

It was the last time in his life that he had ever told the truth. Presumably he had learned better.

He had a remarkable insight about himself. It was *not* about the lawless acts he performed that he felt guilty, for even as a child he had perceived that "bad" meant simply what the grown-ups didn't like. It was his response to the interrogation that made him feel guilty! He hated them. He would not give them the time of day. It was vengeance, it was victory, to construct plausible alibis. And even to get in thicker and thicker in order to make them look like fools!

To his relief, he found that it was even *more* satisfying not to give a damn whether they knew or what they knew. Why hadn't anybody ever told him this charming recipe?

He was moved. He was inspired by the high-born frankness of Meg. He fantasized being entirely dry and frank at the hearing. It was a new world.

After a bit, he decided against this nonchalance, the world being what it was.

5

His immediate problem was to get a job. He answered an ad, and was faced with the form to fill out.

"Here goes," he thought, and lied. But when he handed the page back to Personnel, he asked if he could see Mr. Polk, the manager, because he wanted to know about the actual operation. Mr. Polk happened to be see-able.

"What I really came to see you about," said Harold, "is this. I was just fired from Hutchins after working there nine years, when they found I had a conviction for burglary eighteen years ago on the Coast."

"How in hell did they suddenly find that out?" asked Mr. Polk.

"That's a good question," said Harold, and drew a breath. "I was keeping a little Puerto Rican hustler who got into trouble. The police knocked the shit out of him and he sang."

"What's a hustler?" asked Mr. Polk.

"That's a male prostitute who makes pickups in the bars or on Forty-second Street."

"You ain't a pimp, are you?" asked Mr. Polk. "You don't look like a pimp."

"No, just queer," said Harold.

Polk shook his head disgustedly. "You ought to have your head examined," he said. "What do you expect from trash like that?" He picked up the phone and called for the record.

"I lied on the form," said Harold, suddenly embarrassed.

"I hope you did. You don't look that crazy. . . . My son was just kicked out of Cornell for queer. What do you think about that? Now I'll have to get him into Johns Hopkins."

"Yes, sir," said Harold sympathetically.

"Why are some people always minding other people's business?"

"I don't know, sir," said Harold.

"They talk about the normal suburban family!" cried Polk angrily, banging on the desk. "I never know a one of them that don't have something—a lush, a queer, a junkie, a peace-marcher, a sitter-in in bus terminals in Alabama! Jesus Christ, what a generation!"

The girl brought the form and he looked at it.

"What's lies?" he asked. "Is any of this part lies?"

"No, sir," said Harold. "The lies begin down here. I'm really very competent. Look here—I came out in the top quartile."

"Quartile!" said Polk with disgust. "Never use that language around here. But O.K., O.K., you're hired since we've come this far. Come in Monday." He initialed the form. "I'll start you at twenty more than you were getting."

I wouldn't tell this tale if it hadn't happened.

That night—it was Wednesday—he took Meg to the races as usual. It was the end of November, the last week of the season.

He was extraordinary. Instead of losing, he won. They arrived late, for the third race. The field was already in the hands of the starter. Harold rushed to the window and laid his bet on the horse to place that he had *picked* to place. He did not bet her to win. He did not, as more usually, discard her at the last moment for another horse altogether.

They rushed to the rail to watch, under the brilliant floodlights in the cold and starry night. "Come on, 4! Make a move!" they cried. And sure enough, the mare came storming down the stretch under the whip, and placed. Paying $7.10.

It set the pattern for the evening. With Harold wondering at himself, and Meg pleased. He bet his carefully calculated choices, and more than half of them came home and paid good money; and nevertheless he did not recklessly parlay his winnings, but always kept comfortably ahead. He won over a hundred dollars. Instead of losing.

What impressed him was that he did not find this boring! Rather, his excitement mounted and became hilarious. Contrary to their custom, they sat out a race and had a couple of drinks. (Harold liked to drink only when he was having a good time.) He expected that he would desperately miss the blow in the solar plexus that he was wont to give himself by stupidly betraying his better judgment and gambling heavily on a lost cause, and losing. For years that fever, and the blow that ended it, and the glum feeling of waste in the world, had been a darling addiction of Harold's. Yet tonight he did not crave for it. How was that? On the contrary, he found it stimulating to win, or even to be furious when a well-considered choice was boxed in and could not make it.

The old drivers in their particolored silks looked more honest tonight. The horses were spirited as they sped their scores up and down the gleaming tan under the artificial day. Harold found himself out at the rail watching, next to Meg, instead of tormenting himself at the odds-board under the grandstand and changing his mind.

Meg always remained at the railing watching the horses trot and pace up and down. She did not tire of this. She rarely bet.

Harold looked away from the bright artificial day of the field into the darkness of the sky, and soon he saw the stars whose names he did not know. He was unusually ignorant for an intelligent man who had had some education. He did not know what the Big Dipper looked like. He did not know what a clam or oyster tasted like. This kind of ignorance was one thing that he shared with the kids. He ungrudgingly respected Roger and Jason who knew something.

7

It was quiet on the drive home. Harold did not have his losses to gripe about. Meg was pleased that he had been successful, but she was not one to let on. "I got a job today," he told her offhand. And he turned on the radio.

He was a passionate lover of music, especially of the more Romantic twentieth century composers like Rachmaninoff, Dohnányi, Sibelius. He shivered with delight when he heard Rimsky-Korsakoff. It surprised Meg that he listened to music in the car, for he had no music in his bleak home.

Tonight they tuned in on Elgar's *Enigma Variations,* another of his favorites.

He pulled off the highway at a midnight florist's, to buy flowers for Meg out of his winnings. He was full of old-fashioned courtesies; and this strain of his mother's time and place sometimes came crashing through his compulsive habits, his convict sternness, the places he haunted. Meg thought that he was funny. They chose a big bunch of gorgeous chrysanthemums.

8

At Meg's, he did not drop her off as usual, but came up, as he knew and planned, to fuck.

The baby-sitter, one of Jason's sophomores, left with her books and her thick looseleaf notebook. Harold said that she was a pretty girl, and Meg looked at him mischievously and vanished into the bathroom.

Harold put the flowers in a vase. He was in love with her, she was so beautiful and kind. Her coarse black hair was to him as gorgeous as the orange chrysanthemums. He put his face down into the pungent blooms. He would often have asked her to marry him—he was not bashful—but he was impotent. Tonight he was not going to be impotent, but he knew, wistfully, that Meg would never marry him anyway, because he was not interesting enough.

But he knew that he was not going to be impotent. He almost did not think about it at all. He did not have the premature hard-on that so treacherously spited him and died when he got into bed. Instead, he had the feeling of her warmth beside him in the car, the brasses of the climax of *Enigma,* the pungent smell of the chrysanthemums.

She reappeared, naked, and he was grateful that she was so kind to him. Meg was hairy, her breasts were not firm; just as she was, Harold desired her. He kissed her gravely, and his penis rose.

Fucking her, he felt extraordinary. It was strange—he was not quite in touch with his feelings, but he had no despair that they were going to die. Rather, it was as if somewhere within him, and in possession of his genitals, was a twelve-year-old, a total stranger to him, who was excited and determined to be satisfied. With himself, Harold did not know what to do. He kept kissing Meg gravely, but sometimes his hands flew wildly, out of his control, caressing her breasts and her behind.

Meg thought that he was funny, but she seemed to understand how it was. She was pleased for him, and decided, as she could, to have a good time herself and enjoy an orgasm. She kept laughing, laughing at him, when he tried to kiss her. But he kissed her gravely, and with wild thrashing the boy came off.

She comforted him as if he were the small boy, murmuring approval into his ear, "Such a good Hal! Oh, that was first rate, Hal; that was well done!" and he burst, for the first time in twenty-five years, into awful sobs.

mount kisco

1

Mr. and Mrs., Joanna's father and mother, forbade her to
visit Terry in the hospital where he was being kept for
observation till he went to trial for possession and pushing
of narcotics.

A family showdown was unavoidable, and there was a
formal hearing in Mount Kisco. The newspapers—perhaps
to confuse, by being impartial, the issue of the police bru-
tality at the Times Square demonstration—had played up
the story of the crazy youth in the crowd. The implication
was that many pacifists were crazy youth. By a fatality, he
stood for all. Who subverted the American (Mount Kisco)
way of life. Joanna's name was mentioned, linked with
Professor Davidson. There was a picture of the University
people. According to the Dean's office, Terry had been
dropped for bad grades. *Post factum,* as they did not tell
the press.

Her parents sharpened their razor. If she defied them,
they would cut off her board and tuition. This was a good
threat because she was bright and worked hard. The question was how to know if she disobeyed, for they took it for
granted that she would lie to them.

There was the cynical rudeness in their $75,000 home
that sometimes astounds one in the middle class. (Just as the
slippery integrity of University administrators takes one
by surprise.) The family quarreled coldly, without courtesy,
and called one another foul names. It was hard to understand how they continued living together after saying words
that violated human dignity. Their growing son listened in
on it for the entertainment.

Joanna had deceived them about Terry as long as possible. When they found out that he was at the University,
she lied that she did not have sex with him. Her father
employed a detective to follow her to Vanderzee, and there
was a fierce hearing in which she defied them by describing

in detail how she had sex with him. This led to an uneasy verdict, an agreement not to discuss it any further.

They had settled for making her life at school as inconvenient as possible, rooming her with a Mrs. Gray who promised to be a watchdog. But Mrs. Gray had business of her own to attend to, and Joanna spent a couple of nights a week with Terry. Sometimes her mother phoned at Mrs. Gray's at two and three in the morning and Joanna wasn't there. Sometimes on those nights she wasn't in Vanderzee either. The arrangement was calculated to cause as much deception as possible, as much disruption as possible, and to be as expensive as possible.

It was hard to know what they wanted from the girl, unless her father was carrying on an enraged jealous love affair with her, and her mother was torturing her because of it. If this was so, it was sad. But they misinterpreted their terrible passions as maintaining public decency and their station in life—Mr. was a highway engineer who had become a functionary of the state government—while, one way and another, they and their class were destroying the country, its youth, and Western civilization.

Their belief in the Image was uncanny. They seemed to assume, unlike Harold's new boss Mr. Polk, that there was a Normal Youth that was being lived in all the other ranch houses in Westchester County, as described in the magazine distributed by the chain-store grocery, in the organs of the ten-billion-dollar teen-age market, and in the catalogues of the good colleges. Only *their* family was in disgrace.

Sometimes, however, Joanna's father suspected that there was a general conspiracy, and one worthless youngster corrupted another. *All* the apples in the barrel were rotten. And indeed, Joanna was just as spirited and hard as her parents. Even before she went to college she had joined the conspiracy, and proceeded deliberately to waste herself to preserve herself. At college she explored the drugs, made the scenes, and had sex for variety. But she handed in her term papers on time and was careful not to become pregnant. There weren't enough hours in the day and night for all this, so she kept herself awake on dexedrin.

2

From the moment she sized him up at the jazz festival at Newport, Terry seemed to be just right, an accomplished hipster as an accomplice for kicks, and an interesting philosopher when the kicks became boring. Their introduction was entirely ritual. They singled each other out to spar, and went at it for seven hours—he trying to throw her off balance by keen psychological analysis of her type and refutation of her metaphysics of life, continually attacking, to gain a male ascendancy; and she adroitly making him fall on his face by practical remarks and showing him that she couldn't care less what he thought of her, and so winning his admiration. After this fine tournament, they exchanged love letters between their colleges, which explored in minute detail the nuances of their daily adventures, without mentioning any facts or revealing any feelings. Naturally, such documents required long preparation, and it was months before one arrived and months before it was answered. It was a real cool romance.

To her total surprise, when they met again they were serious with each other. For all his gambits and stratagems, he cared for her. He was happy when she was happy and disturbed when she was wretched. This cast her into confusion. They were a pair of the Wild and the Wasted, as John Oatfield has called them, clinging to each other in the world that was falling apart.

3

He was not what she had counted on, and she began to be embarrassed by him. Far from being cynical, he proved to be naïve. And callow. Many a prospective junior executive was three or four years hipper than Terry. For instance, he did not understand about making the scene. He had friends to whom he was loyal—expecting her to love them as he did—and he dragged them along. But this destroyed the scene, for it is a scene when each person in the company is indifferent to the others, and all are together making the scene. Terry wasn't cool.

The crisis occurred at a literary party. It was a big party, with almost a dozen lions, novelists, popular sociologists, TV producers. But Terry, instead of being objective and witty, insisted on talking about his true problems and quarreling fiercely with the most distinguished author of them all, as if the man cared and might have some wisdom to tell him. Soon he became obnoxious—it was a writer's *duty*, he howled, to solve adolescents' hang-ups! Worst of all, he was ill informed, and the younger set easily made him look foolish, with their detached good sense, often wittily phrased. People, including the author, could not help laughing at him, and he became incoherent. His eyes began to tear.

To her surprise, Joanna was not disgusted with him but felt protective. To her greater surprise, the writer afterward took Terry and herself to a drugstore for coffee and corn muffins and sat up with them till dawn, giving what advice he could. This made her thoughtful.

At a certain moment, she realized that Terry had generous instincts, and she fell in love with him. He sincerely thought that some things were not phony; he was really indignant about hypocrisy, cruelty, and ruthless greed. To be sure, he could not remember any of this one day to the next. But she had a more orderly mind, and remembered.

She began to discover that her major in moral philosophy and literature at the University was *about* something, although the professors did not seem to grasp this. She became interested in the courses, studied the books, and worked hard on her essays.

She was keenly ambitious, to prove to her father that she was not good for nothing.

4

Sexual intercourse with Terry was usually poor, sometimes good. But it was always meaningful, and they exhausted their unsatisfied excitement in angry quarrels.

Unfortunately, she could not see how deeply wounded he was simply by the bad manners that she had learned at home and that she took for granted. When she spoke to him in her hard and cruel tone, she expected her father's cutting retaliation, and hardened herself further to meet it.

What Terry was thinking, however, was that he did not want to marry a young woman who spoke in that tone of voice and said such cynical things about her own parents. How would she treat *him* when he was ill or down? And how would she talk to *their* children?

He did not strike back; she concluded that he was spineless. In contempt, she went to bed with another fellow who was more callous. But the sex was meaningless. There was no one whom she *could* marry but Terry. In their confusion, they would have to find out how to be with each other. They worked at it.

5

As the months passed, however, a more terrible underlying truth began to be revealed. Terry was a fuck-up. He flunked out of the University just as he had flunked out at Columbus. He thought up useful and original projects that fitted his abilities, but he did not carry them out, apparently he could not carry them out. First he rationalized; afterward he went in for bitter speeches of self-reproach like an alcoholic. What was to become of him? And what was to become of her? If she married him, she foresaw her ruin.

He was most pathetic when he was proud of trivial crimes he committed that were all his own, gratuitous acts, as though he were a kobold upsetting a farmer's milk pail, the way a child shits in his pants. No doubt it was better to be able to do this than to be totally inhibited from ever doing it, but it was not much to be proud of.

And now they had locked him up, and the long months stretched ahead. She had no doubt that in his cell he still had it all figured out. What good did that do her?

—Like a storm the loyal love roared into her heart. She could not bear the empty place that he had left in her life.

She remembered his desperate hand grip in the crowd on Times Square, as he ran toward Professor Davidson who was staggering toward them with the blood streaming down his face; and then she lost sight of them both, and the crowd bore her away.

6

"I love this boy!" she shouted at her daddy. "I'll quit school and stay with him! If that's what he wants."

She was remorseful of the nights that she had spent on her essay, which interested her, rather than staying protectively by his side smoking pot with his chums who had come to bore her. She was indignant at herself for the weekends she had fearfully gone home to Mount Kisco to satisfy her parents, as if Terry had ever given her the courage not to go.

Her father was quick to detect the falseness of her tone, and he pounced on her without mercy. "I expect the expression 'I love this boy,' or its French equivalent, comes from one of your *nouvelle vague* movies. Probably the dubbed-in subtitle, your French being what it is. Well, it's your legal right to attach yourself to a boy rather than a man; you're twenty years old. Tell me, how does your boyish friend put up with your contempt? 'I love this boy.' I wouldn't have taken that condescending remark from your mother. I would have slapped her in the face. It would earn a slap in the face from any young man with spunk. Up to now I assumed that Terry was a bad influence on you. Now I feel sorry for the kid. You're a bitch."

At this, Mrs. burst out laughing.

"What's this other remark, the one about school? Did he try to keep you *away* from your classes? I'll horsewhip him, if he ever gets out of jail. That tuition costs me $1,700 a year. My guess," he shrewdly guessed, "is that your boy is envious that his girl gets better grades than he does. That's manly of him. You're doing well in school, better than I hoped. You must have caught on to something there that I didn't count on. Do you intend to give up your career for a dope addict?"

"He's not a dope addict!" wailed Joanna, and fled upstairs, to cry.

Although spirited, she didn't have much stamina. None of these wild kids did. Where would they get stamina from? Even their physical health was poor because they didn't eat and sleep right.

Pretty soon it became clear that Terry was not going to be immediately released. Through his notebook the police had caught a couple of his cronies who, of course, laid it on him, and he, of course, kept his mouth shut. Joanna panicked.

When as best he could, his father's lawyer tried to tangle the jurisdictions and play up the mental aspects, in order to stall and get the charges reduced—now Terry was playing chess in an asylum, a somewhat more pleasant environment—Joanna at once decided that Terry's father and the lawyer were conspiring to have him put away in the asylum indefinitely, where he could not make them any more trouble.

She felt that Terry himself had no will to get out. He was afraid to face the problems of freedom. Like anywhere else, he would adapt to an insane asylum and behave like a big wheel there too. The truth was that she did not want him to be lucid and quiet but to be crazy and exciting and also, somehow, practical.

She visited him in the asylum, but the twenty minutes were worth less than nothing, for he was under maximum security and they spoke through a mesh screen. Especially with Terry there was no way to get into contact, past his role playing, except by a warm embrace. And on the day that she came he was being the young convict, petulant, defiant. He looked whiter than ever.

When anybody talked about Terry, she began to laugh sardonically. It was her mother's laugh. She began to laugh a lot, about everything. Her voice became appallingly jazzy and throwaway, so that it was painful to talk to her. One felt mocked. The lawyer tried to explain what he was doing, and she said, "Don't give me that jazz. All that jazz. Don't give me all that jazz." He was an old man and not used to being talked to like that.

She went to bed with all her former men, including one
or two from the distant past, as if programmatically. But
it was a lot of jazz.

8

Her father could not let her be. It was the pacifist demonstration that got him. How did she come to march in a
pacifist demonstration? He had a good mind, but it had
become so rigid that he felt mortally threatened by any
difference of opinion and he had to put it out of court or
he could not rest.

But pacifist demonstrations were the limit! Just because
they were ludicrous, they were dangerous. As Arthur Krock
said it in the *Times:* In the end it would be this absurd
sentimentality, spreading among youth who considered
themselves idealistic, that would subvert the nation. Like
everybody else in Westchester, Joanna's father ritually held
that the pacifists were dupes of the communists and that
their organizations were infiltrated by communist leaders;
but his real opinion was that the pacifists did not *even* have
organizations. They were headless, like a low form of life.
The sloppy adolescents, wishy-washy ministers, eccentric
scientists, and hysterical women who made up the pacifist
movement could not organize a bridge game. But it spread
like a contagious disease, intangible, miasmic.

American youth were the pawns of subversive professors,
for instance, Jews. In his more frantic moments, he rein-
vented the Protocols of Zion; but he was usually too logical
for this. He prided himself on being a scientific positivist.
But one *fact* he did know, that Joanna and her "circle" were
friends of the do-gooder, the tired man. They quoted him.
They played tapes he had made.

"You have fallen under the influence of sociologists,"
he said hoarsely, "who want to ban the cars. Of sociologists
and psychologists. Second-rate minds. Ban the cars? By God,
did you ever hear such lunacy? Ban the cars!" He was beside himself; he was the deputy highway commissioner.

He gripped hold of himself and said more calmly, in

263

his satiric vein, "Ah. When you were at Wellesley you were in an atmosphere of exact science, and naturally it was too bracing for the level of intelligence you have, so your grades were B— and C. But in New York you get A's on your reports because the University is infiltrated with social-psychologists: $1,700 a year."

He spoke calmly, but his eyes were rolling.

·

9

And his daughter, who hated him but loved him, was alarmed to see him becoming stupid, and she said, "You mechanical man! My poor Daddy. You're getting stupid. My poor Terry, he was so white. Yes, I saw him in his prison yesterday; yes, I did. I don't care what you do to me. But you're sick yourself, Daddy; yes you are. Your job is turning you into a computer.

"You do need help, Daddy. I can't give it to you because I hate you and hope you die, because you have poisoned us. My hippy Terry, he looked so white." She began to weep, but this time her tears did not stop her words, which were indeed thoughts that she was writing for her course in Contemporary American Philosophy. Even as she sobbed, she spoke out loudly between the sobs.

"You said"—she sobbed—"Terry was not man enough to take me out of here. No, he's not." She sobbed. "How could he become a man? In your lousy world"—she sobbed —"do you know what he worked at? Do you? See! you know all about it but you don't even know what Terry did for a living. *He was a TV monitor at night!*" she wailed, and at this thought she really began to bawl.

"When he came back from there"—she sobbed—"he couldn't get an erection. Could you?" She sobbed. "Could you get an erection if you had to watch the TV for four hours?"

"I?" said her father, amazed.

She screamed: "Do you think we're fools to be willing to live as you and Mama do? I want a husband I can re-

264

spect! *My mother is married to a deputy commissioner!"*
She wailed. She could not stop wailing.

"That will do," said her father. "That's quite enough
out of you, young lady."

"Young people these days," she quoted out of her essay,
"we have to make the world out of our own guts. Oh, yes,
the milk is poisoned in Mount Kisco, just like everywhere
else. In Salt Lake City they had to stop the distribution of
milk because of radioactive iodine." She screamed, "I can't
make a baby out of my own guts!"

"What *are* you talking about, girl?" said her alarmed
father. Her poetry was more disturbing than her sobbing.

"There it is! Terry is in jail. All of the rest of them are
grade-grubbers. And Daddy is nothing but a big prick."

When she said this, the little brother, who was listening
to her tirade with fascination, burst into a guffaw. It was
the same laugh as his mother's.

Stricken, his father hit him repeatedly with his clenched
fist, like a maniac, and the boy, who was about Hugh's
age, howled with pain.

plato's ladder

1

I expected to miss the young fellow, and I did. My exhausting days needed him. And as his absence stretched into the weeks, the hair grew an inch white at my temples.

I did not visit Terry in the hospital. There was no point to it, under maximum security, especially for a person like myself who was so starved for touch that without it I wasn't human. If I couldn't touch him, through a mesh screen, my severe and rational conversation would make him only guiltier. My tired face would make him sad, just as my liveliness, when we could touch each other, used to make him happy pleasing me.

It was December; the days were short. But my exhausting days were not short, as I fled from one appointment to another, in my monstrous unpeaceful community, always arriving on time. It was cold, and I couldn't dawdle on the streets. But I am a man of streets.

2

The conference with the Police Department, in the aftermath of the riot, was ludicrous. They had badly damaged their prestige at Times Square, especially on account of Davidson. Just because it was Davidson, at least twenty witnesses had had their eyes on him and saw the brutal maltreatment he received, from which he was still convalescing. The affidavits all came to the same: the attack was unprovoked, the squad had lost its nerve because a professor said "Shame!" The public indignation was unsparingly mocking, and the judges suspended most of the sentences.

Now the police were leaning over backward; they wanted fully to cooperate with future pacifist action! They pointed out how much it was to our advantage to notify them beforehand of our intended spontaneous demonstrations, so that we could make an orderly and dignified showing and also be protected from the hoodlums and counter-demonstrators who hooted "Communists!" This reasoning applied a fortiori to illegal civil disobedience. If the cops were ready for them, the nonviolent protesters could make their exemplary stand in a proper exemplary setting and be carted off to jail without anybody being hurt. There was no doubt, the police agreed, that in a democratic society all citizens had the right, to convene, petition, and protest, and also be arrested if conscience demanded.

Since the police were so accommodating, our spokesmen, too, hastened to be reasonable. We agreed that policemen had to do their jobs. Like any other working stiffs. They had no choice but to cordon us in and drag us off. We were impressed by the statistics of how many traffic cops had their arms and legs broken in a town like New York. And even though they didn't bring it up, we thought that it *was* inhuman to subject them to the outcry of "Shame!" Henceforth, we offered, this word would be forbidden by our discipline. And of *course* the police should be notified in advance, for it was a principle of nonviolent action to respect one's opponent and not catch him off guard. (I was puzzled by the psychology of this, but I report it as it was agreed.)

So we shook hands all around and, spreading out a map of the site, we and the police proceeded to design our demonstration at the British Consulate, for the British had given license to the President to explode bombs off Christmas Island. At the barricades would be one hundred police facing the pickets, thirty on the longer side of the great doorway, twenty on the shorter, and fifty along the side street. The police decided that they would stand two feet apart, legs astride. Three pacifists at a time would walk into the building and try to interview the Consul. When they emerged, another trio would enter. But if after half an hour they did *not* emerge—for of course some people might be inspired to sit down inside and chain themselves to a steam pipe—another trio could enter anyway. Policing inside was up to the British.

267

(When this demonstration actually occurred, the police, be it said to their honor, carried out the Byzantine ceremonial to the letter. But only six or seven pacifists bothered to straggle to the spot and the Consul, a pleasant blond chap, invited all of these in together. When they emerged, warm with tea and cookies, they walked away chatting up First Avenue. For hours the blues stood there, legs astride. It was cold.)

3

I hurried across town to my appointment with Salty, Dr. Gresham Salisbury, who was associated with the hospital where they had Terry. Yes, Salty at once assured me, he had looked in on Terry and Terry was fine; that is, he was crazy like many others, but not curable in that hospital.

He looked at me. "I'll go along with whatever the lawyer thinks is convenient," he said.

"Thanks, Salty." There it was again, they wanted to be good to me. But what *was* good for me? I hesitated. Then, "Don't tell me he needs three or four years to find himself. We know that," I said.

He insistently looked at me. "How long *did* you know him?" he asked.

"Less than a year. More than six months."

He seemed surprised.

"We had unusual advantages!" I said. "We had—a community."

"He told me," said Salty dryly.

"Oh, cut the shit, Salty. What's the worst?"

"The worst?" He pondered it. "The worst is that deep down he thinks you're dead. Not only you."

"No. He wrote me a letter that he loves me. . . . Does he think I'm dead?" I asked sadly.

"He didn't write you, he wrote a letter. He makes you up. He always did. It is a way he has of whistling in the dark—passing the cemetery. The boy is in too much pain to be honest."

"It isn't true," I contradicted him. "He has looked at me in a way that is love! I'm not easy to deceive!" I was not. But I did not want to hear about his pain. I needed his health.

"*Who* looked at you?"—And Salty looked at me. "Who looked at whom?"

I tried to remember the look that Terry gave me. It was like an angel's. It was like the dog's. He was right; it certainly was not a young man's.

"Then I wasn't there either!" I cried. "Neither one of us in the untidy bed! What difference does who make? In the flurry of the afternoon, as it passes. I'll tell you how it was! Awhile we clung to each other abandoned in this city infested by the violent and the cowed. I taught him useless secrets that are the art of life among men, but not here."

"*They were too simple for him,*" said Salty. "This boy is suffering too intensely to risk coming to earth and making sense. My problem is you. Let him alone. He'll come out of there and this time you'll break your heart, overworked as you are. You don't have a community in fact. You can't do it all by yourself. You know—I hope you do—you're a very arrogant man; but who do you think you are, Napoleon? If the gray flannels don't kill him on Madison Avenue, the niggers will get him on Forty-second Street. Let bad enough alone."

"We'll see about that," I said quietly. "Do you have another coming generation?" My mother too died of angina. I did not have a father. I have improvised that. "And is the poor kid in such pain, Salty? You said it two times. Give me the phone." I dialed a number.

I was in a fit of quiet rage. I refused to accept the idea that I was dead, even though this desperate boy thought so. I was raging to raze Mount Kisco to the ground, for Joanna had told me of her father's attack on me, how *I* was to blame because their suburban children with all their privileges were going to the dogs. I spoke to the City Planning Commission and made an appointment for the late afternoon, after I got back from Trenton, to put in my two cents about the proposed Downtown Expressway. We'd see about subsidizing the suburbs any further!

269

4

I went to Trenton to visit Pedro. To tell him that the indictment against him was going to be reduced from murder to manslaughter. (It was certainly a day for cops and jails.)

Oddly, it was Barry Conklin, persuaded by Jason, who had most exerted influence for Pedro. Barry was moved by the story that Jason had told him, and he had really put himself out.

I was startled when Pedro was brought out to me, not by the change in him but by the lack of change, considering what he had gone through. He did not expect a visit from me, Harold would have been more likely—but it was unwise just at present for Harold to extend the official list of his acquaintances. Pedro was uneasy that he would not know what to talk to me about and might bore me. We had been through this before. He put on company manners.

I told him my good news, glad to have it to tell. We had thought that it was cruel not to let him know at once, and I happened to be the best available messenger.

He listened to me gravely and gave no sign of interest at all.

I assumed he had not understood, and I began to spell it out.

"Oh, I know," he stopped me courteously. "This way I might get out in three years with good behavior. Señor Martínez explained everything." I was always surprised by his good English. "Instead of perhaps the electric chair? But that would not be likely. But for life."

I was at a loss at his apathy.

"My behavior is sure to be good," he reassured me. "Unless I become angry again and killed somebody else. . . . Oh, I won't," he assured me courteously. "I don't have any contact with these people here."

In order to say something, I asked him, "How old *are* you, Pedro?"

"I am nineteen," said Pedro.

"Then isn't it better—"

"No, it's not better. It is the same."

He asked for Harold. I had intended to avoid mentioning Harold's troubles, but in the circumstances, to one so desperately honest, I was ashamed not to be frank, and I told him about Ramón.

His eyes flashed. "I could see it coming!" he said in a livelier tone, and he breathed faster. "When I get out I'll break his arm. No, no, don't be alarmed. I meant to, but I never got around to it."

He rapidly asked about the fate of the others in the gang, as if he were still responsible for them. Awestruck, I could see that he did not care one way or another about them, and he had never cared, except to fulfill his station and its duties.

"One way, it's better here," he said. "It is easier to keep off the junk."

The guard tapped him and said, "Two more minutes."

"Thank you! thanks for coming to tell me," said Pedro with sudden animation. "It's better than the electric chair! Connie will sometime come to see me?" He said it as a question.

"Oh, she'll come to see you every Saturday for three years," I said, "just like last week."

"It's always for an hour on Saturday, isn't it?" he asked the guard.

5

It was five o'clock before I got to the Municipal Building and sat down with my pipeline, Assistant Commissioner Edel.

By now my Mount Kisco rage had broadened out—the hideous landscape of the ride from Trenton had not assuaged it—and my soul was gloomy with the latter days of Rome, when the optimates left the center to decay. How could we make decent public schools, segregated 80, 90, and 100 percent, when half of the white middle class had already fled to Westchester, Nassau, Rockland, and Fairfield

271

counties? (The rest of the white kids went to private and parochial schools.) Therefore there was no community for Terry! And White, Negro, and Spanish youth were pitted like fighting cocks—

"*Was will der Mensch?*" said Edel. "Are you telling me that the suburban flight has put us in a box? Is this news? Did you ring me up to tell me to tax Mount Kisco out of existence? Why especially Mount Kisco? And who in the devil is your Terry?"

I liked Edel. I saw him very clearly in front of me, sharply outlined against the dim books of Registry. I no longer quite remembered why I had rung him up.

Suddenly I had got up and taken him by the lapels of his jacket and was shaking him. Not in anger, but just shaking him. To shake him out of something. To shake him into something. His glasses fell off onto the carpet. We were neither of us young men. My glasses fell off onto the green blotter. "*Nu?—Nu?—*" he found some voice, to gasp. It *was* not clear what I wanted, not from the way I was.

His secretary, dressed to go home, appeared in the doorway. "Did you call?" she said.

"No. My friend is trying to help me with my bursitis. Good night. It's a disgrace!" he said to me with sudden anger, "how these people neglect public goods. Do you have any ideas?"

I thought up ideas because I was unhappy. Why else would one think up ideas?

6

In spite of this added mission in a crowded day, I got home in time for dinner. It was laid. They were waiting for me. I poured the wine.

My daughter was home from college, a young lady. She looked splendid. In a couple of years she had made a fine recovery from the polio that had left her crippled. She had willed it and worked at it. "You're looking very well," I said gravely.

Hugh made more sense day by day. At the dinner table he often had a story about the latest of Dr. Monk, the principal of his public school, who did look like a gorilla and ran the school like a jail. But Hugh was able to escape from it at 3:00 P.M., and so far as we cared, he didn't have to go at all, any day he didn't feel like it. But he usually went, for the company.

As I sat at the table, after the weary day, in my loosed limbs I felt the approving praise. "Well done!" it said to me, "O patient, reasonable, and by and large fairly just!" The sparkle of the light in the wineglass was mad with excitement, it exclaimed. It leaped into existence out of nothing. As I tilted the glass and looked into it, everywhere, continually, the sparkles danced, they shone. I saw this without smoking hasheesh. My blood began to tingle in my limbs, I was so dead beat. I felt the muscles in my old face sag.

I understood from experience that my good fortune, such as it was, was precarious. Any day we might be visited by disaster. I was vulnerable to it. I had a recurrent apprehension—but it was not always with me, only sometimes—that it was probable that the powers of the world, whom I hit as hard as I could with my weak strength, would lash back at me with terrible strength.

My wife, these days, was unusually kind and loving to me, as if she had decided to be pleased that long ago she had picked me instead of somebody else. Perhaps it was that being pregnant gave her something interesting to look forward to. I wondered also, more sadly than resentfully, if she was not pleased because Terry was out of the way.

I was wrong about this. For after the kids got up from the table and while we sat a little longer over coffee, she said: "I wish you would stop, dear. You're trying to do too much. It shows. I see now. When there was Terry, you had more peace. Of course he's an impossible snot, but I see now he must have been good to you. You've aged the last month."

I hardly knew what to say to this. The way she said it did not ask for an answer.

7

Finally I had to face the fact, as I sat lonely drawing on my pipe, that none of them who tried so hard to be good to me—not Irving or Salty, and not Meg or Harold, not my wife and not Terry either—could help me in the kind of anxiety I felt, that made my life more painful than was necessary. It was something that I had to do myself, or to cease to do—it came to the same thing. Like everybody else who was alive, I was erotic. I was climbing on the ladder of love. I was pretty high, compared to some, but now I had become timid of the height and was clutching to the wood with a death grip, and did not love.

How accurate Plato's analysis proved to be! I used to think it was only literature.

He said that, as a man grows, he is first attracted to the beautiful bodies he sees; and I had certainly been wondrously attracted to them, though with indifferent success in ever getting to touch them.

But then, he said, a man begins to fall in love with the virtuous characters of people that behave in those bodies and give them the beauty that shines on their faces. It was true. I had found it to be so.

And then, he said surprisingly, a man's eros turns to the institutions and the customs of the city, that educate character and nurture physical beauty; and now his lively concern is with these. I should never have believed it when I was younger! But as I grew up, I found that it was true. My crowded days were this love affair with my city, a thorny adventure, but often I was so busy at it that I didn't know whether I was unhappy or happy, and that meant, I suppose, that I was sometimes happy.

But at last, said Plato, a man begins to have intimations of God in whom the city exists, and he comes to love Him. And presumably God comes across. I had not yet found it so. At this rung I was frozen on the ladder. I did not feel any peace of God, if it is peace that one feels—how would I know? There was a risk that I was afraid to take. I did not trust to let the nature of things be, although it certainly worked out according to its nature, in spite of all my efforts.

amos

1

When they landed him at Idlewild Airport, after a storm-less trip via Rome and Paris, Amos remembered vaguely that he had acquaintances in New York City. He could even, with effort, have made his memories precise, but why bother? since he invested no feeling in them. He thought he remembered that he used to have a wife in this vicinity, but marriage, like other relations grounded in sexuality, certainly had no interest for him, though he enjoyed having an occasional sexual discharge. And he certainly was not going to linger in New York where, people had informed him, prices were out of line and it was hard to get a pleasant room with a bath.

His medical papers were in order and he was out of custody. He was on his own, with all America to choose from. The Israeli Government had generously given him £100 on his departure, and he had $186.47 of his own money left, in his wallet and in his change purse. He had verified the amount on the plane. To go to San Diego, the farthest southwest corner of the country, cost, plane and bus, $117.60. Not that he intended to go to San Diego, but just for instance.

He did *not* want to go to West Virginia, where he was born. That was one part of the country that was excluded, because he had a mother and brothers and sisters there, and family relations certainly had no charm for him. On the contrary. But West Virginia, he had verified on the map, occupied only a small area in the eastern part of the country and was easily avoidable, so to speak.

Amos was thinking, by preference, of a small city, of population 75,000 to 100,000, where he could work at accounting, for which he had a tested aptitude. There must be scores, maybe hundreds, of places like that from coast to coast; but he would have to buy a directory and check the number. The decision was his to make between one of them and another! As he walked about the concourse of the new glassy airport with its ceramic murals in primary colors, it was pleasant, it was mildly exciting, to be free, not under custody, even though he was toting a heavy bag. On his own! Making his own choices!

His memory was really very good, if he made any effort. He had been cuckolded by his mother and cuckolded by his wife and cuckolded by his world his only one; and he used to spend years and weeks trying to deny it, while he kept hearing echoes of wailing. But he truly didn't much care for that kind of thing anymore. He had spent nearly forty years glaring at those he loved! until he stopped loving his world his only one. But now he and she had commenced to live on civil speaking terms, since he didn't care for that so much anymore.

2

No. "The Lord has yet more light and truth to break forth," as John Robinson said to the Pilgrims embarking toward America.

New York City
September 9—New Year's Eve, 1962